SHADOW PEAK
THE FIFTH BUXTON SPA MYSTERY

CELIA HARWOOD

NEUF NEZNOIRS LIMITED

Published by Neuf Neznoirs Limited
Unit 20, 91-93 Liverpool Road, Castlefield, Manchester, M3 4JN.
e-mail: gemggirg@gmail.com

ISBN 978 0 9933261 4 1

© 2019 Margaret Fowler

British Library Cataloguing in Publication Data.
A catalogue record for this book is available from the British Library.

Printed and bound in England by 4edge Ltd. Hockley, Essex
Tel: 01702 200243

For
Durham

CHAPTER ONE

The train to Buxton Spa in the Peak District was crossing the viaduct at Chapel Milton and would shortly be arriving at Chapel-en-le-Frith Central station. The young woman in the window seat, facing the direction of travel, took out a compact from her handbag, flipped it open, and examined her face critically in the mirror. She gave a little pout, and then began powdering her nose and cheeks. She then re-arranged the curls over her forehead and, after a final glance in the mirror, snapped the compact shut and returned it to her handbag. Then she reached for the hat which she had tossed on the seat beside her as soon as the seat had become vacant. It was a straw hat with a wide brim, decorated with a broad pink satin ribbon and a bunch of artificial flowers on one side of the crown. She stood up and turned to face the back of the seat, above which was a mirrored glass panel. She adjusted the hat various ways until she was satisfied with the effect, then sat down again, impatiently. She sighed and looked out of the window. Then she began fidgeting with the handles of her handbag, twisting and untwisting them. Without seeming to observe her, an older woman sitting in the seat nearest the corridor and with her back to the engine, was mentally taking notes: very attractive, quite young, no more than twenty years old, possibly less, makeup made it hard to tell, stylishly dressed but cheap clothes, not very sophisticated, appalling manners, anxious about something.

The two women had boarded the train at Manchester

Central just over an hour ago. The young woman had hurried along the platform looking through the carriage windows for an empty seat. Most of the compartments were already full and there was little choice. When the young woman reached the last of the second class carriages, she stepped up into the train and walked along the corridor until she came to a compartment occupied by a family. The mother and father had taken the middle seats opposite each other. Their two children, a girl of about twelve and an older boy, were sitting in the window seats watching the activity on the platform. The two seats next to the corridor were vacant. The young woman stopped at the door of the compartment and looked in. The family took no notice.

'Oh,' said the young woman, taking a small step forward and looking first at the window seat and then at the vacant seat next to the corridor.

'Would you mind awfully? I can't possibly travel with my back to the engine.'

She looked pointedly at the little girl sitting in the window seat and then at the mother and it was clear from her tone of voice that this was a request not a question.

There was a slight pause while the mother eyed the young woman up and down and then said: 'Molly dear, come and sit here with me and let the lady sit where she wants.' She patted the seat next to her.

'But you said. . .' began Molly. Her mother gave her a stern look.

'It's all right,' said the older boy, standing up. 'Molly can have my seat.' Then, looking at his mother he added, with emphasis on the first word: 'She doesn't mind having her back to the engine.'

The older woman, who had followed the young woman along the platform and into the carriage, was standing in the corridor and had been watching this scene in silence. She noticed the father nod approval at his son and wink at him.

The boy took the seat beside his mother next to the corridor and the young woman, without looking at the boy or thanking him, made a great fuss of arranging herself in the window seat facing the direction of travel, and then, opening the magazine she was carrying, began flicking through the pages. The older woman then entered the compartment and, as she turned to lift her travelling bag up to the luggage rack, the father stood up and helped her. She thanked him and then took the remaining seat next to the corridor, acknowledging the boy opposite with a smile. The family re-settled themselves, the older woman opened a book, and the journey passed in relative silence, apart from the occasional rustle of the father's newspaper and the erratic flicking of the young woman's magazine pages and the occasional tapping of her foot. The older woman thought that she seemed to be impatient for the journey to end.

When the train was approaching Chinley station, the family began gathering their possessions and the father said to the older woman: 'We're getting off here. We have to change for Edale. Would you like me to lift your bag down now for you and put it on the seat? I don't suppose many people will be getting on here so it won't be in anyone's way.'

Looking up from her book, she said: 'Oh, thank you. That is very kind of you.'

'We're on holiday,' said the little girl, as she passed the older woman.

'Then I hope you have very fine weather,' said the older woman. 'Goodbye, Molly.'

The train pulled out of the station and the two women were now the only occupants of the compartment. Neither thought it necessary to speak to the other. In fact, they probably had little in common. The young woman was dressed in a light summer frock of deep pink crepe-de-chine patterned with red flowers and finished with a broad sash of the same material tied in a large bow at one hip. Her jewellery was a pearl necklace and matching bracelet. She wore white, high heeled shoes with a strap across near the ankle. Her light brown hair was a mass of curls. By contrast, the older woman was dressed in a sensible light brown tweed suit, with a dark brown felt hat in a rather manly style, and brown flat-heeled Oxford shoes. Her hair was tied neatly in a bun at the nape of her neck.

Chapel-en-le-Frith was served by two railway companies operating two different railway stations and this train was calling at the central station closest to the town. As the train began slowing down, the young woman opened her handbag and took out a scarf. Then she stood up abruptly and looked at herself in the mirrored glass. She smiled at her reflection then picked up her belongings and went out into the corridor.

The older woman had a ticket for Buxton, the next station, but she closed her book, put it into the pocket of her jacket, picked up her travelling bag, and followed the young woman into the corridor. They each left the train by different doors. The older woman paused on the platform near the train door. She had her ticket safely inside one of her gloves but she went through the motions of looking for it, searching her pockets and then her bag in order to give herself an excuse for remaining on the platform. She watched as the young woman found a porter, summoned him to retrieve her luggage from the luggage van, and then directed him to follow her into the station yard. The older woman now joined the crowd going through the gate, handed her ticket to the ticket collector, and then paused at the entrance to the station as though deciding whether to walk or take a taxi.

When the young woman and the porter emerged from the station entrance, the young woman looked around anxiously. Then she spotted a motor car parked on the far side of the station yard, a two seater coupé which the older woman easily identified as a Lagonda. The older woman watched as the young woman rushed over to the motor car. The man occupying the driver's seat was wearing a motoring coat and goggles and it was not possible to judge his age or identity. He did not bother to get out. Instead, he leaned over towards the passenger side and handed the young woman a motoring coat.

The older woman walked towards the line of taxi-cabs waiting at the station. She got into one of them, asked the driver to wait, and watched the proceedings from there. The young woman put on the motoring coat, draped her scarf over her hat and tied it securely under her chin. As the young woman finished tying the scarf, the porter emerged from the station entrance, wearily trundling a barrow laden with two suitcases. He spotted the young woman, crossed the station yard, and stopped beside the motor car. Realising that there was no luggage rack, he called to the driver: 'Where do you want these?'

'Oh, just have them sent on!' ordered the driver.

'And how would you like me to do that, sir,' asked the porter, icily polite. He sighed because he knew the size of the tip, if there was one, would not cover the trouble he was being put to.

'Use your initiative, man. Get one of those taxi-cabs to take it,' said the driver, impatiently. He started the engine of the motor car. 'Stanley Hotel, Buxton. Here, that should cover it.' He thrust a pound note at the young woman. 'Tell the driver to leave the change at the hotel,' he added. The young woman took the money and, giggling and simpering, handed the money to the porter. 'Get in,' said the man.

The young woman climbed into the motor car and, as it eased forward out of the station yard, she laughed and waved gaily to the porter. He remained standing beside his barrow for a moment, pushed his cap back with the heel of his hand, and shook his head in disbelief. Then, as he turned towards the taxi-cabs, he heard someone call to him.

'Porter,' called the older woman, leaning out of the window of the taxi-cab she had taken. 'Would you come over here, please.' She opened her purse and took out several coins. She said to the porter: 'Here is the tip you were just deprived of. I'm going to Buxton, so this driver will take the luggage.'

The porter touched the brim of his cap deferentially and then looked at the coins in his hand. 'Thank you, Miss. That's very kind of you, I'm sure.'

The porter stowed the luggage into the taxi-cab and gave the driver the man's pound note.

The older woman said to the driver: 'Buxton, please, driver.'

She smiled and settled back in her seat confident that she now had the information she needed and she prepared to enjoy the taxi ride to Buxton which she had just obtained at no expense to her employer.

CHAPTER TWO

Earlier that week, in the last two days of May 1923, Buxton had attracted the attention of the nation's press having been chosen as the venue for the annual conference of the National Liberal Federation. That organisation, a union of the English and Welsh Liberal Associations, had been created to promote liberalism. Its inaugural conference, held in Birmingham in 1877, had been chaired by Joseph Chamberlain and addressed by W. E. Gladstone. This was the precedent that Buxton now had to follow and this year H.H. Asquith, the former Prime Minister and currently leader of the Independent Liberals, was coming to address the delegates. When it had been announced that Buxton would be the venue for the conference, there had been a feeling in the town of anxiety mingled with hope: anxiety about being in the national spotlight, and hope at the prospect of a boost to Buxton's reputation.

For centuries, Buxton had provided visitors with the benefit of its famous water and now also offered medical treatments based on hydrotherapy as well as various forms of entertainment and some first-class sporting facilities. Many visitors came because they enjoyed the clean air and the relaxed atmosphere, a welcome escape from the crowded and dirty industrial towns where they lived. However, like many resort towns which depended on people having the time, the money, the freedom to travel, and the desire to indulge in leisure activity, the town had been badly affected during the sombre years of the War and the nation's subsequent economic decline. Since the War, there had been much discussion amongst Buxton's civic officials, tradespeople, hoteliers, and lodging house keepers as to way to increase the flow of visitors and reclaim Buxton's place as one of the nation's leading spa towns.

The leaders of the National Liberal Federation were coming to Buxton with a similar mixture of hope and anxiety but for very different reasons. It was their ardent hope that, at this conference, the current rift between the two factions of the Liberal Party could be healed. Their anxiety was caused by the looming prospect of a general election and fear that the reconciliation would not be achieved in time. The Liberal Party had been founded in 1859 and for over half a century, control of the government had alternated between the Conservatives and the Liberals but, during the War, the two parties had had to form a coalition in order to retain power. This coalition had been weakened because differences of opinion arose within the Liberal Party over the conduct of the War and, in 1916, the Liberal Party had split into two factions. One faction, the National Liberals, chose to remain allied to David Lloyd George, the Prime Minister. The other faction, the Independent Liberals, chose to leave and joined H.H. Asquith, the former Prime Minister.

When peace was declared in November 1918, Lloyd George had promised to make Britain "a fit country for heroes to live in" but, in the four and a half years since that promise, very little progress had been made towards fulfilling it. The task of reconstruction was enormous. The War had destroyed the lives of hundreds of thousands of young men and brought unimaginable grief and hardship to their families. It had undermined the old certainties: the confidence in authority, the power of the church, and the acceptance of a hierarchical society. It had severely weakened the economy. Industry, the source of the country's wealth, had been disrupted by the depletion of the male labour force and the diversion of production to the goods needed for war. Borrowing to fund the War had left the country with a debt of almost seven billion pounds. Although there was a desire for change, there was no consensus as to the sort of country people wanted Britain to be and the political parties, squabbling amongst themselves and vying for personal power, had robbed the country of the guidance and spirit of co-operation essential for recovery.

In the first general election held after the War, the franchise had been extended to men and some women who previously did not have the right to vote and it had been hoped that the result would be a clear majority for one party. Instead, it was necessary to form another coalition government, now made up of Conservatives, led by Bonar Law, and Coalition Liberals, led by Lloyd George who remained as Prime Minister. This government also proved to be ineffective and in October 1922, the Conservatives withdrew their support. Bonar Law replaced Lloyd George as Prime Minister and a General Election followed a month later in November 1922. The Conservatives and Bonar Law managed to retain power but the political situation continued to be unsettled.

A week before the National Liberal Federation conference was due to begin in Buxton, Bonar Law resigned as Prime Minister, having been informed by his doctor that he had throat cancer for which no treatment could be provided. The following day, Stanley Baldwin was appointed to replace him. Although it had been only six months since the last general election, speculation had already begun as to how soon another one would be called. The Liberal Party desperately wanted to regain power but a divided party could not hope to contest another general election successfully. The traditional rulers, the Conservative Party and the Liberal Party, were both aware that votes split between Liberal Party factions would erode their power and allow the newly formed Labour party to increase its influence. Therefore, the delegates arriving in Buxton earnestly hoped that the rift between the two factions of the Liberal Party could be healed.

Buxton had risen to the challenge. It did its utmost to soothe the delegates and put them into a conciliatory frame of mind. The town had been tidied up, the Pavilion Gardens were blooming, the weather was perfect, the shop-keepers were in an optimistic mood. On the first day of the conference, the delegates gathered at the magnificent Opera House and were welcomed to Buxton by the Mayor. Then the President of the National Liberal Federation opened the proceedings, reminded the delegates that the Liberal Party had to be clear as to its policy regarding the various issues facing Britain, and expressed the hope that they would use the opportunity provided by the conference and the warm welcome and wonderful facilities offered by Buxton to reflect on their current position and strive to reach a resolution.

For two days, various speakers addressed the delegates and their speeches were reported faithfully and at length by the national press and the *Buxton Advertiser*. The address by the leader of the party, H.H. Asquith, was lengthy and covered the issues that had divided the party: the Irish Question; rebuilding the relationship with Russia; the economic recovery of Germany and the security of France; the tenuous and difficult position of the League of Nations; Britain's industrial policy and the balance between trade and labour; the housing question; and the proposal for taxation of land. Mr Asquith concluded by emphasising the need for reconciliation and unity in order for the party to survive.

Those citizens of Buxton who were politically-minded were proudly aware of the town's contribution to the history of the Liberal Party and watched events with interest. Some of the gentlemen, being members of the Party, attended the conference, some read the newspaper reports and spent an evening at the Union Club discussing the issues, and those who had links with the Liberal Party entertained some of the delegates to dinner after the first day of the conference. There was much to discuss and opinion was still divided on the various topics but the general consensus was that the conference had been a success. Following the conclusion of the final session on the Thursday, the mood was optimistic and there was an evening reception at the Pavilion Hall attended by a thousand guests, including Mr and Mrs Asquith, Mr Asquith's daughter Lady Violet Bonham Carter, Lord Grey of Falladon, Lord and Lady Sheffield, and Mr Oswald Partington, M.P., the former member for High Peak.

O O O

Lady Carleton-West, the chatelaine of Top Trees, the largest and most luxurious mansion in Buxton and, in her own opinion, the leader of Buxton society, had used her connections in the political hierarchy to secure herself an invitation to this evening reception. Naturally, her family had been staunch supporters of the Tory party for many generations and it did not occur to her that her presence at the evening reception might be considered out of place or that her views were unlikely to be shared by members of the Liberal Party. Rather, she regarded it as her duty, as the leader of Buxton society, to make the delegates feel welcome and to steer them onto the right path towards a resolution of their differences. She had an opinion on every topic that was being debated at the conference and during the last two days had shared her views confidently among the members of her social circle. She had sent dinner invitations to some of the more prominent delegates but these had been declined "with regret that Party commitments prevented them from accepting."

Lady Carleton-West regarded it as her further duty to share all the details of the National Liberal Federation's evening reception with those in her social circle not fortunate enough to have been invited to the Pavilion Hall. She was confident that they would want to know who had attended, what the ladies present had worn, what Lady Carleton-West had said on the occasion and to whom, and how successfully she had resisted being taken in by all the liberal sentiment expressed there. Generosity compelled her, therefore, to give an evening reception of her own at Top Trees, as soon as possible before interest in the event waned. Accordingly, on the day after the National Liberal Federation reception, she sat down at her writing desk to compose a suitable invitation.

The reception was not intended to have any political purpose and Lady Carleton-West hesitated over what to call it. She decided to postpone that problem for the moment and consider instead the question of a suitable date. She consulted her diary and frowned as she flicked backwards and forwards through the pages and noted the many commitments she already had. She realised that it was going to be difficult to hold a reception as well as perform all her other social duties in the short time available before she and Sir Marmaduke left for London. Their daughter was getting married there. When the date for the wedding had been fixed by Lady Carleton-West and she had chosen the church and the venue for the wedding breakfast, Sir Marmaduke had discovered that, not only was he going to have the expense of a society wedding, he was also going to have all the bother of going to London to attend it. So, he thought he might as well make the disruption to his routine worthwhile by remaining in London for what was left of the Season. He saw no reason why, having done his duty by his daughter, he should not then be able to enjoy the cricket at Lord's, the racing at Royal Ascot, and the tennis at Wimbledon. Then he asked himself why he should not also travel further and take in Cowes Week. Consequently, he and Lady Carleton-West were going to be absent from Buxton for several weeks.

Before she could leave Buxton, Lady Carleton-West had a round of morning calls to make so as to take leave of her many friends. She still stuck rigidly to the Victorian etiquette of her mother's generation and always made these calls or left cards on behalf of Sir Marmaduke and herself when they were going away for any length of time. She deplored the casual attitude which younger people seemed to be adopting, the so-called "modern" informality of coming and going unannounced. Apart from her impending departure, these morning calls were essential for another reason. She wanted to be sure that as many people as possible had all the details of her daughter's wedding to the youngest son of Lord Rampley and a full description of the many wedding presents that had been received from the groom's titled relatives. She had never had such an opportunity to pepper her conversation with references to Sir This and Lady That and she was not going to sacrifice that pleasure for any other engagement, however tempting.

Thinking of these morning calls prompted an idea for the name of the reception she was planning. She realised that all of the people on whom she would have to call would also be on the guest list for the reception, so she could easily combine duty with pleasure and use the reception to serve two purposes. She would call the evening gathering a *Réception Pour Prendre Congé*. Although her absence was not really going to be of a long enough duration to warrant leaving P.P.C cards, she was sure her guests would find the title amusing and she could use the occasion to take leave of her friends at the same time as telling them about both the wedding and her triumph at the National Liberal Federation reception. That settled, she decided on a date, drafted the text of the invitation, and set about composing the guest list. Once the list was finished, she went upstairs to her dressing room and considered the gowns she had ordered from *Maison Christophe* for her stay in London. There was not going to be time to order anything new for the Buxton reception so she needed to find something suitable, and not too grand, from this collection. She selected the least formal of the gowns: an ankle-length draped affair in midnight blue silk printed with a pattern of gold motifs, which Monsieur Raymond, in return for his usual considerable fee, had created especially for her in a style which was very fashionable but cleverly adapted for the fuller figure. Lady Carleton-West felt confident that nothing more was needed to ensure a perfect evening for her guests. Her first task the next day would be to alert her usual caterers for the refreshments, engage a string quartet to play during the reception, and decide on which of her "regulars" she would ask to provide the musical highlights of the evening.

Many Buxton families were spending the evening in the comfort of their own homes in blissful ignorance of Lady Carleton-West's plans for them but this would last only until their *Réception Pour Prendre Congé* invitation was delivered – by private messenger, naturally, not by the public post.

CHAPTER THREE

The office of Messrs Harriman & Talbot, Solicitors, Notaries, and Commissioners for Oaths had been at Hall Bank for many years. It was a busy practice, well-respected by its many clients in both the town and The Park and it consisted of Mr Harriman, the senior partner, Mr Edwin Talbot, the junior partner, Mr Harriman's daughter, Eleanor, a solicitor, and James Wildgoose, the confidential clerk. The Harriman family had once lived in a mansion in the residential area of the town known as The Park but the War had reduced their number making a large house no longer necessary. Edgar, the only son, had been killed in France, followed by Wilfred, the husband of Cicely, the youngest daughter, and then by Alistair Danebridge, Eleanor's fiancé. Mrs Harriman had not recovered from the shock of so many deaths and had died not long afterwards. The house had been sold and the remaining members of the Harriman family had left The Park. Cicely had moved to Oxford House, a property owned by Mr Harriman, where she provided accommodation for visitors and supported herself and her young son, Richard. Mr Harriman had the floors above the Hall Bank office renovated and he and Eleanor, together with Eleanor's Boxer dog Napoleon, had moved there. The organisation of the office was in the hands of James Wildgoose, who had been at Hall Bank for nearly thirty years. The organisation of the household was in the hands of the housekeeper, Mrs Clayton, a war widow with two young sons, who was as cheerful as she was competent. There was a spirit of co-operation and mutual support at Hall Bank which sustained them as they all recovered from the effects of the War. Edwin Talbot, the junior partner, lived with his wife, Helen, and their two boys in a large house on Spencer Road, only a short walk away from the office and they too were part of the Hall Bank community.

At ten o'clock on Friday morning, James Wildgoose scanned the notices in the office copy of that day's edition of *The Times* which had arrived in Buxton by train from London. On behalf of Harriman & Talbot, he had sent an announcement for insertion in that newspaper and he wanted to check that it had been published. He took up a blue pencil and circled the notice in question. An identical notice would appear in the *Buxton Advertiser* the following day. The notices were addressed to "all persons having a claim against or an interest in the estate of Miss Euphemia Godwin of Godwin Hall, Green Fairfield" and invited those persons to send particulars of any such claim to Messrs Harriman & Talbot at the address specified. Four weeks previously, notices had appeared in both of those newspapers announcing that Miss Euphemia Godwin of Godwin Hall, aged fifty-four and the last surviving daughter of Mr Alfred Godwin, had died peacefully at home. The Godwin family had been clients of the Hall Bank practice for several generations and James Wildgoose was well acquainted with the family history and the numerous files and storage boxes labelled Godwin.

One of the many tasks that James Wildgoose performed each day was to check the death notices and note the name of any client of the practice whose Will was stored at Hall Bank. Many clients preferred to have their deeds and other important documents stored for them and, in the basement at Hall Bank, there were rows of locked tin boxes each with the name of the client painted on the top and the side of the box. The boxes were all stacked neatly on shelves according to a cataloguing system devised by James. James knew that Mr Harriman was Miss Godwin's executor and when he had read her death notice, he had taken out his keys for the two locks on the door of the basement and, with caution, descended the narrow stone stairs to the room below ground level and collected the large safe custody box marked Godwin. Most of the deeds and documents relating to the Godwin family were kept at Godwin Hall but Miss Godwin's Will and her personal papers were kept in the storage box. Then James had opened a file and begun the process of collating the information required for the probate application.

O O O

The Godwins had been farming at Green Fairfield for over three hundred years and during that time, Godwin Hall had passed in a direct line from one male heir to another until, in 1846, it came into the possession of Alfred Godwin, the father of Miss Euphemia, the deceased. Alfred was a younger son and had not expected to inherit Godwin Hall. However, his older brother, William, had died in a riding accident only a few weeks before he was due to be married and two years later, following a very bad winter, Alfred's father, George, had died of pneumonia. At the time, Alfred was a bachelor content with his own company and enjoying a small income and a life free of any responsibility. He had accepted this unexpected burden with patient resignation, deciding to make the best of it, and had devoted the rest of his life to improving the farm and producing prize-winning livestock.

At the age of forty-five, it had occurred to Alfred Godwin that he needed to produce a son and heir. He duly found a wife but then discovered that breeding livestock was much simpler than breeding male children. Five daughters arrived but no son. Mrs Godwin, having survived five difficult pregnancies in rapid succession, was advised by her doctor not to attempt any more. Although disappointed, Alfred accepted the lack of an heir with his usual degree of patient resignation. He was truly fond of his daughters and, being a Victorian gentleman, he ensured that they were well-schooled in all the accomplishments and manners necessary for a young lady who was expected to secure her own future by marrying a gentleman with a secure income. It did not occur to him for one minute that a daughter could inherit Godwin Hall.

On his sixty-fifth birthday, Alfred contemplated the future of Godwin Hall. In the absence of a direct male heir, Godwin Hall would pass to the descendants of his uncle, Charles Godwin, now deceased, who had been a colonel in a regiment stationed in India. Uncle Charles had not married until the age of fifty-two. His first child was a son, Alfred's much younger cousin, Thomas, who was born in 1850 and at the age of eight, was sent from India to a boarding school in Kent. When he left school, Cousin Thomas had chosen not to return to India, had secured a post as a minor civil servant, and had never ventured further north than London. Alfred and Cousin Thomas had never met or even corresponded. In his turn, Cousin Thomas had produced one son, Ernest, who was Alfred's cousin once removed, and was about the same age as Alfred's eldest daughter. Alfred knew even less about Ernest than he knew about Ernest's father, Cousin Thomas.

Because Ernest would inherit Godwin Hall, which was Alfred's only source of income, Alfred feared for the future of his much younger wife and his two unmarried daughters. Not wanting to leave them unprovided for, Alfred had consulted his solicitor, Mr Harriman of Hall Bank. That Mr Harriman was the current Mr Harriman's father. The current Mr Harriman was still an undergraduate at Oxford at the time. Mr Harriman, senior, had considered very carefully the deeds creating the entail on Godwin Hall, which ensured that the property would pass to male heirs only, and he had then considered the documents relating to Alfred Godwin's marriage settlement.

After considering the problem from all angles, he suggested a course of action which Alfred approved. He sent a proposal to the various trustees and to Alfred's heir, Cousin-once-removed Ernest, still living in Kent. With the consent of the trustees and to the relief of Ernest, who had no desire to become a gentleman farmer and absolutely no intention of ever travelling to the North, Mr Harriman, senior, drew up an agreement and drafted a Will for Alfred which provided for the appointment of a farm bailiff on Alfred's death and a life interest in Godwin Hall for his widow and then for each of his two unmarried daughters, one of whom was Miss Euphemia.

During the forty years since Alfred Godwin had executed his Will, Alfred had died, eventually to be followed by his widow and then his youngest daughter. Mr Harriman, senior, had also died and been replaced as executor and trustee of the settlement trust by the current Mr Harriman, now the senior partner. The original farm bailiff appointed after Alfred Godwin died had also died and had been succeeded by his son, family connections being very strong in this part of the world. So, for the last eighteen years, in accordance with the provisions of her father's Will, Miss Euphemia Godwin, the last remaining daughter, had been in sole possession of Godwin Hall. Together with her bailiff, Mr Robert Nall, Miss Godwin had continued her father's programme of stock breeding and the farm had prospered and everybody in the local community had forgotten that she was not the owner of Godwin Hall.

O O O

Four years ago, Mr Harriman had received a letter from a firm of solicitors in Kent informing him that Alfred's heir, Cousin-once-removed Ernest Godwin, had died in the Spanish influenza epidemic and that their client, his son and only child, Hedley Godwin, was now the rightful heir and intended to pursue his claim to Godwin Hall. The letter also stated that Hedley Godwin intended to take up residence in Buxton so as to become familiar with the locality and the farm. Mr Harriman was undecided as to whether this was a prudent move on the part of the heir apparent or a threat but he passed the information on to Miss Euphemia Godwin. However, Hedley Godwin failed to arrive. Nothing further was heard either from him or his Kent solicitors. Miss Godwin assumed that he had changed his mind and she and Mr Nall went on managing the farm as usual. That is, until six months ago. On New Year's Day, Hedley Godwin had taken rooms at Mrs Broomhead's lodging house in The Square.

Buxton attracted thousands of visitors from all stations in life and provided accommodation to suit all budgets: large hotels, inns, private hotels, guest houses, lodging houses, or a single room in a private house. Many people came for their annual holiday and stayed for a fortnight or a month. The families of merchants and manufacturers from Manchester or Liverpool, or their wealthy widows, came for the summer to escape the heat and grime of their own towns. When visitors arrived, they wished to know who else was in town and whether any of their friends or acquaintances had arrived and, by long-standing custom, the *Buxton Advertiser* published each week a list of visitors under the names of the hotels or lodging houses at which they were staying. Many titled people, retired military officers, and politicians came to Buxton and their arrival was noted by the residents of The Park. Cards were left at their hotel and invitations to local events and dinner parties were also sent.

Accordingly, six months ago, the name of the heir to Godwin Hall had appeared in the list of visitors and those who always looked at the list to check for the names of any acquaintances, noted the local name, Godwin, and made enquiries. To those who acknowledged his arrival in Buxton, Hedley Godwin let it be known that he was interested in horse riding, fishing, and shooting and he very quickly found himself part of a group of like-minded young men. He was invited to join them in their pursuit of sport and pleasure and to become a temporary member of the gentleman's Union Club. Therefore, although he had rooms at The Square, he was rarely there. He was frequently out of Buxton for a day's sport and when the weather was unfavourable he could generally be found in the bar of the St Anne's Hotel, conveniently located just around the corner from his lodgings or, in the absence of an engagement for dinner or a party, he would resort to the bar of the Union Club, even more conveniently located across the road from where he was staying. Rowdy or drunken behaviour was frowned on at the Union Club, it having been formed by gentlemen for the pursuit of more cerebral activities so, later in the evenings, Hedley and his friends would progress to the Milton's Head in Spring Gardens where they could play cards and carouse until closing time. After two months, when his social life had been arranged to his satisfaction, Hedley Godwin called on Miss Godwin with a letter of introduction. He had set himself the task of captivating her with flattery and charming manners. Mr Harriman, as a member of the Union Club, was aware of the arrival of Hedley Godwin but they moved in very different circles and had not been introduced.

O O O

Mr Harriman had learnt of Miss Godwin's death from the

farm bailiff. Robert Nall had called at Mrs Broomhead's house in the Square early in the morning on the day after Miss Godwin died. Mrs Broomhead informed Mr Nall that her lodger had left the previous afternoon saying that he intended to travel to Kent. Mrs Broomhead did not know Hedley's address in Kent and had no idea when he was likely to return, although she believed that he did intend to do so. Mr Nall, uncertain as to his current status and at a loss as to how to proceed, had called at Hall Bank to ask Mr Harriman for advice.

After expressing his sadness at Mr Nall's news, Mr Harriman informed Mr Nall that he, Mr Harriman, was Miss Godwin's executor and assured Mr Nall that, as such, he would now be able to make all the decisions that Mr Nall needed. He explained that it would be some time before a grant of probate could be obtained and that, as Godwin Hall was still a working farm, he would be very pleased if, in the meantime, Mr Nall would remain at Godwin Hall and carry out his duties as usual. Mr Harriman added that he was confident that that was what Miss Godwin would have wanted. Mr Nall readily agreed to the request and returned, greatly relieved, to Godwin Hall.

On the death of Miss Godwin, it was time for Harriman & Talbot to deal with the next chapter in the long history of Godwin Hall. Mr Harriman made a temporary arrangement for funds to be advanced to Mr Nall so that he could pay the men's wages and meet any other necessary farm expenses. He wrote to the Kent solicitors informing them of the situation and asked them to contact Hedley Godwin. Then, he asked Eleanor to take carriage of the application for probate.

CHAPTER FOUR

At ten thirty on Friday morning, Eleanor closed the file she had been working on and, followed by Napoleon, went downstairs to see James, who was in the process of copying a letter into the letter book. While Eleanor took her hat and coat from the hall peg and put them on, Napoleon sat on his haunches and watched, hoping to hear the word *walk*. He listened attentively to Eleanor's conversation with James but his hopes were not realised. Unfortunately, Eleanor had an appointment at Godwin Hall. She had arranged to call on the housekeeper, Mrs Lomas, to discuss the inventories which needed to be prepared for the probate application.

'I've had the motor car brought round from the garage, Miss Eleanor,' said James. 'It's at the front door.'

'Thank you, James.'

'Here are the copies of the previous inventories that were in the Godwin safe custody box. One for Mr Nall to revise and one for Mrs Lomas. It must be getting on for twenty years since they were last needed, so they may take a little while to bring up to date.'

'Yes, it's not a task I should welcome. Let's hope they keep good records up at the Hall,' said Eleanor as she put the documents into her satchel. 'I'll be about an hour I should think. Will you keep an eye on Napoleon for me?'

'Certainly,' said James, reaching to scratch Napoleon behind his ears. Napoleon leaned in against James' leg, watched Eleanor leave, and abandoned hope of a walk.

Eleanor went out to the motor car, stowed her satchel, put

on her motoring coat to protect her clothes from the dust of the unmade roads over which she would have to travel, and set off for Fairfield. She drove slowly down Spring Gardens because it was busy with horse-drawn carts and un-predictable pedestrians still not fully accustomed to motorised vehicles, then she picked up speed as she crossed the river, and began the steep climb up Fairfield Road. Fairfield was only half a mile from Buxton, on the north side of the river Wye which formed the boundary between the two towns.

As she drove, Eleanor reflected on the fate of Fairfield. Until thirty years ago, it had been independent of Buxton. It was in a different parish and governed by its own town council from its own town hall. Eleanor could fully understand why some Fairfield residents resented the fact that their town had been forced by the government to become part of a larger district controlled from the Buxton Town Hall. She also saw the irony of the situation. Fairfield, which had a much longer history, was now overshadowed by Buxton and their roles had been reversed.

Before and after the Norman invasion, these two areas had been part of a vast hunting forest reserved for the king. Gradually, as the forest was encroached upon by settlement, illegal at first and later legitimate, the two neighbouring settlements developed for different reasons. Fairfield was a well-developed farming community which once covered a much larger area than Buxton and supported a population three times that of its smaller neighbour. By 1255, Fairfield had its own chapel and, not long afterwards, a church dedicated to St Peter, whereas Buxton had no substantial buildings until the sixteenth century. Some of the Fairfield farms had existed since the fourteenth century, and some farming families could trace their history back many centuries. There were still a dozen or more farmhouses and cottages, which dated from the sixteenth century. Fairfield had been considered significant enough in 1783 to receive a visit from John Wesley, the preacher and founder of the Methodists.

By contrast, for most of this time, Buxton was merely a handful of crofts strung out along a packhorse route with a Well dedicated to St Anne and its fortunes fluctuated according to the popularity of the water at the Well. Buxton briefly attracted the attention of the ladies and gentlemen of Queen Elizabeth I's court, largely due to the occasional presence of Mary Queen of Scots at the Old Hall during her imprisonment. Then, the wife of Queen Elizabeth's successor, James I, preferred to go to Bath instead and Buxton returned to relative obscurity. Until the end of the eighteenth century, the poor condition of the roads deterred all but the determined traveller. It was only after the fifth Duke of Devonshire had The Crescent built in 1789 that Buxton again became popular with visitors but its most significant development and current prosperity had only begun sixty or so years ago as a result of investment by the sixth Duke.

As Eleanor drove towards Fairfield, she progressed backwards in time. The wide curve of the lower part of Fairfield Road had only been built in the 1790s to allow horse drawn carriages to avoid the much steeper gradient of the original road, it being suitable only for single horses or trains of pack-horses. Towards the top of the hill, Eleanor reached St Peter's church, the 1620 Vicarage, and the other houses clustered around The Green. Then, as she turned east into Waterswallows Lane, she reached the oldest part of the town. To her left was the southern edge of Fairfield Common, an area of grazing land recognised since at least the beginning of the thirteenth century and large enough to have accommodated a very popular racecourse in the early nineteenth century. Now, most of the area was occupied by one of England's first golf courses.

25

Lining the south side of this road, the short stretch of the town's original main street, was a mixture of former civic buildings, houses, and the town's original cottages and crofts. Further along she reached Town End, a cluster of houses amongst a grove of sheltering trees, and then the landscape opened out into gently rolling hills and lush green fields edged by the grey, dry-stone walls so characteristic of the area. Here, Fairfield could even match Buxton's Grin Low with its own Bronze Age burial mound, Great Low, excavated in 1895 by local antiquarian, Micah Salt and known to the local children as the haunted Skellybob Wood. Now the road meandered between fields dotted with grazing animals and stone barns and, on either side, the grass verges and stone walls were brightened by splashes of white from the Hawthorn, Elderflower and Cow Parsley, in full bloom at this time of year. Eleanor was now approaching Green Fairfield, an area of larger farms, many centuries old, and she turned right off the main road to follow the lane which led to Godwin Hall.

O O O

The oldest part of Godwin Hall was known to date from the sixteenth century. However, the first written record of the family dated from 1705 when a Mr James Goddwyne, yeoman farmer, of Goddwyne Farm, Fayrefeld gave evidence at the inquest into the death of a shepherd, lost on the moors in a blizzard. The family had prospered and it was in the early nineteenth century that Godwin Farm, then in the possession of Miss Euphemia Godwin's grandfather George, had been much enlarged and elaborately furnished to become Godwin Hall. The house was now the centrepiece of a thriving rural business, surrounded by a variety of solidly built and well-maintained barns, sheds, and stables, as well as a coach house and a dairy.

To people from other English counties, calling what had begun as a small farmhouse a Hall might seem a little misleading or even pretentious. The house was quite modest compared with the grand stately homes built since the late eighteenth century by wealthy landowners of other counties, who added the word *Hall* to give the name of their new residence an air of greater antiquity. In the case of Godwin Hall, the use of the word was both historically and architecturally accurate. Like many early farmhouses in the area, the original house had been built on the same principal as a medieval hall. Stone built and oak framed, it was a long rectangular building with a through passage which divided the building into two parts: at one end was a large, high ceilinged hall which served as the living and sleeping quarters for the family and their servants; the other end was a shelter for their livestock. Over time, the hall had been divided horizontally to form two floors, a staircase was added, and the upper floor was reserved for the family for sleeping and the storage of provisions.

Successive generations of the Godwin family had banished the livestock and added larger sections to their original building, using whatever architectural style was current at the time. By the Georgian era, well-proportioned extensions had been added to the front of the building as well as a stable block and coach house. It was beginning to look rather grand. The Victorian Godwins had added large bay windows, attic rooms, decorative chimneys, a conservatory, and an extension which contained a billiard room.

CHAPTER FIVE

Eleanor's arrival at Godwin Hall was heralded by the barking of the dogs and the housekeeper, Mrs Lomas, alerted by them and the sound of the motor car engine, was already at the front door. She came forward to meet Eleanor.

'Good morning, Miss Harriman. Welcome.'

'Good morning, Mrs Lomas. How are you?'

'I'm very well, thank you, Miss Harriman. Let me take your coat.'

'Thank you,' said Eleanor, as she took off her motoring coat and handed it to Mrs Lomas, who shook it energetically to get rid of the dust and put it in the motor car.

'Mr Nall is expecting you. He's in his office on the other side of the yard, if you wouldn't mind stepping this way. He would have seen you in the business room, as usual, but we didn't think it right under the circumstances.'

'Oh, is that where . . .'

'Yes,' said Mrs Lomas.

'Of course,' said Eleanor and followed Mrs Lomas around to the side of the house.

'I'll leave you with Mr Nall. Would you care for a cup of tea, Miss Harriman, when you have finished with Mr Nall?'

'Thank you, Mrs Lomas. That will be most appreciated. The roads are very dusty at the moment with all this dry weather we have been having. I'll come back to the house when I have finished here.' Eleanor turned to the bailiff. 'Good morning, Mr Nall. How are you?'

'I'm doing just fine, Miss Harriman, thank you, although

it feels right strange running the farm without Miss Godwin. I can't get over the fact that she's gone. She were no age. And as full of energy as a woman half her age.'

'Yes,' agreed Eleanor. 'It is a great pity. And I know she was looking forward to success at the Show again this year. I believe she expected to do well.'

'Oh, aye. We've some great beasts this year. Bound to win.' Mr Nall shook his head, sadly. 'Though it's not much good now though, is it?'

'Oh, will you not be showing them?'

'Do you think I could?' Mr Nall's eyes lit up at the thought of adding yet more ribbons to the trophy room. 'No-one's suggested it and I didn't like to ask because I thought maybe it would seem disrespectful like.'

'I'm sure no-one will object, except perhaps your fiercest competitors. I think Miss Godwin would approve, don't you?'

'I'm sure she would.'

'Perhaps you would like to telephone my father and ask him what he thinks? If he gives you permission, no-one can object.'

'I'll do that, Miss Harriman. That would be grand. The lads 'ud be right pleased 'un all.'

'Now, speaking of the lads,' said Eleanor, 'Their wages have been taken care of and I have here a list of their names and amounts for you to check.'

'Thank you, Miss Harriman. We don't need the indoor staff now but I've got to keep the lads on and I can't ask them to work for no pay. Though I'm sure they would if needs be. They thought a lot of Miss Godwin.'

'We all did, Mr Nall, and it will be difficult to get used to Godwin Hall without her.'

'Aye, it will that.'

'It will be some time before probate is granted so my father has arranged for the accountants to pay the wages as usual in the meantime. If you would just send your list to him at the Hall Bank office each time, he will authorise payment. Unfortunately, we shall have to prepare an inventory for the farm for the probate application and I have brought with me this, which is the most recent one. It will be quite a bit out of date I should think. I shall leave it with you so you can have a look at it and get some idea of what has to be done and then you can let me or my father know what help you need. Now, unless there is anything else, I'll go and see Mrs Lomas. I'm afraid I have an inventory for her as well.'

'There's nothing more for the moment, thank you, Miss Harriman. I'll say good day and get back to my work.'

'Goodbye, Mr Nall. Good luck with the Show.'

Eleanor crossed back to the house and Mrs Lomas said: 'I'm afraid the main rooms are in a bit of a jumble at the moment. They're not needed at the moment and we're not sure what's to happen, so the rooms are being cleaned and then we'll shut them up until they are needed again. Perhaps you wouldn't mind coming into the housekeeper's room to take your tea.'

'Thank you, Mrs Lomas, I would feel rather like an intruder in the main part of the house now that Miss Godwin's not here.'

Mrs Lomas nodded. 'Oh, I know just what you mean.'

When they were seated in the housekeeper's room and tea had been served, Eleanor said: 'This must be a very difficult time for you, Mrs Lomas. You have been with Miss Godwin for a long time.'

Mrs Lomas nodded and then sipped her tea, unable to speak. Then, when her voice was under control, she said 'Yes, I've been here at the Hall twenty-five years, eighteen since Miss Euphemia was in charge. And never a cross word. She always made it very clear what was wanted and how it was to be done, quite firm she was, but she didn't hold back with expressing her appreciation when people gave satisfaction. Reasonable and fair with everyone who served her.'

'She was very well respected,' added Eleanor.

'Oh, she was,' said Mrs Lomas. 'I know she was thought by some of the local worthies to have opinions too strong for a woman but she was a real lady, nevertheless. Knew when to speak out and when to mind her own business. She had the respect of all the farmers hereabouts and she did a lot of good in the community as well. Her father would have been proud of what she has achieved with the farm. He was right to leave Miss Euphemia in charge.'

Like many people in Fairfield, Eleanor was too young to have known the older members of the Godwin family and had only ever known Euphemia Godwin and then only as Miss Godwin. However, the older people had continued to refer to her as Miss Euphemia as though they still needed to distinguish between her and her sisters. Everyone thought of Miss Euphemia as the owner of Godwin Hall and had forgotten that she only had a life interest in it. They had certainly not contemplated a time when some "foreigner" would come from the south and lay claim to it. Eleanor anticipated that there would be a lengthy period of adjustment in the local community.

'We only ever associate Godwin Hall with Miss Godwin, don't we?' said Eleanor. 'She had such a strong personality that there never seemed to be the need for anyone else. To me, as a child, she was quite formidable but very kind and I can still remember the first time I met her. I was quite young. My sisters and brother and I used to enjoy the children's parties she gave at Christmas.'

'Oh, she did enjoy those. The Hall always looked so lovely decorated with greenery and candles and the big Christmas tree, a great log fire blazing in the fireplace, and the smell of spices everywhere.' Mrs Lomas was lost in the past for a moment and then she sighed and said: 'I don't know what's to become of it now. It's all been so sudden.'

Eleanor said: 'Yes, it was very sudden. I was not aware that Miss Godwin was ill.'

'Oh, but she wasn't! She's never had a day's illness in her life. She didn't believe in it. That is why it was such a shock.'

'So, may I ask, how did it happen?'

'Well, respiratory failure the doctor said, but I don't know what that means or what could have caused it. She didn't have a cold or anything like that although she did complain that her feet were cold from sitting in a draught that morning.'

'And there was no warning sign?' asked Eleanor.

'No, she was right as rain all morning, had her lunch and, as usual, enjoyed it. After lunch, she went into the business room. It was her day for looking over the monthly accounts so I knew she would be in there most of the afternoon and wouldn't want to be disturbed. She always rang for tea when she was finished and we knew to leave her in peace until then. So, after lunch was cleared away, Doris laid out the tea things ready and then she and I got on with our other work. We were quite busy cleaning out the pantry that afternoon, turning out the store cupboards, and putting fresh paper on the shelves. I didn't notice the time and it was a quarter past five before I realised that Miss Euphemia hadn't rung. I wasn't sure what to do because she didn't like being interrupted when she was checking figures. I thought there must have been a problem with the accounts and she was taking a bit longer than usual to sort them out so I waited. Then it occurred to me that perhaps she had already finished the accounts and gone out with her horse without wanting her tea. You can get out from the business room directly into the yard, you see. She still hadn't rung by half past, so rather than risk disturbing her I went round to the yard so as I could look in through the business room window and check if she'd left. And that's when I found her. I called Mr Nall to help. He was just in the stockyard, thank goodness, and he came straightaway. We called the doctor, of course, but we could see that there was no hope. She was quite cold.'

'And you hadn't heard her call for help at all?'

'No, I don't believe she did call but then Doris and I were in the pantry so we probably wouldn't have heard if she had. She just looked like she'd fallen asleep. Dr Morley took a while to get here because he was up at Redgate farm delivering Mrs Swann's latest and he said he wouldn't have been able to do anything anyway, even if he'd got here sooner. He said there was no sign that Miss Euphemia had been in pain or struggled for breath or anything like that. Dr Morley said she wouldn't have suffered, which was a blessing. She just slipped away.'

'And is Dr Morley the family's doctor?'

'Oh, yes, for many years. He treated Miss Florence, that's Miss Euphemia's younger sister, when she was ill before she passed away. But, as I said, Miss Euphemia, hardly ever needed him. I can't remember the last time he came, since before that last visit, I mean. That's what makes it so strange. There was no warning. One minute she was having lunch, large as life and the next minute she was gone. You never know, do you?'

'No. We none of us know.'

'And we don't know what's to become of the farm either.'

'Well, it will take some time to prepare the application and all the other paperwork, then we shall have to wait for probate to be granted. No decisions can be made until then and, in the meantime, Mr Nall will be in charge. He's keen to keep preparing the cattle for the Show and he's sure they are going to be prize winners again this year.'

'That is good news. Miss Euphemia would approve of that.'

'Now, that brings me to the reason for my visit today. Can

I leave you with this inventory which I believe was last revised when Miss Godwin took charge of the farm. We shall need an up-to-date list and there probably will be quite a few things to be added. If you have any questions or if any difficulties arise, please don't hesitate to telephone me and ask for help.'

Eleanor put on her motoring coat, said good-bye to Mrs Lomas, and drove slowly back to Buxton, enjoying the sunshine and the scenery.

CHAPTER SIX

While she was at Godwin Hall, Eleanor had very much sensed the absence of Miss Godwin's guiding hand and she had heard rumours about Hedley Godwin. She was not feeling particularly optimistic about the future of Godwin Hall but she consoled herself with the hope that if Mr Nall continued as bailiff at least the farm would survive. Eleanor had not been able to go to Miss Godwin's funeral so she had not yet met Hedley Godwin. Miss Godwin was very well-respected and Fairfield was a close-knit community so the funeral was well attended. There was a service at St Peter's church, followed by interment in the adjoining graveyard, and then refreshments at Godwin Hall for the mourners. Eleanor and Mr Harriman had intended to go the funeral service and interment but not to Godwin Hall afterwards. That would have required only a short absence from the office for both of them and could have been managed without any difficulty. However, that plan had been changed.

Hedley Godwin had not been seen in Buxton since Miss Godwin's death and he was believed to be still in Kent but, after the date of the funeral had been announced, the Kent solicitors wrote to inform Mr Harriman that their client would be in attendance and that he expected that, according to custom, Miss Godwin's Will would be read at Godwin Hall after the funeral. Mr Harriman was uncertain as to what Hedley Godwin thought to gain by this request. As Miss Godwin had only a life interest, Godwin Hall did not form part of her estate. Her bequests were made out of her personal estate and her Will was really no concern of Hedley Godwin. There were no surviving close relatives and the only beneficiaries were a few charities and Miss Godwin's employees, all of whom would be contacted by letter, so there was no need for the Will to be read formally.

Mr Harriman wondered if Hedley Godwin thought that Miss Godwin was very wealthy and hoped that he, as the heir, would be remembered in the Will with a large bequest. He was about to be disappointed. Mr Harriman was afraid that Hedley Godwin might react or try to abuse his position by interfering with the funeral arrangements or asserting rights at Godwin Hall that he did not yet have. Mr Harriman decided, therefore, that he should attend the wake to ensure that all went smoothly. That meant that Mr Harriman would be out of the office for a considerable part of the day. Edwin had to go to Manchester for the hearing of a client's claim in the County Court and would be out of the office all day, so Eleanor had to remain at Hall Bank to look after the office instead of going to the funeral as she had planned. Thus, her introduction to Hedley Godwin had been postponed.

On the evening after the funeral, Mr Harriman had given Eleanor a vivid description of the events of the day and shared his impression of Hedley Godwin. Mr Harriman's report did not fill Eleanor with hope for Godwin Hall. Mr Harriman had concluded by saying:

'I could not find that Hedley Godwin was particularly interested in either Godwin Hall or the farm. He has had no experience of farming and appears to care very little for learning about it. He wanted no information about the property and asked only about the income he could expect and how soon he would be entitled to receive it. When I attempted to explain the source of his income and the requirements of farm management, he cut me off by saying that he wasn't at all interested in those details because he intended to leave Mr Nall in charge of the farm and the breeding of livestock. He is interested only in horses and has plans to expand the existing stables. He informed me that he would be sending me details of the building programme he has in mind so that I can work out the cost and make the necessary funds available. And, of course, he wants to begin his project immediately. I'm afraid I foresee some difficulties in dealing with Mr Hedley Godwin in future, including the difficulty of remaining polite.'

Eleanor thought about this conversation as she drove back to Buxton. She decided that she needed more information about Mr Hedley Godwin and she knew who could probably supply it. She arrived at the junction at the end of Spring Gardens and instead of crossing over Terrace Road and returning to Hall Bank, she turned the motor car to the right into The Quadrant and, at the top of the hill, pulled up and parked outside Philip Danebridge's showroom.

O O O

Philip Danebridge was the cousin of Eleanor's fiancé, Alistair Danebridge and they had met after Alistair was killed in France. Philip had returned from the Front with lungs damaged by poison gas, and had taken some time to recover both from his injuries and from the loss of Alistair, his closest boyhood friend. Eleanor, shaken first by the death of her only brother and then of her fiancé had been in no better mental state than Philip and the two friends had sustained each other during their process of recovery.

'Hello, old thing,' said Philip as he opened the showroom door for her. 'Welcome to the world of refined taste and tranquillity. I'm always pleased to see you, of course, but you usually appear here when someone has ruffled your feathers. Are you in need of unruffling?'

Eleanor laughed. 'Oh dear, I'm becoming predictable. But, no, as it happens, no-one has done any ruffling.'

'Well, come in anyway.'

'But I do have a purpose in coming here.'

'Ah, well before I consider that, you must come and admire this exquisite rosewood Regency games table I have acquired. It has just been delivered by the carrier. I found it last week at a house clearance tucked away in a corner. I only discovered it by chance and no-one else seems to have noticed it so I got it for a very reasonable price.'

Philip pointed at a small oval table standing in the aisle. He drew Eleanor's attention first to the table-top and its delicate inlay pattern and then he demonstrated the several drawers and panels that slid or hinged open to accommodate games of cards, chess, and backgammon.

'It is a beautiful piece,' agreed Eleanor, when they had examined all of the table's features, and were standing looking at it. Eleanor turned to Philip and said: 'You're thinking of keeping this, aren't you?'

'Now I'm becoming predictable,' said Philip, laughing. 'That will never do. Yes, I'm seriously considering it, I must admit, but I ought not to.'

'Why ever not, if you like it so much?'

'Because in this showroom I am constantly surrounded by temptation; it is a hazard of the profession. In order to be financially viable I must make my head rule my heart. I have to let pieces go no matter how beautiful they are, and no matter how much I like them or dislike the customer.' He paused and adjusted two of the backgammon checkers which had slipped out of place. He sighed and added: 'With this piece, I confess, I really am struggling to let go.'

Eleanor watched as Philip carefully closed the various drawers and re-assembled the piece back into a side table. He picked up a polishing cloth from a nearby hook on the wall and rubbed the table gently to remove his finger marks.

'I can see why you like it so much, but it is more than just a piece of furniture to you, isn't it?'

'Yes, it is. It is a very cleverly constructed work of art made by a master craftsman.'

'Then, instead of avoiding temptation, why don't you just avoid making a decision?'

'What do you mean?'

'It's easy. Put the table right at the back of the showroom where no-one else will see it. Then no-one will make you an offer and, consequently, you won't be in a position where you have to decide whether or not to sell it. If there is no decision to be made, there isn't any temptation to be resisted, so you can just go on enjoying the table with a clear conscience.'

'Only a legal mind would come up with a devious justification like that. You should be at the bar!'

'There's nothing devious about it at all. It's a perfectly sound suggestion.'

'I'll think about it. Anyway, I noticed that you did not come on foot, what have you been doing this morning that required the motor car?'

'Ah, yes, that reminds me why I came here. I need information. You're a man-about-town and a member of the Union Club, do you know young Mr Godwin, the heir to Godwin Hall?

'Tall, dark-haired fellow, very fashionably dressed, first name, Hedley?'

'I don't know about his appearance but he is certainly called Hedley.'

'Yes. He's new in town and only a temporary member but I certainly know him. He's the sort of person you can't help noticing. He only arrived here a few months ago but he's already made his presence felt. One of those "hail-fellow-well-met" types. Offers to stand you a drink, orders one for you and one for himself, then once you've been served, spots someone else he knows, grabs his own glass and goes off saying "I'll just have a word with old so-and-so" leaving you alone with the chit. Luckily, I was put wise to that little game by a friend of mine so I've never been caught having to pay for Godwin's drinks but I've heard others complain when they receive their monthly account.'

'Ah, I see. He's of the family black sheep variety, would you say?'

'Definitely. Why do you ask? Are you following a lead? Or looking for a new tennis partner?'

Eleanor laughed. 'Neither. My interest in him is purely curiosity.'

'I'm relieved to hear it,' said Philip.

'My father is Miss Godwin's executor and I've been out to Godwin Hall to see the farm bailiff and the housekeeper. That's why I needed the motor car. I'm wondering what Hedley Godwin is likely to do with Godwin Hall and whether he will stay and run it. He seems more interested in horses than livestock and is reputed to have no experience of farming.'

'I know you can't give me any details, client confidentiality and all that, but I'd say you should probably expect the worse. I've heard plenty about him. He seems to be the sort of chap everyone has a story about, and not a complimentary one at that. He's certainly a bully and he's known to be a gambler, even rumoured to cheat at cards, although I hasten to add that I have no proof of that. He's always short of cash so I imagine he would want to get his hands on what's due to him pretty quickly.'

'Oh, dear. I hope Miss Godwin didn't get to hear about any of this before she died. It would have upset her terribly. She would have wanted someone responsible and settled to inherit Godwin Hall.'

'Yes, she would. I also heard that, being short of ready cash, Hedley Godwin is very fond of heiresses. Apparently, he was engaged to one before he left Kent. That may even have been why he left there. The heiress was described to me by a fellow at the Club as, and I quote: "Lady Isabella Ford-Hawes, pronounced Forres, aged eighteen, came out last Season, filthy rich but horsey-looking and still on the books." And don't look cross, I'm just quoting not giving my opinion. I gather Godwin thought he was engaged to Lady Isabella until her parents disabused him of the fact. As soon as they got to hear of it, Mama packed Isabella off to relatives in France and Papa showed Hedley the door and also, legend has it, a pistol.'

'Goodness,' said Eleanor, frowning. 'What complicated lives some people do lead. So, with Hedley Godwin it's probably worse than I thought.'

'Probably. Of course, what I have told you about Lady Isabella might all be a rumour that has been embellished with every telling but it is certainly the tale being told at the Club and Godwin doesn't seem to have denied it. The version of the story I heard was that he was intending to tap into the young lady's inheritance to pay off a very large gambling debt he had in Kent and, his hopes in that direction having been dashed, he came north to Buxton in order to avoid some rather unpleasantly insistent creditors.'

'So, he doesn't have any money of his own?'

'It seems not. His father was a minor civil servant who died and left Godwin with almost nothing. I heard recently that Godwin had a new target for his financial ambitions. He had his eye on the Preece-Mortimer girl and thought he was making some progress there but when he heard that the father's baronetcy was pending he rather cooled on the idea and decided to await developments.'

'Hah,' said Eleanor. 'I don't like his chances there. Mrs Preece-Mortimer will be aiming for something higher than Hedley Godwin for a son-in-law, even with Godwin Hall. I haven't met the daughter but I gather she is very attractive so she will no doubt be sold off to the bidder with the highest ranking title. Mrs Preece-Mortimer will insist on it because she is very keen to improve her own social standing and there are plenty of titled gentlemen short of cash since the War who would willingly take her daughter with the right dowry.'

Philip laughed and shook his head. He said, with mock severity: 'Lella, you are dragon! And a cynical one at that.'

'Not at all,' said Eleanor, frowning and pretending to take offence. 'I'm being purely objective. Anyway, it's true. Mrs Preece-Mortimer is most anxious to improve her status and she was quite put out when she heard that Lady Carleton-West had managed to bag the youngest son of a lord for her daughter. And Lady C.'s making jolly sure he doesn't escape. The engagement was only announced at the end of January but the wedding is in London in a fortnight.'

'That will be a bit of a set-back for Mrs Preece-Mortimer, I agree.'

'Since the confrontation with Lady Carleton-West at the charity concert in January, Mrs Preece-Mortimer has been very quiet and there have been no further clashes. I suspect she's been biding her time until Mr Preece-Mortimer succeeds to the baronetcy. Socially, that would put her on an equal footing with Lady C. and she would regard that as giving her the right to be even more bossy and overbearing.'

'Perish the thought!'

'Don't worry. The baronetcy may be in doubt. I heard a rumour yesterday that Mr Preece-Mortimer's claim to be the heir of Sir Richard Preece-Mortimer of Fenton Butler has been challenged.'

'Drum roll as the mysterious challenger enters the lists, clad in a suit of black armour, visor down, identity unknown.' Eleanor laughed as Philip added: 'Carrying a shield, of course, blue with a silver chevron. No, I mean azure and argent, don't I?'

'Yes, and your mystery black knight is, in fact, a distant cousin. Mr Preece-Mortimer's claim is through his father and his grandfather but the cousin alleges that Mr Preece-Mortimer's grandfather omitted to marry Mr Preece-Mortimer's grandmother until after Mr Preece-Mortimer's father was born, thus making him ineligible to inherit. So, unless Mr Preece-Mortimer can produce the paperwork to disprove this allegation, he may lose his claim to the baronetcy.'

'I imagine that, at this very moment, archives everywhere are being frantically searched on behalf of Mrs Preece-Mortimer,' said Philip, 'and a fearful amount of dirty linen will have to be washed in public if the challenge proceeds. Mrs Preece-Mortimer will not be happy about that.'

'No, she will not, and she will be even less than happy with the result of the laundering. So, it's possible that Lady C. may still triumph. And I must admit that I'm rather glad. Much as I find her exasperating, she means well and she does do some good in the town. Mrs Preece-Mortimer seems to me to be only interested in her own affairs.'

'I think you are probably right.'

Eleanor looked at her watch. 'I must go. Thank you for the very useful insight into the life of Mr Hedley Godwin. I appreciate your help, although I didn't find your account of him very comforting. And I must say that for men who think that women are the only gossips, the gentlemen at your club seem to do a very good trade in it.'

'There's gratitude for you,' said Philip.

'I'll leave you to get on with moving your Regency table to the back of the showroom, shall I?' Eleanor smiled sweetly at Philip, inclining her head to one side and raising her eyebrows to emphasise the question. 'Before it catches someone's eye.'

'Go!' ordered Philip, laughing and pointing to the door. 'Daughter of Eve!'

'Not at all. Besides I don't need a serpent to blame for my ideas. I take full responsibility for them myself and for my very sensible suggestion for resolving your dilemma.' Eleanor turned and moved towards the door, adding over her shoulder. 'Oh, and I'd advise you not to use Adam's defence. It wasn't very successful.'

'Out!' said Philip, as he opened the door for her.

'Are we still playing tennis tomorrow?'

'Certainly, I'll call for you at a quarter past two.'

CHAPTER SEVEN

At lunch time when Eleanor went into the dining room, Mr Harriman and Edwin were already there. With a mischievous look, Mr Harriman handed his daughter a square white envelope made of good quality paper, saying: 'This was delivered by messenger while you were out.'

Eleanor saw that the envelope was addressed to her father and then turned it over. When she saw the crest on the back she groaned as she always did when such an envelope arrived.

'Lady Carleton-West, oh dear,' she said. She took out a stiff white card on which Lady Carleton-West's invitation to the *Réception Pour Prendre Congé* was written. She read the card and said: 'My only consolation is the fact that the title of this reception seems to herald the impending absence of our hostess. Perhaps it will be an extended absence and there will be no more of her committee meetings during the summer. I am overcome with a feeling of hopelessness whenever I get a summons to attend one.'

'But Eleanor you always come back with such entertaining anecdotes. You know you secretly enjoy them,' teased Edwin.

'Hah! You don't have to sit through them, though,' said Eleanor. 'And her receptions are not much better than her committee meetings. I suppose the usual crowd will be there.' She smiled at Edwin. 'And I'm willing to bet that you are going to have to endure this reception too. Helen has probably opened your invitation this morning in your absence, and you'll find it on the chimneypiece when you get home.'

'You're probably right,' said Edwin, mournfully. 'Now I'm the one who needs cheering up. What's Mrs Clayton offering us today, I wonder.' He lifted the covers off the dishes on the sideboard and said: 'Ah! Ham salad. And devilled eggs, excellent. I can vouch for the freshness of the lettuce because I brought some from home this morning. What can I help you to, Eleanor? A little of everything?'

'Yes, please, Edwin.'

'What about you, Harriman. The same?' asked Edwin as he handed Eleanor her plate.

'Thank you,' said Mr Harriman, with a nod.

When they had seated themselves at the table, Mr Harriman said: 'You know Lady Carleton- West better than we do, Eleanor, what do you suppose this reception is all about?'

'I've not heard. I should think it will be the usual. A lot of idle gossip and some indifferent music from one of her latest protégés.'

'At least, Lady C. always puts on a decent supper,' added Edwin, 'Don't forget, though. Lady C.'s daughter is getting married soon, so perhaps it's related to that. The wedding is in London, isn't it? A titled affair as well.'

'So I believe,' said Mr Harriman. 'I suppose we should organise a wedding gift. I'd better speak to James.'

'Yes. I imagine that it is expected,' agreed Edwin. 'That reminds me, Harriman, what about the visit by the West Indies Cricket team. They are due to play against the Derbyshire County Cricket Club First Eleven on the twentieth and I was talking to one of the members of our Cricket Club when I was at Court this morning. He told me the club needs two hundred pounds to cover the expense of preparing the ground at The Park and maintaining it for the three days of the match. They were hoping for support from local businesses but so far they haven't raised even half that. They haven't got much longer and they're getting a bit concerned. I said I'd speak to you and see what we can do.'

'That's less than three weeks. It's an awful lot of money to raise in such a short time,' said Eleanor.

'Yes, it is, and the publicity from the tour will be very good for the town so it will be worth it. I can't understand why there is not more support. I think the cricket will attract just as much attention in the national press as the National Liberal Federation conference did. Possibly more considering it is sport and not politics.'

'I think we can manage something in the way of support,' said Mr Harriman. 'I'll speak to James about that as well. I'm glad you raised it.'

'Excellent,' said Edwin. He turned to Eleanor and said: 'How did you get on at Godwin Hall, Eleanor? Are they managing, do you think?'

'Well, the house feels deserted, of course, but the farm is running as usual and Mr Nall seems to be coping very well. Although, it must be difficult for him, not knowing what the heir is going to do.'

'Yes,' said Edwin, 'I certainly hope young Godwin keeps him on. He'd be a fool no to. He knows every inch of that farm and he cares a great deal about it. He and Miss Godwin made a formidable team.'

'That reminds me,' said Eleanor. 'Mr Nall is going to telephone you, Father. He wants to know if he could show some of the livestock at the Show as usual and I suggested that he should ask you what you thought.'

'I don't see any reason to object,' said Mr Harriman.

'Oh, he will be pleased. Miss Godwin has always been very successful in the past.'

Mr Harriman asked: 'Was Hedley Godwin at the Hall? I've heard nothing from him since the funeral.'

'No, he wasn't at the Hall while I was there.'

Mr Harriman said: 'According to the solicitors in Kent, Mr Hedley Godwin came here with the intention of becoming familiar with Godwin Hall but he doesn't seem to be there very often. From what I've heard he spends a great deal of time out with his sporting friends.'

'I asked Philip about him and what I learned did not inspire confidence,' said Eleanor. 'I do hope Mr Godwin is not just going to take the income and let the Hall fall into disrepair. Miss Godwin would not be very pleased.'

CHAPTER EIGHT

On Monday, Mr Hedley Godwin had an appointment to see Mr Harriman and was due at the Hall Bank office at twelve o'clock. Leaving Napoleon in her office, Eleanor went downstairs on the pretext of giving James a draft letter. He was sitting at his desk copying a court document.

'This is a letter in the Matheson matter, James. I'll leave it here on your copying pile.'

'Very good, Miss Eleanor,' said James, absently, still focussed on his task.

Eleanor lingered at his desk and James looked up. He gave Eleanor a wry smile and said: 'Is there something else I can do for you, Miss Eleanor? Or are you just curious to see the heir to Godwin Hall?'

Eleanor smiled: 'I have to confess that I am curious.'

'As am I, Miss Eleanor.'

'He telephoned to make this appointment, didn't he? Were you able to form any opinion of him?'

'I did not form a very favourable impression of his telephone manner,' said James, cautiously. 'Abrupt, possibly even discourteous, is how I would describe it. Perhaps he is not comfortable using the instrument. Some people aren't.'

'Did he say what he wanted?'

'No. He simply insisted on seeing Mr Harriman. It was last Friday when he telephoned and he expected to see Mr Harriman immediately. He was most displeased when I suggested today, that being the first appointment time Mr Harriman had available. I had the impression that he thought

I should rearrange Mr Harriman's diary to suit him and that I was inconveniencing him unnecessarily by not doing so.'

'Hmm,' said Eleanor.

'From my desk, the view of the front hall is unimpeded,' observed James, his tone impartial, 'and while I show Mr Godwin into Mr Harriman's office, the desk will be unoccupied.'

'Ah, yes. So it will,' said Eleanor, equally impartially.

James resumed his copying and Eleanor continued to hover. The grandfather clock in the hall struck the hour but Hedley Godwin did not arrive.

Eleanor waited a few minutes, undecided as to whether to wait a little longer or return to her office and then said: 'My curiosity is still burning, James, but I can't just stand here being idle. Please give me something to do.'

James laughed. He pointed to a pile of papers. 'Well, there are some letters and documents in that tray there which need to be sorted so that they can be filed. Would that be suitable?'

'Excellent,' said Eleanor, seizing the pile of paper.

By the time she had finished sorting the papers, Hedley Godwin had still not arrived so Eleanor began to put the sorted pages into their files. Eventually, the front door opened so abruptly that it banged against the door stop. James took out his watch and looked at the time: nineteen minutes past twelve. He frowned as he pocketed the watch, left his desk, and moved into the entrance hall. Eleanor slipped behind James' desk.

'Godwin, to see Harriman,' said Hedley looking at James, his tone harsh, his manner brusque. He removed his hat and, instead of keeping hold of it, tossed it carelessly onto one of the pegs in the hallway.

'Good morning, Mr Godwin,' said James, calmly, the model of politeness. He continued in a smooth, calm voice: 'Mr Harriman is expecting you. I shall let him know you are here, if you would care to take a seat.' James indicated a chair in the waiting area and went into Mr Harriman's office, closing the door behind him.

Hedley Godwin did not sit. Instead, he paced up and down impatiently, looking at the floor and turning abruptly on his heel at each change of direction. On the third turn, he looked up and suddenly noticed Eleanor.

'Is he going to be much longer?' he said, crossly.

Before Eleanor could answer, James came out of Mr Harriman's office, held the door open, smiled, and said: 'This way if you please, Mr Godwin.'

Hedley Godwin turned and moved quickly to the door. As James closed the door after him, Eleanor moved away from James' desk. She looked at James, her eyebrows raised in disbelief. James, shaking his head, resumed his position behind his desk and did not comment.

'Thank you, James. I've seen enough and I'll leave you with the pleasure of ushering Mr Godwin out,' said Eleanor as she headed for the stairs. James smiled, rolled his eyes, and returned to his copying. Eleanor added: 'I shall tell Mrs Clayton not to bother with tea for our client. The social niceties would clearly be a waste of time as far as he is concerned.'

'Very good, Miss Eleanor,' said James.

O O O

Eleanor and Edwin were already in the dining room when Mr Harriman came in for lunch. Eleanor had described to Edwin, the manner of Hedley Godwin's arrival at the office.

'Well, Father,' said Eleanor. 'Did you enjoy your meeting with the heir of Godwin Hall.'

'Arrogant young pup!' grumbled Mr Harriman, as he picked up a plate and helped himself to the chicken and salad set out on the sideboard.

'What did he want?' asked Edwin.

'Only fifteen hundred pounds,' said Mr Harriman.

'He asked you to give him fifteen hundred pounds?' asked Edwin.

'Oh, yes,' said Mr Harriman, as he sat down at the table. 'He said he would be obliged if I would arrange for him to have an advance on his inheritance. He produced a document which he said showed the details of the building programme he has in mind for the Hall. He said that he was sure the bank would accommodate him and he expected me to arrange for the funds to be available immediately as he had someone lined up already to start the work.'

'What on earth is he planning? What kind of stables cost fifteen hundred pounds?' said Edwin.

'And you refused, of course,' said Eleanor.

'Yes, and when I explained to him that the main asset of the estate is the farm and that it does not have that amount or, indeed, any amount of ready money available, he told me that I was just making excuses and that, if I was inclined to, I could easily raise the funds he wanted. Apparently, all I need to do is sell the livestock.'

'Phew!' said Edwin, pulling a face. 'That's arrogant all right.'

'Then he announced that if I would not arrange for the loan he needed he would have no alternative but to move into Godwin Hall and arrange things for himself, which he said he would do by the end of the week.'

'I suppose he thinks he could sell the livestock more easily if he was on site,' said Edwin.

'And probably most of the furniture, pictures, plate and other valuables in the Hall itself,' said Mr Harriman.

'So what did you tell him?' asked Eleanor.

'I explained to him his current status with respect to Godwin Hall and sent him away with a flea in his ear,' said Mr Harriman.

'I don't blame you,' said Edwin. 'I would have done the

same.'

'Did he say what his building programme was all about?' asked Eleanor.

'Oh, yes. He has great plans for Godwin Hall, wants to breed horses instead of cattle or sheep. He intends to turn Godwin Hall into a stud farm and wants the money for building more stables and for fencing off training paddocks.'

'He's a fool,' said Edwin. 'It's taken years to build that farm up. He'd be throwing all that away. Can't he see that Godwin Hall is a success just as it is. He'd be mad to change it. Anyway, there's no call for horses now.'

'Oh, he plans to breed racehorses, not working horses,' said Mr Harriman.

'That's even more foolish that I thought,' said Edwin.

'Fortunately, there will be a delay before probate is granted and the new trust deeds are prepared,' said Mr Harriman.

'Maybe you can take as long as possible before filing the application,' suggested Edwin. 'That might give Godwin time to come to his senses or at least give Mr Nall the opportunity to talk him round.'

'Perhaps not,' said Eleanor. 'I think there might be a more immediate need for money and for a different purpose than he is letting on. Philip told me that Hedley Godwin is rumoured to have debts, some of them from gambling. There's even a story that he came north to avoid some unpleasant creditors who were pursuing him in Kent.'

'So you think he wants the money to pay off his debts and has no intention of investing it in the farm, with or without horses?' asked Mr Harriman.

'Yes,' said Eleanor, 'some of it at least. I don't know how much he owes.'

'Miss Godwin must be turning in her grave,' said Edwin.

'I suppose Philip got his information from the Club,' said Eleanor.

Mr Harriman said: 'I don't have much to do with the younger members there so I haven't come across Godwin. I imagine his set keeps later hours than we older members do.'

'Philip doesn't go to the Club very often,' said Eleanor. 'Perhaps I should ask him to take a sudden interest.'

'It certainly sounds as though a little investigation into the affairs of friend Godwin might be warranted,' agreed Edwin.

'I think you're right,' agreed Mr Harriman.

O O O

Later that evening, Eleanor and Napoleon were just leaving Hall Bank for their after-dinner walk when a large Bentley pulled up at the kerb and Philip jumped out.

'Evening, old thing, I've just come back from Derby and I thought I'd call in on the off chance.'

'We're just off to the Pavilion Gardens. It's such a lovely evening. Will you join us?'

'Delighted to. I didn't mean to be this late. I was more successful with the bidding than I anticipated and I had to sort out transport for the pieces I had bought and then I got waylaid by a potential customer. Hello, old chap.' Philip bent down to greet Napoleon. 'Can we detour through the Winter Garden? My mother was there yesterday with a friend and she said the flower display is wonderful at the moment.'

They walked to the end of Hall Bank and continued along The Square until they came to the entrance to the Pavilion Gardens next to the Opera House. Eleanor always enjoyed strolling through the Winter Garden and she still had a vivid memory of it from her childhood: the swish of a long silk gown as her Victorian grandmother, a few paces ahead, stopped to peer through a lorgnette at an unusual plant. The Winter Garden was a relic of the Victorian belief in the benefits of exercise and fresh air no matter what the season. They had a habit of building huge public glass houses in which ladies and gentlemen could stroll during inclement weather. These glass houses also accorded with the Victorian penchant for collecting new plants from warmer climates that would not survive outdoors in England, and Buxton's Winter Garden was filled with a staple of large exotic plants and shrubs forming a backdrop for seasonal displays of flowers.

The spring flowers which, all last month, had filled the whole of the glass house with their heady scent were giving way to summer flowers whose attraction was their vibrant colour and appeal to the sight rather than the senses. Eleanor and Philip dawdled through the glass house and then emerged onto the terrace. There was still another hour of daylight so they took possession of one of the wooden benches. Napoleon stretched out on the grass and all three of them settled down to watch the passing parade of residents and tourists strolling and taking the air in the approved Victorian fashion.

'I saw Hedley Godwin today,' said Eleanor.

'Oh, where was that?'

'He came to the office to see Father and made himself very unpopular.'

'That sounds in character.'

'We are really concerned about his plans for Godwin Hall. He wants to abandon the farm and breed horses instead.'

'Does he, by Jove? I suspect he knows more about betting on them than breeding them. That would require rather a lot of capital and it seems that Hedley Godwin is not particularly well endowed in that department. On the contrary.'

'Quite,' said Eleanor, 'and Father and Edwin are worried that his plans for Godwin Hall are unrealistic. I think Miss Godwin would be extremely distressed at having her years of hard work tossed aside.'

'I think you are right. It doesn't seem fair, does it?'

'No. Father is the executor and the trustee so, at the

moment, he is in control and it will be a while before he has to hand over to Hedley but he will have to eventually. And there is also the question of the entail to be dealt with. If it seems necessary to protect the future of the farm, Father will have to argue very strongly in support of it being continued. I know it probably sounds absurd but I feel that, if at all possible, we should be taking action to protect the farm and preserve Miss Godwin's legacy.'

'No, it's not absurd. I agree with you wholeheartedly, but what can you actually do if Hedley Godwin is the rightful heir?'

'I'm not sure. The trouble is that, at the moment, we are just speculating. We don't actually know much about him, apart from the fact that he is rather unpleasant, very ill-mannered, and the subject of gossip. We need to know more, what his plans really are, whether he plans to live at Godwin Hall or put in a manager and go back down south. And, more importantly, if what you have heard about him having debts and chasing heiresses is true, whether he plans to use the income from Godwin Hall to pay these debts because that could be very detrimental to the farm. And, it would be useful to know just how much money he actually owes.'

'Hmm. I see your point.'

'The problem is that, from what I can gather Hedley spends most of his time at the bar of either the Club or St Anne's Hotel or is out with his sporting chums and, as these activities are exclusively male preserves, I cannot join in any of them, not as a spy or even for the purpose of research.'

'I have a feeling that I know where this is leading.' Philip glanced sideways at Eleanor.

'I'm sure you do,' said Eleanor, 'so what do you say? Could you spend an evening or two at the Club and see what you can find out about the man and his plans? Without arousing his suspicions, of course.'

Philip sighed dramatically for effect. 'I can think of a

better way to spend an evening than in the company of Hedley Godwin and his friends, even an evening listening to that notorious musical wonder, Miss Constance-Lavinia Poskitt, seems positively uplifting by comparison, but you are very persuasive Miss Harriman. I shall see what I can glean.'

'Thank you, Philip. I do really appreciate your help.'

CHAPTER NINE

After the office had closed on Tuesday afternoon, Mr Harriman, Eleanor and Napoleon were strolling along Broad Walk on their way to Oxford House for tea. Broad Walk was on the other side of the Pavilion Gardens from The Park where many of the large Buxton mansions, including Top Trees, had been built either in the latter half of the nineteenth century or the first ten years of the new one. The Park was purely residential and consciously exclusive; Broad Walk was for visitors.

Originally it was a winding gravel footpath which followed the contours of a river terrace and led to a bath house, the Tonic Bath, fed by a cold spring. Then, it was widened, straightened, and surfaced to provide a promenade in front of the row of large Victorian houses built in the mid-nineteenth century by local investors under supervision from the Devonshire Estate as part of the Duke's plan to provide good quality accommodation that would attract more visitors to Buxton. When the weather was favourable, Broad Walk was a popular place for visitors to stroll, meet friends or greet acquaintances, sit and read the newspaper or engage in one of Napoleon's favourite activities, which was watching people. Along the edge of Broad Walk opposite from the houses, there was a row of railings which marked the boundary of the Pavilion Gardens. About halfway along Broad Walk, at its junction with Fountain Street, was the entrance to the Gardens. Here there was a large booth where visitors to the Gardens paid for entry or showed their day, weekly, or season ticket.

At the moment, it was sunny and Broad Walk was busy but clouds were building towards the south and rain was expected. Oxford House was towards the end of Broad Walk away from the centre of the town and Eleanor and Mr Harriman were just passing the Stanley Hotel, with Napoleon a little way up ahead as usual, when Eleanor noticed a couple walking towards them. The woman stopped and said: 'Oh, Robert, isn't he adorable.' The woman was carrying a straw hat decorated with ribbon and artificial flowers. She put the hat on the ground and extended her hand towards Napoleon saying: 'Here, boy.' Napoleon, always willing to make a new friend, approached her and stood still while she stroked him along his back.

When Eleanor and Mr Harriman had caught up with Napoleon, the woman looked up and said: 'Is he yours?'

'Yes,' said Eleanor, noticing that the woman was quite young, probably no more than twenty, and very attractive.

'What's his name?'

'Napoleon. He's famous for taking up more territory than he's entitled to.'

The woman looked puzzled. 'He's very handsome.'

'I think so,' said Eleanor. 'So does he.'

The woman laughed and crouched down so that she was level with Napoleon's face and she fondled his ears. 'Hello, Napoleon,' she said. 'I love dogs. I should just adore to have one of my own.'

From the appearance of the couple's "holiday clothes" and the leisurely way they had been strolling along, Eleanor judged them to be visitors. The man was expensively dressed in spotless and well-pressed cream trousers, a striped blazer, spectator shoes in brown and white, and a Panama hat. The young woman was wearing a summer frock of deep pink patterned with red flowers and finished with a broad sash tied in a large bow at one hip. The man appeared to be considerably older than the woman and Eleanor thought that perhaps the woman was his daughter.

'Are you visiting Buxton?' asked Eleanor.

'Yes,' said the woman. 'We're staying at the Stanley Hotel.'

The man said, rather abruptly: 'Come along, dear, or we shall be late.'

'Oh,' said the woman, looking a little surprised and standing up immediately. The man took her arm, raised his hat and, bowing slightly to Eleanor and Mr Harriman, steered the woman away.

Eleanor, Mr Harriman and Napoleon continued on their way to Oxford House. The Harriman family had always been close and they enjoyed spending time together. Richard had won the fifty yard dash at his school's sport competition the previous day and was anxious to show off the ribbon stamped with the words "First Prize" that he had been awarded. Mr Harriman was very fond of his eight year old grandson and, being conscious of the fact that he now lacked a father, spent time with Richard whenever he could. Philip Danebridge, and more particularly his Bentley motor car as far as Richard was concerned, was always welcome at Oxford House. Philip had promised to call in as soon as he had closed the showroom.

After greetings all round, the family settled down at the tea-table chatting and enjoying the food Cicely had prepared. Napoleon flopped on his side next to Eleanor's chair to snooze and, from time to time, open one eye to check on the progress of consumption and the likelihood of his being invited to share in it.

When Richard had finished eating, he said to Cicely: 'May I leave the table, please. I should like to go and keep watch.'

Eleanor and Mr Harriman exchanged puzzled glances but said nothing.

'Yes, you may,' said Cicely, 'but please go and wash your hands first, they look rather sticky.'

Richard nodded as he got down from the table and then disappeared, followed by Napoleon.

'He's been reading *Treasure Island*,' explained Cicely, 'and he's been gripped by pirate fever. He's keeping a lookout for the seafaring man with one leg, the man Billy Bones was afraid of.'

'Oh, I see,' said Mr Harriman, 'the man who is going to deliver the black spot.'

'Yes,' said Cicely. 'Richard and his friend, Thomas, have been playing pirates at every opportunity recently. The other night, I was preparing to go to bed and I went into Richard's room to make sure he was asleep and there he was, wide awake and sitting up at the window. It was about ten o'clock and when I asked him why he was not in bed fast asleep as he was supposed to be, he said he was keeping a look out. That was his explanation. Then, yesterday at breakfast, he told me that he had seen a mysterious stranger but the stranger had two legs, so it couldn't be the man with the black spot.'

'Well, that's a relief,' said Eleanor.

'No, not really, because Richard said that meant Billy Bones still needed him to keep watch.'

'And did Richard describe this mysterious stranger that he had seen?' asked Mr Harriman.

'Oh yes, in detail. Not very tall, wearing a long dark coat and a hat and walking very slowly along Broad Walk. He disappeared out of sight and then after a minute or two, Richard saw him come back again, still walking slowly. The man made two more such passes along Broad Walk and then was seen no more.'

'The description doesn't sound very much like a pirate,' observed Eleanor.

'No,' said Cicely, 'but according to Richard we are all still in danger so that requires him to still keep watching.'

Mr Harriman was smiling and shaking his head. 'His imagination is very lively, isn't it? It will run away with him one of these days.'

'I think it already has,' laughed Eleanor.

'Well, like you, I thought it was just his imagination,' said Cicely, 'and I told Richard that he was not to get out of bed again in the middle of the night because he needs his sleep. The school holidays haven't started yet. I didn't expect to hear any more about this mysterious man but now I'm beginning to wonder if there is something to worry about. I heard Richard in the kitchen this morning talking to Ellen. He was telling Ellen about keeping watch and I went in, intending to shoo him out because Ellen was supposed to be preparing the breakfasts for the guests. I expected Ellen to tell him he was making things up but she didn't. She agreed with him. She said she has seen someone walking along Broad Walk exactly as Richard described. She'd been coming home from the pictures on Saturday night.'

'So the mysterious stranger may actually exist,' asked Mr Harriman.

'It seems so. Richard's description certainly fits with Ellen's description.'

'This all seems a bit odd, don't you think?' said Eleanor. 'Lurking on Broad Walk late at night. It isn't the sort of thing we're used to in Buxton.'

'It certainly is not,' said Cicely. At that point, the front doorbell rang. 'That will be Philip,' said Cicely.

'Or Billy Bones' nemesis, the one legged seaman,' said Eleanor.

O O O

Eleanor, Napoleon, and Mr Harriman had stayed longer at Oxford House that evening than they intended. That was because there had been a long discussion after Richard had gone to bed. The school holidays were due to begin in three weeks' time and Richard was going to stay with his grandparents at Wyvern Hall. Mr Harriman had agreed to take him on the train as far as Shrewsbury and Nanny Gilchrist, Wilfred's former nanny, was going to meet them there and take Richard the rest of the way. Cicely had spent some time telephoning to Wilfred's mother discussing train times and other arrangements and consulting Mr Harriman as to when he would be available. Then, when the travel plan had been sorted out, Cicely told Eleanor and Mr Harriman that Wilfred's parents were still pressing her to agree to Richard going to Wilfred's old school and wanted him to start at the beginning of the new school year. Cicely was not keen on Richard going to boarding school so far from Buxton and there had been a long discussion about what to do for the best. It was twenty to eleven by the time Eleanor, Mr Harriman and Napoleon left Oxford House to return home.

It had rained quite heavily earlier in the evening but the sky had now cleared. They were just passing Grosvenor Mansions when Napoleon stopped to sniff at something on the ground at the edge of the path. As she caught up with Napoleon, Eleanor saw that it was a strip of material and she picked it up and moved under the nearby gas lamp in order to see it better. It was wet from the rain. At first, she thought it was a scarf then she realised that it was a belt made of pink material dotted with red flowers. She remembered the frock worn by the young woman they had met on their way to Oxford House earlier that evening.

Eleanor said to Mr Harriman: 'Remember the young woman who stopped to make a fuss of Leon when we were on the way to Cicely's. I think this is her belt. It matches the frock she was wearing.'

'Yes, I remember the woman but I don't recall what she was wearing.'

'She said they were staying at the Stanley Hotel, didn't she?' Eleanor frowned: 'The woman said the man's name. What was it? Oh, I know. She referred to him as Robert.'

'I think that's what she said. I'm not sure. If they are at the hotel, I suppose the reception clerk would know who he is,' said Mr Harriman.

'It didn't look like a terribly expensive frock but even so, if the belt matches, it would be a nuisance to lose it. The frock wouldn't look right with another belt.'

'Perhaps the owner will come back and look for it. You could hang it on the railings so that it can be seen easily.'

'Yes, or I could go back to the Stanley Hotel, I suppose, and leave it at reception. It's getting late, though. I could take it tomorrow morning when I take Leon out for his walk.' Eleanor hesitated. 'No, that's too much bother. I'll take it now.'

'I'll come with you,' said Mr Harriman.

They retraced their steps and Mr Harriman said: 'Shall I take it in while you wait here with Napoleon?'

Eleanor laughed: 'No, it might look a bit odd if you try to return the belt of a lady's frock. It could lead to awkward questions. Perhaps I should take it.'

Mr Harriman laughed and waited with Napoleon.

When Eleanor returned, she said: 'Well, the man behind the desk was not very co-operative but he clearly knew the woman in question and he agreed to return the belt to her. So that's our good deed done for the day.'

o o o

'Good morning, Mrs Clayton. How are you this morning?' said Eleanor, on Thursday morning, as she passed the kitchen on her way to the dining room for breakfast. Napoleon followed and took up his usual position in the hall from which to supervise Mrs Clayton as she prepared the food.

'Good morning, Miss Harriman,' said Mrs Clayton, as she looked at Napoleon and defied him to cross the threshold into her kitchen. 'Better than some,' she said cheerfully. 'They found a young woman dead in the Gardens early yesterday morning. Alf was called to do the collection.'

After Mrs Clayton's husband had been killed at Gallipoli in 1915, she and her two young sons had gone to live with her brother, Alf, and his family. Alf was an undertaker and coffin maker so Mrs Clayton generally had first-hand information as to who in the town had died.

'Oh dear. The poor woman.'

'The gardeners found her when they went in first thing to tidy up. She was lying in one of the lakes, well, the one she was in is only a pond really. Young she was. No more than about seventeen or eighteen, Alf said. All dressed up as though she'd been out somewhere for the night.'

'But how did she get into the Gardens? They're closed at night.'

'Well, whatever was she doing there at all?' said Mrs Clayton.

'More to the point, what was she doing in a lake?'

'Exactly. According to Alf, the doctor said she drowned but how can that be? The lake's not deep enough. It's only for ornament. Not like the boating lake.'

'Which lake was it?'

'The one at the end near the Old Hall.'

'No, that's not very deep, not more than a foot or so. Do you know who she was?'

'No. Alf said he didn't recognise her. He knows a lot of local people, of course, with the sort of business he has. But there's a good many visitors in town at present. It could be one of them.'

'I've just realised. We were at Oxford House that night and we walked back along Broad Walk, of course. I wonder if the young woman was in the lake then or whether it happened later on. We'll just have to wait for the post mortem, I suppose.'

'Alf didn't say if the doctor knew what time she died.'

'Perhaps we'll hear more during the course of the day.'

'I expect we will, Mr Harriman being the Coroner. Now, I'd best get on otherwise Mr Harriman will be down wanting his breakfast and it won't be ready. I'm a bit behind this morning.'

Eleanor laughed. 'Then I shall leave you in peace, although Napoleon won't.'

'Oh, he knows his place. The tea's on the table already. It's just made.'

'Thank you, Mrs Clayton,' said Eleanor as she turned to go into the dining room.

CHAPTER TEN

Harriman & Talbot followed the practice then common to solicitors and kept "bankers' hours" and the Hall Bank office was open to the public only between the hours of ten in the morning and four in the afternoon. For the first hour in the morning and the last hour in the afternoon, James took all the telephone calls and the three solicitors were left in peace either to work on their files, consider legal problems, or research the law. At the end of the day, the three solicitors generally collected in Mr Harriman's office for a chat before Edwin left to go home. It allowed them to keep up to date with the work of the practice and the needs of their clients and it also allowed them time to discuss any relevant new Court decisions or changes to legislation that might affect their work.

Just after half past five on Thursday, Eleanor had gone down to Mr Harriman's office. Edwin was already there. It had been a particularly busy day and Eleanor had been the only one in at lunch time so they had not had chance to catch up with the news about the young woman found in the lake.

Eleanor asked: 'Has there been any information about the young woman who was found in the Pavilion Gardens yesterday?' asked Eleanor. 'Mrs Clayton mentioned it to me just before breakfast and she'd heard about it because her brother Alf was involved.'

Mr Harriman said: 'Oh, yes. I received notification from Superintendent Johnson about an hour ago. Apparently, they have not been able to identify her yet.' He picked up a document from his desk and read from it: 'June 6th 1923. Location, northern-most lake, Pavilion Gardens. Found by gardeners, seven a.m., lying face down in shallow lake. Female, approximate age eighteen to twenty, height five feet four inches, light brown hair, eyes brown, fully clothed: no coat, pink dress with red pattern, costume jewellery necklace, handbag found in the lake very wet but contained no identification. Dr Patterson examined the body at eight a.m. Preliminary estimate of time of death between 10 p.m. and 2 a.m. Preliminary cause of death, drowning but subject to P.M. scheduled for Friday. No other cause or suspicious circumstances observed. Enquiries continuing as to identity of deceased.'

Eleanor said: 'I notice that the woman was wearing a pink frock with red flowers. You don't suppose it's that woman we met on Tuesday on the way to tea with Cicely do you, Father? She fits that description and we did find that belt on Broad Walk that I thought matched her frock.'

'It's possible, I suppose,' said Mr Harriman. 'I'll let the Superintendent know and he can check at the Hotel to see if the woman is still there, just in case.'

O O O

On Friday evening, Mr Harriman drove with his two daughters up to Top Trees in The Park for Lady Carleton-West's *Réception Pour Prendre Congé*. He did not particularly enjoy such occasions but since he and Eleanor had moved from The Park to their much smaller house at Hall Bank and could no longer entertain, he was grateful for the opportunity that they provided of maintaining contact with his former neighbours. As usual, the carriage drive at Top Trees had been decked with Chinese lanterns. All of the windows on the lower floor at the front of the mansion were ablaze with light and the music of a string quartet floated out from the open windows.

The Harriman party was welcomed at the front door by Ash, the Carleton-West's butler and directed to the larger of the two drawing rooms. The string quartet, framed by two potted palms, was positioned in one corner of the large hall to entertain those waiting to enter the drawing room and be welcomed by Lady Carleton-West, alone. Sir Marmaduke had already taken refuge in his study. Eleanor knew most of the people present and spoke to those closest to her. She surveyed the scene and had to admit that it did look elegant. The brilliant colours of the ladies' frocks and the sparkle of their jewels contrasted dramatically with the sombre black and white of the gentlemen's evening wear. Lady Carleton-West greeted the Harrimans very graciously, as she did all her guests, as though they were the only people present and were doing her a great honour in attending. As they moved into the drawing room, Cicely was claimed by some friends and she moved away to join their group. Eleanor noticed that the Pymble sisters were amongst the crowd nearest the door. They were dressed identically as usual in black satin evening gowns of a style last fashionable at least forty years ago. They were the elderly cousins of the vicar, good-natured and generous to a fault but notoriously single-minded and indefatigable when it came to one of their good causes or charity projects. Eleanor watched with amusement as the two ladies spotted her father and bore down on him, one on each side, so as to capture him in a pincer movement that the Duke of Wellington himself would have admired.

'Oh, good evening, Mr Harriman and Miss Harriman,' said Miss Pymble, the elder twin.

'Good evening,' echoed Miss Felicity, her junior.

'Good evening, Miss Pymble, Miss Felicity,' said Mr Harriman and Eleanor, in chorus.

'I trust you are both well,' added Mr Harriman.

'Oh, yes thank you, Mr Harriman,' said Miss Pymble.

'We're very well, thank you, Mr Harriman,' said Miss Felicity, 'and it is so fortunate for us that you are here this evening.'

Eleanor tried not to smile. She knew what fate had in store for her father.

'You see, we would really value your advice,' said Miss Pymble.

'It's about Miss Godwin, you see,' added Miss Felicity.

'We wouldn't want you to think that we are being uncaring asking about this so soon after her passing.'

'But it really is very important, otherwise we would not think of troubling you,' said Miss Felicity.

'But you see, on the day that dear Miss Godwin departed from us, we were all at a meeting with the vicar of St Peter's discussing our joint project for the Girls Friendly Society. Both parishes have decided to combine and hold a fête to raise funds for a camping trip.'

'And Miss Godwin was good enough to come to the meeting and she very generously offered to hold the fête at Godwin Hall and we discussed whether or not that would be a suitable venue,' added Miss Felicity.

'And Miss Godwin said that if it was decided to hold the fête at St Peter's instead, she quite understood.'

'It being a more central location and more convenient.'

'But she said, if that was the case, she would gladly make a donation to our fund instead,' said Miss Pymble.

'And then, of course, only a few hours later, she was gone,' added Miss Felicity. 'and with you being her executor, we thought . . .'

'Perhaps you could advise us, Mr Harriman,' concluded Miss Pymble.

'I see, ladies,' said Mr Harriman. 'Then, perhaps if we were to go over there where it is a little quieter, we can discuss this further.' He turned to Eleanor, winked and said: 'Do you mind?'

'Not at all,' said Eleanor smiling and shaking her head. She watched as Mr Harriman skilfully steered the two elderly ladies through the crowd to the edge of the room. Eleanor turned and, seeing Dr. Catherine Balderstone standing alone by the large window which looked out over the town, she made her way over to join her friend.

'Good evening, Catherine. Are you being unsociable or can anyone join you,' she asked.

'Good evening, Eleanor,' said Catherine, turning and smiling at Eleanor. 'No, I'm just trying to avoid people who want to share their symptoms with me.'

'A professional hazard, I'm afraid. It's the same for solicitors.'

'Yes, I saw your father being kidnapped by the Pymble sisters as soon as he entered the drawing room.'

A maid approached them and offered them champagne. They stood in comfortable silence watching the guests mingle. There was a lull in the level of conversation and they heard Lady Carleton-West speaking to a group of newly arrived guests. 'You will no doubt have read the report of the Federation's reception at the Pavilion Hall given by the Honourable Oswald and Mrs Partington last week. She was the Honourable Clara Murray before her marriage, of course, one of Viscount Elibank's daughters. And you will recall that he was the member for High Peak before the War although naturally Sir Marmaduke did not vote for him. Our family has always voted Tory so we don't know them socially. His father owns the paper mill at Glossop although he was one of the members of parliament knighted when Mr Asquith resigned. I felt it was my duty to be at the reception for the sake of the town. And we know Lord and Lady Sheffield socially, of course, even though our politics differ.'

Eleanor and Catherine exchanged glances and stifled their laughter. 'Isn't she a fearful old snob?' said Catherine.

'And as usual Lady C. is expressing her opinions with

complete disregard for the political and social sensitivities of her audience,' agreed Eleanor. 'I suspect there are several Liberal supporters here this evening who have infiltrated her guest list without her realising it.'

The ladies and gentlemen who considered themselves the social elite of Buxton tolerated Lady Carleton-West and were willing to remain unoffended by her opinions as long as she provided them and members of their family with social occasions at which good food and drink were served, and they could enjoy meeting their friends at no expense to themselves, which was no small bonus given the cost of entertaining since the War.

Eleanor and Catherine caught snatches of the narrative as Lady Carleton-West continued: 'As I said to Mr Asquith, something must be done, our politicians have been so misguided recently . . .and that dreadful man Lloyd George. At least he had the decency to stay away. . . the effrontery of of the man attaching himself to our Conservative party just to keep in power, and selling honours to raise money for his own political ambitions. Chapel of course, not Church of England. I should have known what to say to him if he had attended. At least Mr Asquith is a gentleman and knows how to behave and he expressed his gratitude to me when I gave him my advice at the reception. I said that he really should consider. . . '

The background level of conversation increased temporarily as other guests moved into the space between Lady Carleton-West's group and the two friends. They were then only able to catch disjoined phrases of Lady Carleton-West's monologue. 'Mrs Asquith is quite extraordinary. Very ready with her opinions. One of the Souls, apparently. . . self-indulgent nonsense! All that boasting about being artistic and more sensitive than the rest of us. Tosh! She's the daughter of a baronet and ought to know better.'

Catherine said to Eleanor: 'I believe Mr Asquith has been

quoted as saying that " women have no reason, very little humour, hardly any sense of honour, and no sense of proportion," and I wonder if it is true.'

Eleanor laughed. 'The quotation or his opinion?'

'Well, if it is his opinion, I doubt whether Lady C.'s assault on his senses would have done much to change it. I do know that he was against allowing women to vote so perhaps the quotation is true.'

'And as I understand it, he was against that because he was convinced that all women are conservative by nature and he was afraid that they would vote for the Conservatives and not for his party and that would have upset his career.'

'And he was wrong, of course, and that served him right for generalising about women,' said Catherine.

'There's such a lot of self-interest involved in the decisions made by politicians, isn't there?'

'Absolutely. I do get tired of all this political turmoil and uncertainty, though. I very much hope we shall be spared another general election. What the country needs now more than anything is stability and firm government, not all this squabbling between the political parties and worse, squabbling within the parties themselves.'

'I couldn't agree more,' said Eleanor, 'but, at the moment, it does not look as though your hopes will be realised. From what I read of the speeches reported in the *Advertiser*, Mr Asquith's motivation in attending the Federation conference was to urge the two factions to unite because he believes that there will be another general election. And, of course, the Liberal party can only win it if it is united.'

'Good evening, ladies. You both look very charming as usual but, if I may say so, also rather sombre. Has Lady C. been overwhelming you with her reminiscences or are you thinking of the musical offerings by Miss Constance-Lavinia Poskitt which are still to come. I believe we are threatened with a performance from her later in the evening.'

Eleanor and Catherine both laughed as they greeted Philip.

'You are a welcome sight and guaranteed to relieve our gloominess,' said Catherine. 'And you look very smart too,'

Philip, as usual, was effortlessly immaculate in evening clothes which had been tailored to perfection. 'Thank you, Catherine,' he said, with a bow. 'One does one's best.'

Eleanor smiled at Philip. 'We were actually talking about politics and the prospect of another general election.'

'No wonder you looked so glum,' said Philip.

'We couldn't help overhearing Lady C.'s view on the Federation reception she invited herself to. That's what started us on the subject,' said Catherine.

'Yes, I heard about her storming of the reception,' said Philip. 'You heard about the incident with Lord Grey, I suppose?'

Eleanor and Catherine both looked at Philip and shook their heads.

'Ah, then let me enlighten you. Apparently, Lord Grey, *the* Lord Grey of Falladon, expert fly fisherman, author of a well-respected book on the subject, and much admired in fishing circles for the depth of his knowledge of the subject and his expertise with the rod, was at the reception, chatting amiably to some chaps about his favourite topic. Lady C. overheard him and she leapt in with both feet and lectured him on the advantages of our local fishing. She suggested that he might enjoy a day on the Wye and said that, if he cared to call at Top Trees, Sir Marmaduke would be only too pleased to arrange a day's excursion for him and give him some tips.'

'Oh, no!' said Eleanor and Catherine in unison.

'Fearful cheek, really, but somehow she always manages to carry it off,' said Philip.

'Yes,' said Eleanor. 'One really does have to admire her effrontery.'

'Or complete absorption in her own affairs,' added Catherine.

'You know she sent an invitation to the Preece-Mortimers for this evening, don't you?' Philip added, 'My mother heard it from her bridge partner.'

'Keeping the enemy within sight, I suppose,' said Catherine.

'They are supporters of the Liberal Party,' said Philip, 'but weren't invited to the Federation reception.'

'Ah, so showing off and letting them know how these things are done,' said Eleanor.

'And making sure they know Lady C.'s daughter is marrying into the nobility,' suggested Catherine.

'The Preece-Mortimers are not here though, are they?' said Eleanor.

'No,' said Philip, 'They "very much regretted that they had another previous engagement and were disappointed not to be able to accept." That's also according to my mother's bridge partner.'

'The feud between the two ladies is all very trivial and silly really,' said Eleanor.

'As trivial and silly as the differences between our politicians but vastly more entertaining,' said Philip. He added: 'And Lady C.'s receptions provide such a wonderful opportunity to pick up all the local scandal and gossip.'

'Ah, yes, that reminds me, Eleanor,' said Catherine. 'I want local gossip. I imagine that, as Coroner, your father will have been kept up to date with the latest on the young woman who was found in the Gardens on Wednesday. Has she been identified yet, do you know?'

'Oh, yes. I heard that someone had been found in the Gardens. What happened to her?' asked Philip.

'The medical evidence suggests that she drowned,' said Catherine. 'I suppose she could have stumbled in the dark and fallen into the lake. I say "lake" but it's only ornamental, more of a very large pond really, isn't it?'

'Yes, hardly deep enough to drown oneself in. So not likely to be suicide, then,' said Philip.

'No,' agreed Catherine, 'but one can drown in a surprisingly small quantity of water if one is unconscious at the time.'

Eleanor said: 'It's an odd place to go if she intended to harm herself.'

Catherine said: 'And Dr Patterson estimated the time of death at between about 10 p.m. and 2 a.m. A jury is bound to wonder why she was in the Gardens alone and late at night.'

'So who was she?' asked Philip.

'There's been no formal identification yet,' said Eleanor.

'I gather she had nothing with her for the police to go by,' said Catherine.

'No,' said Eleanor, 'I wondered if it might be someone staying at the Stanley Hotel that I had seen on Broad Walk earlier that day. She fitted the description and she was wearing the same kind of frock. She was with a much older man whom I thought might be her father. He seemed old enough but she called him Robert, so I suppose he wasn't. He seemed a bit overbearing. The police did go to the Stanley Hotel and the receptionist said the husband was still at the hotel but the wife had left. I don't know whether the police questioned him.'

'So, it might be her?' said Catherine.

'Possibly, but the manager at St Anne's Hotel reported this morning that one of his waitresses had not turned up for work so it might be her. She went off duty at nine thirty on the evening the young woman drowned and hasn't been at work since. He's going to the morgue tomorrow to see if it is his missing waitress. What he did say though was that she was strikingly beautiful and, if it is the waitress, he would not be likely to mistake her. But the young woman I saw on

Broad Walk was also certainly very attractive.'

'How old was the waitress?' asked Catherine.

'Eighteen, according to the manager,' said Eleanor.

'And do you know her name?' said Catherine.

'Lily Penlington. She came from Sheffield originally according to the manager but he didn't know much about her.'

'Not part of that scheme Lady C. had for the unemployed girls from Sheffield? I gather only one or two girls actually came to work in the hotels,' said Philip.

'No, she's been here for about a year,' said Eleanor.

'Well, if it is her, what a pity she didn't stay in Sheffield,' said Philip. 'She would have been better off.'

'It seems so,' said Eleanor.

Philip frowned: 'Actually, there is a waitress at St Anne's Hotel whom one would certainly describe as beautiful. I don't know her name but I've seen her when I've been at the hotel for lunch with clients. I'm afraid that all the other waitresses are rather plain by comparison.'

Catherine was looking troubled. 'I wonder,' she said, 'if she . . .'

'In fact,' continued Philip, 'I thought I saw her the other evening. I was on my way to Manchester to see a chap with rather a good collection of miniatures for sale. She was on the platform at Stockport. She was looking into the carriages as we stopped and I thought she must be meeting someone off the train.'

'I don't think that could have been her,' said Eleanor. 'The young woman was found on Wednesday morning. You went to Manchester on Wednesday evening, didn't you?'

'Oh, yes. You're right. Then, no, it couldn't have been her. It was definitely Wednesday evening that I went to Manchester. It must have . . .'

'Ladies and gentlemen!' boomed Ash. 'May I have your attention.'

All eyes turned in his direction. He was standing next to Lady Carleton-West and when the conversation had died down, Lady Carleton-West said: 'If you would kindly make your way into the music room. I am happy to announce that Miss Constance-Lavinia Poskitt has graciously agreed to entertain us with selections from La Bohème.'

'Oh Lord,' groaned Philip, sotto voce. 'Save me.' He rolled his eyes, put his hand to his forehead, and bowed his head.

'There, there,' said Eleanor, patting Philip's shoulder. 'Close your eyes and think of supper.'

Philip looked at her in despair: 'How can I possibly think of anything when that woman is squawking?'

Eleanor noticed one of the maids standing nearby and took a glass of champagne from the tray that the maid was holding.

'Here, drown your sorrows,' said Eleanor as she handed the glass to Philip.

'Oh, you are a life-saver. Do you happen to have any cotton-wool for my ears as well?'

'Ask Catherine, she's the doctor. Let's just stand as far back as possible. I think that is the only remedy.'

CHAPTER ELEVEN

The church of St Mary the Virgin, which replaced a temporary building, was completed in 1917. It was built on Dale Road to serve the growing number of households in that part of the town. Although the style of architecture chosen for the interior of the church was along more traditional lines, the designers, Currey and Thompson, very boldly decided not to use, for the exterior, the pseudo-gothic style of ecclesiastical architecture generally in favour at the time. Instead they preferred the recently developed Arts & Craft style which was more commonly used for houses. It was a bold move.

Their design was unusual, simple but elegant, and refreshingly different. A nod to the gothic style is provided by the large perpendicular style west window which allows the interior to be flooded with light and by the buttresses although they are not traditional in form. The dominant and unusual feature that they gave the exterior of the building had the characteristic steep roof of Arts & Craft buildings. It sweeps down almost to the ground and has cleverly inserted curved dormer-style windows. Surrounded by a large garden, which again was in keeping with the style of the Arts & Crafts movement and its attachment to nature, the design could be seen to advantage from all sides. The partnership commissioned for the design was based in Derby and consisted of two architects: Percy Heylyn Currey and Charles Clayton Thompson. Percy Currey had a close connection with Buxton because he was the nephew of

Henry Currey, the architect employed by the Duke of Devonshire to design many of Buxton's nineteenth century buildings, including The Quadrant, the Natural Baths, and the Pump Room.

St Mary's was only six years old and desperately in need of funds for additional furnishings and equipment. The churchwardens, of whom James Wildgoose was one, had decided to hold a garden party. Months of planning had gone into this event and everyone at the Hall Bank office had followed its progress with interest and, of course, they all intended to be there. The committee had a very small budget and were well aware that many of the people who would attend the garden party would also have very little to spend. For the cost of hiring a marque or two, the church's garden would provide an inexpensive venue. Costs and prices were kept to a minimum by asking members of the congregation to supply both labour and produce. There were plenty of bargains to be had and prizes to be won: guessing competitions, prizes for the best cakes, the largest or ugliest vegetables, and, for the children, the best colouring in. There were stalls laden with all manner of home-made products. For the price of a penny, there was all of the usual entertainment: hoopla, a coconut shy, a bran tub. There was also a fancy dress parade for the children and races for both the children and the adults: egg and spoon race, three-legged race, wheelbarrow race, and sack race. The weather was perfect and a large and enthusiastic crowd had gathered.

The organisers had very wisely arranged for the fancy dress parade to take place before the races, correctly anticipating that parents who had cleverly crafted their children's costumes, largely from cardboard, crêpe paper, scraps of material, and old sheets would not enjoy watching their handiwork being destroyed in the course of boisterous games and races. At half-past two, the master of ceremonies announced that the parade would begin in five minutes and invited the children to begin forming a ring.

Eleanor and Mr Harriman watched with amusement as various characters from novels and comics walked past them. For Richard and his friend, Thomas, there was only one possible choice of costume and Cicely had turned them into a pair of very convincing pirates. They were in the process of making sure their eye patches were in place when Rupert the Bear and Zorro arrived, followed by their parents, Edwin and Helen Talbot. There were greetings all round and admiration for everyone's creative effort.

As the Burbage Brass Band began a stirring march, the children assembled and, when the marshals had managed to capture all the strays and the circle was complete, the parade began. The judges, three ladies in flowery hats sitting at a trestle table, made notes, pointed with their pencils at various characters, and whispered their opinions to each other. As they circled, Richard and Thomas lunged at each other with swords and tried their best to look wicked, Zorro flicked his cape dramatically, which caused Rupert the Bear to battle to keep his scarf in place. Cicely and Eleanor were amused by the disdainful looks that the two rough pirates were giving to the character who was walking in front of them, a very pretty little girl about six years old dressed as Snow White. She was smiling sweetly and seemed to be catching the eye of the judges. Unlike most of the costumes which were homemade and improvised, hers had clearly been specially made by a dressmaker. Eventually, the judges had seen enough and the marshals stopped the circle. The band continued to play while the judges consulted each other and reached their decision. They signalled for the band to stop and handed a sheet of paper to one of the marshals.

'The First Prize goes to Snow White,' called the marshal. 'Miss Florence Sydenham.'

As Snow White stepped daintily forward to receive her prize, Cicely said to Eleanor: 'I wonder if that's Mrs

Crawford-Barnes' granddaughter. Her daughter, Mildred, married the Honourable Reginald Sydenham. Remember how anxious Lady Carleton-West was to have him as a guest at her reception when the engagement had been announced.'

'I do and I seem to recall that the Honourable Reginald was wealthy and dull in equal measures,' said Eleanor, turning and glancing at the crowd. 'Mildred's over there with her youngest sister, Daphne.'

'The Second Prize goes to Captain Barnard, aviator. You'll all remember how he thrilled us last year with that air race from Croydon Aerodrome to Glasgow City and won the King's Cup. Master John Critchlow. Here's your prize, although it's not a cup I'm afraid.'

Eight year old Master John Critchlow came forward. He was wearing a sheepskin cleverly fashioned into a flying jacket, a close fitting leather helmet and goggles, borrowed from his older brother, and he carried a model bi-plane. Cicely and Mr Harriman watched as Richard and Thomas looked on in admiration at the aviator's outfit, nudged each other and whispered together.

Mr Harriman said: 'I don't think it will be long before pirates are out of fashion at Oxford House.'

'Has Richard still been keeping watch for the one legged seaman, Cicely?' asked Eleanor.

'Not very diligently but the two legged mysterious stranger is still around. Richard did see him again yesterday evening.'

Before Eleanor could comment further, the marshal announced: 'And the Third Prize goes to Zorro. Master Frederick Talbot.'

The Harriman party all congratulated the Talbot party, admired the prize and then decided what to do next. The four boys wanted to try their luck at the various tests of skill until it was time for the races. Mr Harriman and Edwin agreed that they had fulfilled their family duties for the day and went off for a round of golf.

O   O   O

Eleanor, Cicely, and Helen had decided to get something to drink and had just reached the refreshment tent when Philip arrived.

'Hello, all,' he said. 'I'm sorry I'm late.'

'Hello, Philip. We were wondering where you'd got to,' said Eleanor.

'I was delayed by a customer. I've just come from the showroom.'

'I'm afraid you missed the children's fancy dress competition, said Cicely. 'Frederick Talbot won third prize.'

'So I've gathered. I met Zorro and his friends as I came in and I heard all about the aviator who came second. That seems to have captured their imagination. When I saw them, they were entering themselves in various races. They expect to triumph and they are also quite confident that you and I, Eleanor, are going to compete in the adults' three-legged race.'

'Their confidence is misplaced,' laughed Eleanor. 'Not even the egg and spoon race. We were just about to get some lemonade. Will you join us?'

'Delighted,' said Philip. 'There are deckchairs over there, you sit down and I'll get the lemonade.'

When Philip returned, he said: 'We have thirty minutes before the races begin so I suggest that we go and look at James' vegetable stall after we have finished our drinks.'

'Good idea,' said Helen. 'We've all brought large bags and I suspect Mrs Clayton is intending to buy her kitchen supplies for next week from his stall.'

Philip sampled the lemonade and said: 'Ah, that is excellent. I was thirsty after that customer. He's been in and out of the showroom three times this week trying to make up his mind between two rather expensive Dresden vases as a present for his wife. He's staying at the Stanley Hotel. He called into the showroom just as I was about to close and said he had definitely made a decision. Then we had to sort out the paperwork but I did not want to miss the sale. I was sure you would understand.'

'Of course,' said Cicely. 'We all know about having to earn a living. Oh, that reminds me, Helen.' Cicely turned to Helen and began a conversation about a guest who had arrived that morning at Oxford House who knew the Talbots.

Eleanor said: 'There's Mrs Clayton.'

Philip stood up and waved. 'Mrs Clayton, come and join us. We're just having lemonade, would you like some?'

'Thank you, Mr Danebridge, that is kind of you but I had some a short while ago. I can certainly recommend it.' Mrs Clayton was carrying a large shopping bag. 'I've just been to the cake stall. The church ladies are very competent bakers. And, of course, I've been to see Mr Wildgoose and his vegetables. Alf's carrying that bag back for me, thank goodness.'

'We're heading there next,' said Eleanor.

'What did you buy?' asked Philip.

'Asparagus and some early potatoes, a lettuce, radishes, oh, and some gooseberries that will make a lovely pie. Alf's very partial to gooseberry pie.'

'James has an allotment,' said Eleanor to Philip. Then she said to Mrs Clayton: 'Did you enter James' guessing competition?'

'Oh, yes,' said Mrs Clayton.

Eleanor turned to Philip and Helen as she explained: 'James told us that there was a debate at the churchwarden's meeting as to whether or not they could legally hold a raffle. Father's advice was sought on that point but then there was a further debate as to whether or not raffles were a form of gambling and, if so, whether the church ought be encouraging that sort of thing. So Father suggested they should stick to guessing competitions instead on the grounds that they required skill rather than luck.'

'And then,' added Mrs Clayton, 'there was the difficulty about what to guess. I suggested the weight of a marrow and Mr Wildgoose said not to be silly, the marrows wouldn't be ready until autumn.'

'What did he finally decide to use?' asked Eleanor.

'How many peas in the jar. A big jar, at that,' said Mrs Clayton.

'Very clever,' said Eleanor. 'Although considering the difficulty of guessing the number of peas, I would suggest that the competition might involve just as much luck as a raffle.'

Philip laughed. 'I realise these discussions are most erudite and absolutely vital but I wonder how you ever have time to do any legal work.'

'I sometimes wonder that too, Philip,' said Helen.

'Ignore them, Mrs Clayton,' said Eleanor. 'Where are you off to now?'

'I'm on my way to find my boys. They've gone to enter their names for the races.'

'Ours are all doing the same,' said Cicely, 'and, of course, we are expected to go and cheer them on.'

'We're going over to the races after we've been to see Mr Wildgoose's stall,' said Eleanor. 'Why don't you join us, Mrs Clayton.'

'Well, yes, thank you. I shall. That would be very pleasant,' said Mrs Clayton.

'Good. We'll meet you at the finish line in about half an hour,' said Eleanor. She stood up: 'Shall we head for the vegetables?'

'I think I'll go and look at the cakes on the way,' said Cicely. 'I'll get something to take back for tea for Richard and Thomas.'

'I'll come with you,' said Helen. 'We'll meet you at the vegetable stall, Eleanor.'

As Philip helped Eleanor up from the deckchair, he said: 'If you would care to turn slowly and look behind you, you will see Hedley Godwin demonstrating his skills.'

Eleanor turned and looked at a coconut shy a few yards away. Hedley, in shirtsleeves was aiming balls very vigorously at the coconuts without any great success and a young woman was standing beside him laughing and holding his jacket. Then he stopped, turned to the young woman and shrugged. He took his jacket from the young woman and put it back on, offered his arm to her, and the pair walked away, still laughing.

'The coat holder was Mrs Crawford-Barnes' youngest daughter, Daphne,' said Eleanor. 'Mrs Crawford-Barnes was at the prize giving for the fancy dress competition earlier. I wonder if she knows Daphne is with Hedley Godwin. I'm sure she wouldn't approve. Daphne must be his new target since if he's stopped pursuing the Preece-Mortimer girl.'

'You have to give him credit for trying but I think he may be wasting his time there.'

'Yes,' said Eleanor. 'Even when he inherits Godwin Hall, he will not be considered a suitable marriage prospect for the daughter of a wealthy Manchester merchant. Miss Godwin lived a very frugal existence and devoted all her money to maintaining the farm and furthering the breeding programme and there is not much to spare. I imagine Daphne Crawford-Barnes expects to have a grander way of life than that and if she doesn't, I am sure her mother does.'

'He's obviously still hoping for an heiress who will provide a source of income but I don't see that relationship progressing very far.'

'No, neither do I.' Eleanor laughed. 'In fact, if Mrs Crawford-Barnes catches sight of the way her daughter is behaving, I doubt it will last the afternoon. Let's go and see

James and his vegetables.'

Later on, while they were at the finish line for the races, Eleanor saw Daphne Crawford-Barnes being very firmly chaperoned through the gate and out of the garden by Mrs Crawford-Barnes. Hedley Godwin was nowhere in sight but, from the set of Mrs Crawford-Barnes' shoulders and the stiffness of her backbone, it was clear that there was no prospect of his seeing Daphne again. As she was watching that scene be played out, Eleanor caught a glimpse of a man in the crowd who looked familiar. At first, she couldn't place him and then she thought that it was the man she and her father had met on Broad Walk on their way to Oxford House. He had a woman with him again today but Eleanor was sure it was not the woman who had stopped to admire Napoleon.

CHAPTER TWELVE

Just after lunch on Sunday, Eleanor's friend Dr Catherine Balderstone telephoned to ask if Eleanor was free because she would like some advice. Eleanor and Napoleon were about to go for a walk so Catherine agreed to join them and the two friends arranged to meet at the top of Spring Gardens. Eleanor suggested that they walk up to Corbar Woods but Catherine said she needed their conversation to be private and the woods were likely to be very popular on a Sunday afternoon so they decided instead to walk up Manchester Road and then follow the roads that formed the outer perimeter of The Park. Napoleon alternated between trotting ahead and lagging behind. He paused to sniff thoroughly anything that attracted his attention and then bounded past them into the lead again.

After they were clear of crowds, Catherine said: 'Eleanor, I need your advice and I'm sorry if I am burdening you with a responsibility you won't want but, you see, I may have information that concerns the young woman found in the Gardens. It's a bit delicate, not the sort of information that anyone would want made public so I don't want to go to the police unnecessarily. But if it is relevant, I should do so. I find myself in a quandary as to what to do.'

'Hmm. Is it a question of patient confidentiality?'

'Yes, so that's why I need your advice. I thought you would know how best to proceed.'

'Tell me as much as you feel is appropriate and then we can decide.'

'Right. Well, I understand that there has been a formal identification of the young woman found in the Gardens.'

'Yes, Mr Gregory, the manager at St Anne's hotel is certain that it is his missing waitress.'

'I also understand that the police have not been able to find any information about the young woman and are trying to locate her family.'

'That's correct,' said Eleanor. 'Superintendent Johnson told my father that Mr Gregory had only the address of her lodgings here in Buxton and no other information about Lily other than that she came from Sheffield and had given him an address there. The police in Sheffield went to the address but no-one there knew anything about her.'

'Superintendent Johnson arranged for one of his officers to visit all the surgeries in town in the hope that if Lily Penlington was a patient we might recognise her photograph and be able to provide some information about her or the name of her next of kin. The police officer visited our surgery on Friday. I was out making a house call at the time and he showed the photograph to Mrs Ardern, the receptionist. Mrs Ardern has been with the surgery for years and has an amazing memory for names and faces. When she saw the photograph, she was puzzled because she thought she recognised the person in it but she didn't recognise the name, Lily Penlington. She sat there racking her brains until she could place the person in the photograph and then looked through our records.

'When I got back to the surgery, she told me what had happened and gave me the record card to look at. It was for a new patient and she was not called Lily Penlington. I had seen her only once and that was four weeks ago. She certainly was very attractive. She was aged eighteen, employed as a waitress, and she said she was married. She gave me an address on London Road, a lodging house. I read through my notes of the consultation and I saw that I had made a note that she seemed very nervous. On her first visit, I had asked her to make another appointment to see me in three weeks' time but she didn't return. I thought back to the reason for her visit and now I wonder if she is actually Lily Penlington, the dead woman, and her nervousness was due to the fact that she was lying about her identity.'

'And you are wondering whether or not the information you have about this patient is relevant to the police enquiry?'

'Well, yes, if my patient is, in fact, Lily Penlington although that is not the name she gave me.'

'Even if she was lying to you about her identity, I'm not sure that it would be relevant to the current enquiry.'

'Well, no, it's not the lie that is troubling me. There's a bit more to it than that. I have to consider my duty of confidentiality towards my patient. I need your opinion so, if you don't mind, I am going to take you into my confidence and by doing so I shall burden you as well with the knowledge I have.'

Eleanor laughed. 'Go ahead. We might as well be in this together. At this stage, you don't need to tell me the name that she gave you so that can remain confidential.'

'Right, well, as I said, the woman said that she was married and that she needed advice. She looked frightfully uncomfortable and I thought she was going to ask me about some marital difficulty which, unfortunately, does make patients very embarrassed but what she said was: "I've stopped being unwell." Of course, as a doctor one gets familiar with all sorts of euphemisms so I asked her how long it was since she last felt "unwell" and she told me and then burst into tears. Then she said: "If it's a baby I have to know. It's very important. Please can you help me?" She looked so desperate, so I asked if she was worried that her husband would not be pleased. I was hoping that talking about him would reassure her and calm her down but that just made her more upset. Then I had to explain to her that she was right to be concerned but that we would have to wait a little longer before we could be sure. I'm afraid medical science is appallingly ignorant on this topic, and it really is a disgrace. By the time we are in a position to give a confident diagnosis, it has become all too evident to the woman herself what condition she is in. She does not need our opinion.'

'Is there no test you can administer?'

'I wish there were, but no, there isn't. You would not believe the extraordinary symptoms that have been, and sometimes still are, used for the diagnosis of pregnancy. I am ashamed to say that we are no more advanced in this field than the medieval quacks of previous centuries whose methods were not far removed from witchcraft.'

'So, is it safe to assume from the fact that your patient did not come back to see you, that it was a false alarm?'

'Possibly, but if this patient is the woman in the lake, obviously she can't come back to keep an appointment. Sometimes young women come to me for advice and, before I have even asked the question, they rush to tell me that they are married. When they do that, I am immediately suspicious. Often, they are unmarried women who have got themselves into trouble and want me to get them out of it. I do not give them advice of that kind so I am always very careful. I pay particular attention to them to make sure they are telling the truth.

'This patient was wearing gloves so I could not see if she was wearing a wedding ring. It is easy to give a false name and to say that one is married when one is not and, of course, I do not ask for any proof. I have wondered whether I should tell the police about this consultation. This sort of information about a patient really should be kept confidential. If I reveal it and then, at the inquest, your father is satisfied that she is not the young woman in the Gardens, I shall have breached my duty of confidentiality for no reason but, worse, I shall have disclosed information about my patient which would make people think less of her. And yet if the information is relevant it ought to be disclosed.'

'But in what way do you think it might be relevant?'

'Well, if young woman in the Gardens is my patient and the death is unexplained, I wondered if this information might help to explain it in some way. I'm not sure exactly how. The false name and her obvious distress suggest that she was not married and, if so, the consequences for her of a pregnancy would not be pleasant. In her situation, many women have killed themselves. She may even have wanted to, although it seems unlikely that she did. But what if she came to harm because she confronted the father, for example, and maybe insisted he marry her, or she threatened to blackmail him either into marriage or into paying her money.' Catherine paused. 'Oh, in my head this all sounds quite plausible but when I describe it out loud it all just sounds like wild imagining, doesn't it? I'm probably just making a suspicious mountain out of an otherwise innocent molehill. That's what comes of spending too much time with you. Just ignore me.'

'No, if Mrs Ardern thought she recognised the person in the photograph, I think you were right to follow this up. Do you recall anything else about your patient?'

'As I said, she was very attractive, the sort of face you'd remember, as Mrs Ardern clearly did. If I looked at the record card, I could tell you her weight and height but apart from her appearance I don't recall anything else distinctive about her.'

'Well, it seems to me that, at the moment, the information you have may not be relevant and she may have given you a false address. Now that you've told me, I shall know if it does become relevant. As we find out more about the young woman, I shall be able to decide and, if the information is relevant, I will let you know. Then you can decide what to do. So I think, at the moment you can safely say nothing.'

'Thanks, Eleanor, that's a relief. Now we can enjoy the rest of our walk.'

CHAPTER THIRTEEN

On Monday evening, when Eleanor and Napoleon came in from their walk in the Gardens, they found Mr Harriman in the sitting room reading a document. Napoleon acknowledged Mr Harriman, shook himself, and then sprawled on the hearth rug, still a focal point for him even in the summer months with no fire.

Mr Harriman said: 'Eleanor, if you have no other plans for this evening, I would very much value your opinion on this report by Dr Patterson. It's his post mortem report on Lily Penlington, the young woman who was found in the Gardens. I have found it rather perplexing.'

'Certainly,' said Eleanor, as she settled herself in one of the armchairs to listen. 'I'm only too pleased to do so.'

'See what you make of this,' Mr Harriman said. 'This is what Patterson says at the beginning: " The deceased was found lying prone in about twelve inches of water with the breathing passages submerged. The body was fully clothed and positioned so that the head was towards the centre of the lake and the feet, without shoes, were approximately two feet in from the edge of the lake. I have, therefore, to consider first of all whether or not the cause of death was drowning and, if so, whether or not any underlying natural disease was the catalyst for that drowning. If not, whether there is evidence of any other reason for drowning to occur." Are you with me so far, Eleanor?'

'Yes, I think so. I see what you mean. When someone is found with the head submerged in water, that seems to us as lay people to be fairly straightforward but obviously it is quite complicated. To a medical man, at least.'

'Apparently so. I'll skip all the details of the analysis of organs, etc., and just get to the main conclusions. He says: "Fluid was present in the lungs as was pulmonary oedema consistent with drowning but these findings are also consistent with other diagnoses. Cerebral anoxia was also evident which can occur whether the deceased was conscious or unconscious at the time when the body entered the water and the breathing passages became submerged. A small quantity of algae was found in the mouth and airways. Water had entered the stomach. These facts in themselves are not conclusive evidence of drowning and, therefore, have to be considered in the context of an absence of any other cause of death." I think that you can see why I was struggling to comprehend the report.'

'Goodness, yes,' said Eleanor. 'I thought drowning was a much simpler affair than that. Either there is water in the lungs or there is not.'

'It would seem to be more complicated than that,' said Mr Harriman. 'The report goes on to say this:

"The circumstances, in particular the low water level, suggest that the deceased was unconscious either at the time she entered the water or very shortly thereafter. If the deceased was unconscious when she entered the water, there is no evidence to suggest that the unconscious state was induced by alcohol or drugs. These have been tested for. The deceased may have entered the water as a consequence of syncope or a fall caused either by collapse or tripping. There is no evidence of any clinical reason for collapse, such as heart attack, or epileptic episode. There is a small patch of very slight bruising on one side of the forehead consistent with a fall resulting from syncope. Given the position of the body and the distance between the deceased's feet and the edge of the water, I consider it unlikely that she tripped and fell at the edge itself. In addition, in the event of a fall, one would expect some evidence of an attempt to stop the fall or to right oneself once having fallen. I found no such evidence.

"Having eliminated these clinical causes, it is necessary to consider whether what I might term mechanical causes of unconsciousness were present and I shall refer to each in turn. The deceased's head may have been held underwater for a sufficient amount of time for her to become unconscious or until death occurred. However, this would require some force and there was no evidence of any force having been applied to the deceased of the kind one would expect in such circumstances or of there being any effort on the part of the deceased to resist such force. Similarly, there is no evidence to suggest that the deceased was dead before entering the water. There is no evidence of trauma, such as a blow to the head. There is no evidence to suggest that she was dragged into the lake, either unconscious or conscious. No grazing of the knees or heels, for example, no bruising on the arms, and no evidence of drag marks on the grass beside the lake.

"Turning now to the distance from the

water's edge at which the deceased was
found, it might be considered inconsistent
with her having tripped and fallen into the
water, and I considered the possibility that
she had been pushed from behind. I find
that, given the lack of appropriate evidence
of bruising or other injury, it is not safe
to reach a conclusion that she was pushed,
on the other hand, I cannot confidently say
that she was not.

"I have concluded that a diagnosis of
drowning is appropriate and that drowning
due to unconsciousness brought about by an
underlying natural disease can be excluded.
If the deceased was unconscious when she
entered the water, there is no evidence to
suggest that the unconscious state was
induced by alcohol or drugs. I am unable to
make any conclusion as to the cause of the
drowning."

'And that,' concluded Mr Harriman, 'is where the learned
doctor leaves us.'

'Hmmm,' said Eleanor. 'I can see why you were at a loss.
I feel quite abandoned myself. The doctor seems quite
confident about his conclusions but it does not provide you
with a great deal to go on as far as a verdict is concerned.'

'No, his report seems to concentrate more on what did not
cause the young woman's death than what did or might have
done.'

'I agree. He eliminates a lot of possibilities but puts forward no explanation, not even a suggestion as to a possible
cause. The report is all completely neutral. Does this mean
you will have to choose between accident or misadventure?'

'I'm not sure that even those mild conclusions are going

to be appropriate at this stage. A finding of accidental death is somehow more acceptable than a verdict of misadventure.' Mr Harriman sighed. 'A verdict of misadventure always seems to me to be an unsatisfactory choice, weak and inclusive. If I conclude that a person has died because of some ill-advised action on their part, I always feel that I should at least be able to identify what that action was. But in this case, I can't see a way forward either in terms of accident or misadventure. As it stands at the moment, I simply cannot reach a conclusion. There is nothing on which I can base it. We simply do not know what the young woman was doing when she died, unless Superintendent Johnson can come up with any more physical evidence from the scene itself.'

'May I look at the report?' said Eleanor. Mr Harriman got up from his chair and Napoleon opened one eye in order to check that no-one was leaving the room. Mr Harriman handed the pages to Eleanor and he sat in silence while she glanced through them.

'There is just one thing that strikes me,' she said. 'Dr Patterson refers to the distance between the edge of the water and the feet of the young woman. Does that, perhaps, merit more significance than he has given it?'

'In what way?'

'Well, he mentions that the young woman was not wear-ing shoes,' said Eleanor. 'Surely that is significant in itself. Then he says there is no evidence that she tripped and fell. That leaves two alternatives. Either she walked voluntarily into the pond, in which case one might expect her to remove her shoes first. Or, she entered it involuntarily, in which case one might expect her to be still wearing her shoes. Either way, shoes ought to be present.'

Mr Harriman frowned: 'Yes, I see your point. Or, if involuntarily, one or both shoes might come off but be found lying in the pond.' He paused, then added: 'Or lying beside the pond.'

'Or, might have been removed later by the hand of another party.'

'But why?'

'To give the impression that the young woman had walked into the lake voluntarily.'

'But if that was the objective, wouldn't the shoes have been left lying beside the pond?'

'Yes. So, perhaps they were removed deliberately to make it difficult to draw a conclusion as to how the young woman entered the water. So where are the shoes? I think we need an answer to that question, don't you?' said Eleanor.

Mr Harriman nodded. 'It's too late to disturb the Superintendent now but, first thing in the morning, I shall telephone and ask him about the dead woman's shoes.'

CHAPTER FOURTEEN

In the morning, Mr Harriman had telephoned to Dr McKenzie saying: 'Look here, McKenzie, there's something troubling me about the post mortem report on the young woman found in the Gardens. It's Dr Patterson's report, I know, but I'm told that he's not going to be available until the day before the inquest and I'd very much appreciate talking to you about it before then, if you can spare the time. I'll send the report over for you to read if that is all right.'

Mr Harriman and Dr McKenzie were old friends. They had shared many dinners and winter evenings together at Hare Wood, the Harriman's former home in The Park, enjoying a crackling fire and a good single malt, as they discussed and unravelled the puzzling problems which had arisen during the course of their professional lives. They were comfortable in each other's company and able to speak their minds. For the last few years, both Eleanor and Philip had been guests at some of these dinners and had joined in the discussions. Dr McKenzie had known Eleanor since she was a child and had shared her father's pride in her progress from articled clerk to solicitor. Dr McKenzie had a meeting to attend that evening at the Devonshire Hospital and agreed to drop in at Hall Bank on his way there.

Just after eleven o'clock, Mr Harriman came into Eleanor's office, pulled up a chair, acknowledged Napoleon, and said: 'No shoes.'

'Hmm,' said Eleanor, 'that is interesting.'

'I telephoned to Superintendent Johnson earlier this morning and raised the question of the shoes, and he sent one of his men to ask the two gardeners who found the body whether they saw or removed them. He has just now telephoned me to say that the gardeners saw no shoes beside the lake. If they had been removed, it must have been before the early hours of the morning because the gardeners don't recall seeing any signs that anyone else had been there. There was a very heavy dew that morning and if anyone had been there within the few hours before dawn, the marks of their presence would have been visible on the grass.'

'So where are the shoes? One might walk in the Gardens without shoes, on the grass perhaps, but it is unlikely that the young woman walked to the Gardens without shoes.'

'I agree,' said Mr Harriman. 'Even if she was driven to the gates in a motor car, one would expect her to be wearing shoes.'

'So, if we assume that she was wearing shoes and we know that they were not with her when she drowned, what are we to conclude? There are not many choices, are there?'

'No. We may yet avoid an open verdict but the Superintendent has suggested an adjournment. He wants to make further enquiries and I agree with him although I am not sure what he hopes to find.'

'Perhaps something will turn up,' said Eleanor.

Mr Harriman saw the glint in his daughter's eye and was not deceived by the disinterested tone of her voice. However, he made no comment.

'I asked Dr McKenzie if he would be good enough to come and discuss the post mortem report with us and he has agreed to come here at about five thirty.'

'That is excellent news,' said Eleanor. 'I shall look forward to his visit.'

O O O

Dr McKenzie gave the borrowed copy of the post mortem report back to Mr Harriman.

'It's good of you to come, McKenzie,' said Mr Harriman. 'I really could do with your expertise on this report.'

'Not at all, if I can be of assistance. We have been able to help each other out over the years. What's troubling you?'

'There are several points that I need clarified. Have you had chance to read the report?'

'Yes,' said Dr McKenzie.

'This is a bit delicate, I know, given that it's not your report. Please don't think that I asked you here to criticise Dr Patterson's work or question his findings. At the moment, based on his report, it seems that a verdict of accident or misadventure will not be justified and an open verdict will be the most likely but the post mortem report left me feeling that we haven't yet asked all the right questions. I don't want to pre-empt the inquest or go putting ideas into people's heads by raising issues that might be irrelevant. That will just delay things unnecessarily but I want to be quite sure that, before the inquest, every avenue has been considered. There seems very little evidence to go on but Eleanor has raised an interesting issue which we shall come to presently.'

Dr McKenzie raised an eyebrow and smiled at Eleanor. 'I see,' he said.

'Yes, Eleanor has a few unanswered questions actually and I should like to be satisfied on one or two points myself as well. So, we would greatly appreciate having the benefit of your medical knowledge to interpret the facts that we have so far. I should like to try to build a picture of what might have happened.'

'Very well,' said Dr McKenzie, nodding. 'Where would you like to start?'

'Let's look at the report first of all and then move on to the facts,' said Mr Harriman. 'We have a cause of death but no reason for that cause, if you see what I mean. In fact, the report seems to remove all of the reasons for drowning without giving any guidance as to why that occurred.'

'I agree with you there but I must emphasise that drowning can be difficult to diagnose and that is the case whether the deceased was found in six inches of water or dragged out of a raging torrent. One cannot just say "the deceased person was found in water, therefore, the cause of death must be drowning." The symptoms of drowning, such as pulmonary oedema or cerebral hypoxia, are common to other conditions as well. Dealing with a case of drowning is no different from diagnosing any other condition. One always has to consider whether or not there might have been a combination of factors involved. A careful process of elimination is required and all the evidence must be considered. Dr Patterson has followed that process to the letter and he is satisfied as to the evidence of drowning. I agree with his reasoning and his conclusion on that point.'

'Good,' said Mr Harriman, 'so we can be confident that the cause of death was drowning. Now we must consider the other medical evidence that is available. Point one. We have a young woman in a shallow ornamental pond. Are we satisfied that, based on the external evidence, or in this case the absence of external evidence, when her face entered the water she was unconscious and her breathing passages remained in the water long enough for her to drown?'

'Correct, so far. In other words, there is clinical evidence consistent with drowning,' said Dr McKenzie. 'She must have been unaware that she was drowning because the report states that there is no evidence that she struggled or tried to remove herself from the water.'

'Then, Point two, Dr Patterson says he found no evidence that her unconscious state was caused by any underlying clinical condition. So we need to ask what then caused her to be lying prone and unconscious in the water. Was it from choice, accident, or compulsion?

Dr McKenzie said, smiling: 'I think we can safely eliminate choice as an alternative. One does not set out to kill oneself by lying down in a shallow ornamental pond. As a method of suicide it is patently unreliable.'

'Precisely, so let us look at the second alternative: accident,' said Mr Harriman. 'To be fatal in shallow water, the accident, such as a fall, needs to be of the type that renders the victim unconscious. Dr Patterson has eliminated the clinical causes of a fall and also the physical evidence argues against the young woman having fallen into the pond.'

Eleanor joined in at this point: 'In fact, when one considers the distance that the woman's feet were from the edge of the pond, the position of the body seems to argue against inadvertence of any kind.'

'I agree,' said Dr McKenzie.

'Which,' added Mr Harriman, 'leads us back again to this: if she was conscious when she entered the water, how or why did she become unconscious?'

Eleanor said: 'Dr McKenzie, is it true that if water is present in the lungs of the deceased it is safe to conclude that the person was alive when he or she entered the water?'

'Generally speaking, yes,' said Dr McKenzie, 'and the converse is also true, the absence of water in the lungs may suggest that the person was already deceased. However, there are anomalies, particularly if the person is alive but unconscious on entering the water. Also, the lungs may fill with water if the body has been submerged for a period of time even if the person was dead on entering the water. However, in this particular case, I think we can safely dismiss that. There is no evidence that the body was submerged for any great length of time.'

'Hmmm,' said Eleanor. 'So, you think we should rule out the possibility that the young woman was already dead when she entered the water?'

'I think it is most unlikely,' said Dr McKenzie. 'On the clinical evidence, I think it is safe to eliminate that possibility.'

'So, if we forget the cause of death for a moment and ignore the medical issues,' said Eleanor, 'could we look at the non-medical facts that we have? If we reconsider our first two alternative explanations, that is, choice and accident, we could conclude that first of all she made a choice. She took off her shoes and walked into the water voluntarily and was conscious at the time. But then she suffered some sort of accident and became unconscious. It still leaves us with the question: why? Why she went into the lake in the first place, and why she became unconscious.'

'Yes,' said Dr McKenzie. 'I am beginning to understand your dilemma. The clinical evidence as to the cause of death seems to be quite straightforward but also inadequate. It leaves some of the facts unexplained.'

'Exactly,' said Mr Harriman. 'Most of the facts.'

'So, it would be prudent to consider the third alternative: compulsion,' said Dr McKenzie, nodding slowly.

'For completeness if nothing else,' agreed Mr Harriman. 'Although I admit that Dr Patterson has not found any relevant evidence to support such a theory.'

'No,' said Dr McKenzie, 'the facts recorded by Dr Patterson do not support compulsion.'

'And the woman was not interfered with in any way.'

'No,' said Dr McKenzie. '*Virgo intacta.*'

'And no evidence of force being used, such as the woman's head being held under the water,' said Mr Harriman, 'and no evidence of any blow that might have caused her to be unconscious.'

'Dr Patterson detected none,' said Dr McKenzie, 'and I could see nothing to suggest it.'

'When Eleanor and I were discussing the report last night, Eleanor noticed that there was no mention of the woman's shoes. That struck us both as being rather odd. I spoke to Superintendent Johnson this morning and he confirmed that the woman's handbag was found in the lake but that she was not wearing shoes and no shoes were present at the scene.'

'So what significance have you attached to the absence of shoes?' said Dr McKenzie.

Eleanor said: 'I have been thinking of possible explanations and I have had a few ideas but I am uncertain as to whether or not they fit the medical evidence. Could the woman have been rendered unconscious by some means without there being any evidence to show how that was done?'

'You're thinking perhaps that she was rendered unconscious, then dragged into the pond, and left with her face under the water, and subsequently drowned?' asked Dr McKenzie.

'Yes, although I was thinking carried into the lake rather than dragged because Dr Patterson said there was no evidence to suggest that she had been dragged there,' said Eleanor. 'I have the impression that he favours the idea that she entered the lake voluntarily.'

'Yes. I had that impression. But you are suggesting that a third party might have caused her to become unconscious?' asked Dr McKenzie.

'I am suggesting that it might have happened that way. I would just like to know if it is possible because, if so, perhaps that ought to be considered,' said Eleanor.

'So, let me get this clear. You're suggesting that she might have been rendered unconscious, carried to the pond, and left with her head in the water while still unconscious?'

Eleanor nodded: 'Yes.' Then she frowned. 'I think what I'm asking is this. Is it possible to make someone unconscious without any marks being left on the body? And would the person be unconscious for long enough to drown if they had been left lying in water?'

Dr McKenzie considered these questions for a moment, then he nodded. 'To answer your first question, yes, it would be possible to cause someone to become unconscious without using any great degree of force. It can be achieved if the assailant has the knowledge and applies pressure to the appropriate point of the victim's neck. However, there is a delicate balance between using the minimum amount of force so as to avoid bruising and the amount of force required to keep the victim unconscious long enough to move her into the pond. I suppose it would not take very long to move a victim who is lightly built and does not weigh very much.' He paused, then added: 'And, if the victim showed signs of coming round before the move was completed, one could always administer the same degree of pressure again without risking bruising.'

'So, once the victim was in the water, would she need to be unconscious for very long in order to drown?' asked Eleanor.

'No. Drowning can occur very rapidly, even in shallow water,' said Dr McKenzie. 'Within a few minutes.'

'So there would be no need to use force to hold the victim's head below the water?' she continued

'No.'

'And the evidence of unconsciousness would be masked by the evidence of drowning?'

'Yes. Cerebral hypoxia would be present initially followed by cerebral anoxia as the victim drowned.'

'And if the victim was carried to the pond, her shoes may have fallen off,' said Eleanor.

'Or been removed to give the impression that she had entered the water voluntarily,' said Dr McKenzie, 'but then why not leave them at the water's edge?'

Mr Harriman turned to Dr McKenzie: 'While Eleanor is thinking about that, I think a glass of whisky is in order.' He held up the whisky decanter and Dr McKenzie nodded.

'Sherry for you, Eleanor?'

'Yes, please,' said Eleanor. 'Thank you for giving up your time this evening, Dr McKenzie. Our discussion has been most informative and you have clarified a number of points that were troubling me.'

'I second that,' said Mr Harriman. 'I think I can see a way forward. Further investigation is certainly justified and I shall talk to Superintendent Johnson tomorrow. The question of the missing shoes needs to be addressed if nothing else.'

Eleanor said: 'Suppose there was a third party involved and the young woman was taken towards the water against her will, and one of the shoes came off in the process and was lost. Or it fell off at the side of the pond. It would look very suspicious, don't you think, if she was found wearing only one shoe and one shoe was missing or was found at the water's edge? So, perhaps the third party got rid of the shoes.'

Mr Harriman looked at his daughter and smiled. 'Sometimes, my dear, I wonder how it is that you can so readily imagine suspicious circumstances when other people, like Dr Patterson, see none. At other times, I marvel at the agility of your mind. I am thankful for both.'

Dr McKenzie laughed and raised his glass to Eleanor.

Eleanor smiled at them both and said to her father: 'Well, you said yourself that you regarded a verdict of misadventure as weak and inconclusive. A little further investigation might at least save you from having to bring in a dull verdict.'

CHAPTER FIFTEEN

Eleanor and Philip, with Napoleon by their side, stood at the edge of the ornamental lake in which Lily Penlington had drowned and watched the ducks as they variously swam about without any obvious purpose, upended themselves to feed, or scudded across the water, wings flapping and necks extended, to express their disapproval of a rival. Taking advantage of the lengthening days, they had been walking in the Pavilion Gardens after dinner.

Stretching two thirds of the way along the eastern side of the Gardens, were two interconnected artificial lakes which were formed by diverting and damming a branch of the river Wye and creating a small artificial cascade to take the water from the southern lake down to the lower lake to the north. The southern lake was the boating lake. The northern-most lake was divided into two sections by a bridge. The section south of the bridge was secluded, being inaccessible on one side, and was largely enjoyed by fish or ducks. The section north of the bridge was the shallowest section. In the severest winters in the nineteenth century, it could be partially drained so that it froze to form an ice rink. Compared with the two other sections of the lake which were in a more natural looking setting, this northern section appeared more like an ornamental pond with curved and indented hard edges. It was in this ornamental lake that the young woman had been found.

'How was your chat with Dr McKenzie yesterday? Did it resolve anything or was it a curate's egg?'

Eleanor laughed: 'It was a very good egg. He was most helpful and our discussion certainly clarified the post mortem report but it has left us with a few questions. Worse still, it has suggested to me a possible explanation as to how she died.'

'Let's go and sit over there,' said Philip, pointing to a park bench, 'and you can tell me your theory.'

'Well, this is just a starting point, nothing more, but Lily must have been somewhere near here before she died, walking towards the lake or standing beside it just as we did a few moments ago. It's sort of a natural thing to do, isn't it? The ducks attract one's attention. Or she may even have been sitting on this seat. It must have been some time after ten o'clock at night. So the first thing I asked myself is, why was she here and was she alone?'

'At that time of night, it seems unlikely that she would be alone, doesn't it? Girls of her age are more likely to be with a group of friends. Unless, of course, she was with a group and there'd been a falling out.'

'That's possible, I suppose. Perhaps she was sulking and went off on her own.'

'Surely there would have been other people in the Gardens as well.'

'Probably not, it had rained quite heavily earlier in the evening so that had probably discouraged most people. And the band performance had been cancelled so there was no reason to stay.'

'But that still doesn't explain how she came to be in the pond, does it? It is simply not credible that she would have lain down in the water and drowned herself. But, don't let me distract you. Tell me your idea. Let's assume someone else was involved, what happened?'

'All right. Suppose you decide to dispose of me. Obviously, you don't want to leave any incriminating evidence. We are close to the lake and you strangle me but not fully, just enough to make me faint but not enough to kill me. While I am unconscious you carry me to the lake and lay me down in it. It's deep enough for my nose and mouth to be under the water. I stay unconscious just long enough to drown.'

'But even if I don't strangle you fully, wouldn't there be evidence, bruising or some such?'

'According to Dr McKenzie, not if you know what you are doing and use only enough pressure to cause me to pass out.'

'A sort of half-strangle rather than a full one.'

'Yes. Something like that. Do you think the average person would know how to half-strangle a person?'

'I don't know about half-strangle but you can certainly make someone faint quite easily. It's an old schoolboy trick. We used to play it on the new boys at my school. If you get behind the person and hold them in a particular way, the blood supply to the brain slows down and they pass out.'

'School boys do the oddest things,' said Eleanor.

'I'm sure your brother Edgar would have known of it. You are probably lucky he didn't try it on you and your sisters during the school holidays.'

'It sounds rather unpleasant so I'm not going to ask you to demonstrate it on me.'

'All right. Let's try to reconstruct this,' said Philip. 'In order for this to work, the half-strangulation would have to occur fairly close to the edge of the lake. If you were sitting alone on this park bench, say, and I came along and found you here, I would have to persuade you to stand up and walk towards the lake with me before I half-strangled you.'

'Yes, because if you half-strangled me here and then had to take me to the lake I might regain consciousness before you got me into the water.'

'However, my task would be much easier if we were walking together towards the pond because you would be off-guard.' Philip stood up and walked towards the path leading to the lake. Eleanor and Napoleon followed. 'So let's imagine we have walked along the path and we have reached this point. I half-strangle you causing you to faint. Then I drag you to the lake.'

'No, because there were no drag marks.'

'Hmm, so I must have carried you.'

'Then you must have walked a couple of steps into the lake in order to put me where I was found,' said Eleanor.

'I don't have time to stop and take off my shoes so I get them and my feet wet?'

'That wouldn't matter because wet footsteps are not going to show up on the grass in the morning, are they?'

'No, but I'm not going to be very comfortable walking to wherever it is I walk to next.' They stood staring at the lake.

'Wait a minute,' said Philip. 'What about this, we are standing by the lake and you are looking at the ducks, or just staring into space, anyway you are not paying attention. I come up behind you and take the opportunity to half-strangle you, you faint and, as you lose consciousness, you stagger forward into the lake.'

'You would have to catch me and lower me into the lake, though, because there was no evidence of a fall such as bruising.' Eleanor thought for a minute and then said: 'That could certainly work as a method of disposing of me. But if that is what happened I would still be wearing shoes. And the really odd thing that I noticed from the post mortem report was that Lily wasn't wearing any shoes.'

'Oh. Let me think about this.' Philip turned to go back to the park bench. Napoleon sat and contemplated the people wandering in the Gardens. Philip sat with his eyes closed imagining the scene. 'So, when they find you in the lake, you have no shoes. If you'd walked into the lake voluntarily you would most likely have kicked them off first. But if I have carried you into the lake, you would still have them on.'

'And if I have no shoes on, where are they? Why are they not on the grass or on my feet?'

'If I wanted to give the impression that you had walked into the lake voluntarily, I would have made sure the shoes were left on the grass beside the lake, wouldn't I?'

'Yes, even if the shoes were still on my feet when you put me in the lake. You would have taken them off me.'

'So, what has your fertile brain concocted as an explanation for this riddle?'

'Well,' said Eleanor. 'When Leon and I were walking in the Gardens at lunch time, I saw a woman pushing a pram and a toddler walking beside her. The woman noticed that the child had lost a shoe and went back a few paces to look for it. Then she put the shoe back on the child's foot. It reminded me of when Richard was small, too small to dress himself and someone had to put his shoes on for him. He wouldn't help at all; he'd just let his foot go limp and it would hang at an angle. Manoeuvring his foot into the shoe was always difficult. Also, if they were sandals, you had to undo the strap to get the sandal back on. Getting his shoes off was never a problem, even the sandals. They would just slide off. So, going back to our imagined scene. You half-strangle me, I faint and go limp, you pick me up and one of my shoes falls off.'

'I carry you to the lake. After I have drowned you, I notice that you have only one shoe on and I think that might look suspicious.'

'Or, maybe you don't notice but, as you are walking away, you trip over my abandoned shoe. And you go back and try to put it on my now limp foot. It's not easy and you get impatient so you give up and you take off the other shoe instead. Then you think, wrongly as it turns out, that if I have no shoes on, it will look as though I went into the lake alive and of my own volition. On a whim. To paddle or something.'

'That's possible, I suppose.' Philip laughed. 'Maybe I want to give the impression that you were overcome with the grief of spurned love and walked into the lake, like poor mad Ophelia.'

'But why wouldn't you just put the shoes down on the grass or, better still, toss them randomly to give the impression either of distraught abandonment or madness. Surely, taking the shoes away arouses suspicion.'

'That's definitely a sticking point, isn't it?'

'Maybe you heard someone coming and didn't have time to do anything convincing with them. You had to disappear quickly, still with the shoes in your hands.'

Philip said: 'Or maybe I just wanted people to think that you walked there barefoot because you were being Ophelia. I don't know. I give up.'

'So do I,' said Eleanor as she stood up. Napoleon was immediately on his feet anticipating action. 'I'm probably imagining something that never occurred but I can't help having this nagging feeling that there is something we are missing. As Father said when we were talking with Dr McKenzie, I seem to be able to imagine suspicious circumstances when other people see none.'

'Well, old thing, that has proven to be of benefit in the past,' said Philip, as he too stood up. 'Let's keep walking, shall we? If you forget about the problem for a bit, maybe the facts will sort themselves out in your head.'

'Good idea. Let's walk down to the tennis courts and see who's playing.'

They walked away from the lake and turned in the direction of the courts. After they had gone about fifty yards, Philip suddenly stopped.

'No wait!' he said.

Eleanor and Napoleon both stopped. Eleanor looked at Philip in alarm thinking that something was wrong.

'Something has just occurred to me. Maybe you are right

about the half-strangulation. It's a method that doesn't require a weapon or any prior preparation. It could be used on the spur of the moment. Perhaps I hadn't planned to do away with you and you made me very angry for some reason. I react without thinking about what I am doing and I dispose of you in the lake and then, when the sudden burst of anger is over, I realise the consequences of what I have done. I think I had better try to make it look as though you had fallen into the lake by accident and then I notice you are wearing only one shoe and that doesn't seem right and, as you suggested, I try but can't get the other shoe back on. My mind is racing and then all I can think of is to take the other shoe off and leave them both on the grass. And then I think, if I do that, the shoes will have my fingerprints on them, the use of fingerprints by the police now being common knowledge. I shall have no explanation for my fingerprints being on your shoes. I panic and I take the shoes away with me, intending to get rid of them later.'

Eleanor looked at Philip stunned. 'That is brilliant!'

'I thought so,' said Philip modestly. 'Allow me to present it to you as a gift.'

'Thank you. You know, if a third party was involved, that could very well be what happened.' Eleanor frowned as she thought about what Philip had said. 'And the fingerprints on the shoes! Of course. Why did I not think of that?'

'You don't seriously expect me to answer that question, do you?' said Philip, laughing.

Eleanor pulled a face at him. 'Of course, fingerprints can be wiped off but if you wipe them off, my fingerprints are going to be wiped off as well, and you realise that the absence of my fingerprints on my own shoes will arouse suspicion. So, which alternative would it be best to choose? To wipe or not to wipe? That is the question.'

'And if one is in a panic, one is not going to stand there calmly soliloquising to an imaginary audience and trying to find a logical solution.'

'You're right. So, disposing of the shoes is the best choice. Yes, it is a brilliant suggestion.'

'Or,' said Philip, 'having made the choice in a blind panic, I later realise that it was the best thing to do because it creates confusion as to what actually happened. Witness our present agonising indecision.'

'Either explanation will do.'

'Good. So now all you have to do is work out what made me angry enough to half-strangle you. In the meantime, shall we go and watch the tennis? Come on, Napoleon. Let's go.'

CHAPTER SIXTEEN

On Friday morning, after Edwin Talbot had arrived at the office, the three solicitors sat in Mr Harriman's office discussing the inquest on Lily Penlington that was to take place that afternoon.

'I'm not expecting to take lay evidence this afternoon,' said Mr Harriman. 'Superintendent Johnson and I have agreed that I shall just take evidence of identification and deal with the medical evidence.'

'I think that is the wisest course, Harriman,' said Edwin. 'There may be nothing in this business with the shoes but, as you say, it would be prudent to allow time for some further investigation. There seem to be some loose ends that do need to be tidied up. Although I can see that Eleanor regards them more as leads to be followed up.' He smiled at his former articled clerk. 'And she does have a habit of producing answers.'

'I would really like the opportunity to speak to some of the waitresses at the St Anne's hotel,' said Eleanor. 'Just to get an impression of what Lily was like but I don't suppose Superintendent Johnson would welcome my interference.'

'No, he wouldn't,' said Mr Harriman, firmly. 'However, I know Superintendent Johnson has taken statements from some of the people at the hotel and he will provide them to me this afternoon so you can read them then if you like.'

'Thank you,' said Eleanor. 'I shall look forward to that.'

'In the meantime,' said Edwin, 'we all have other work to do. I'm in Court this morning. What have you got on,

Eleanor.'

Mr Harriman said: 'After my recent encounter with Hedley Godwin, I'm fairly confident that he will not be able to find the money to begin carrying out his proposal to build stables at Godwin Hall. However, I want to be sure that he's not interfering in any way with the operation of the farm or purloining property, so I've asked Eleanor to go and see Mrs Lomas, ostensibly to talk about the inventory for the house but, in reality, so that she can check on the general state of affairs.'

'Yes, I've planned to go this morning as soon as I've finished drafting that claim for Mr Bailey. I'll leave it on your desk, Edwin.'

'Right you are. Then I shall see you both this afternoon.'

o o o

When she reached the top of the lane that led to Godwin Hall, Eleanor slowed the motor car to a horse's trotting pace and contemplated the lush greenness of the fields dotted with lazing sheep, the verges of the lane full of Cow Parsley, wild herbs, and grass and she revelled in the feeling of optimism and well-being that summer brings, particularly after a harsh winter. When she reached the carriage drive of Godwin Hall, she was greeted by the dogs. After Miss Godwin's funeral, the house had been shut up. The rooms had been swept and dusted, the furniture was covered in dust sheets, curtains or shutters were closed, and only a few rooms were left in use. Most of the indoor staff had been let go because they were no longer needed. Godwin Hall looked and felt deserted.

After Eleanor and Mrs Lomas had greeted each other and commented on the weather and the state of the countryside, Mrs Lomas said: 'Would you care for tea, Miss Harriman, although I must apologise. We're not set up for visitors now all the best rooms have been shut up. There's only the business room open now, although it still doesn't feel right to be in there.'

Eleanor said: 'Thank you, Mrs Lomas. A cup of tea would be most welcome. If Mr Nall is in his office I'll just go and have a word with him first.'

'Certainly. He will appreciate that. He was hoping to see you. This way, Miss Harriman.'

As Eleanor followed Mrs Lomas around the side of the house and across the yard, they passed a motor car, a black Crossley, parked in the yard. Mrs Lomas said: 'Mr Hedley Godwin is here at the moment but I believe he has gone out with one of the horses.' Eleanor did not comment but made a mental note as she followed Mrs Lomas to the bailiff's office. Mrs Lomas continued: 'Mr Nall will ring for tea and take you back to the business room when you finish your talk with him, Miss Harriman.'

Mr Harriman had approved Mr Nall's request for permission to enter Godwin Hall's cattle in the Show and Eleanor began by asking about their progress. Mr Nall was full of enthusiastic optimism and he expressed regret that Hedley Godwin had not shown any interest in their prospects.

Eleanor said: 'I've not heard that he has any experience of farming.'

Mr Nall nodded slowly. 'He doesn't seem all that interested in any of the livestock. Doesn't seem to know much about them. He's only asked about the horses.'

'Does he come to Godwin Hall very often?' asked Eleanor.

Mr Nall shook his head: 'Only when he wants to ride or talk about the stables he reckons to build.'

Eleanor spent some time chatting to Mr Nall about the state of the farm and making a note of things that needed Mr Harriman's attention. Then, she made her way from the stockyard to the business room. Mr Nall had rung for tea and

Mrs Lomas appeared almost immediately with a laden tray.

Eleanor said: 'Mrs Lomas, please sit down and join me. There are some things I need to ask you about and also I should like to hear how you are getting on with the inventory and whether or not you need any help.'

After Mrs Lomas had reported on the progress of the inventory and they had discussed the tasks still to be done, the conversation returned to the absence of Miss Godwin and the future of the Hall.

Eleanor said: 'I gather from Mr Nall that Mr Godwin has plans to expand the stables. Does that mean that he intends to live at Godwin Hall?'

'Oh, I don't think so,' said Mrs Lomas. 'He just seems to want somewhere to keep horses. I believe he plans to buy some. He's mentioned keeping Mr Nall on as bailiff and letting the house to a tenant.'

'I suppose for a single gentleman letting the house is the most sensible proposal,' said Eleanor.

Mrs Lomas sighed: 'Yes, I suppose so, although Miss Godwin didn't see the need. She was quite happy here, even after the rest of the family had gone and she was by herself.'

'I suppose,' said Eleanor, 'when one has grown up at the Hall and spent all one's life living here, going to live somewhere else would be unthinkable. Much better to stay on, even if one is alone.'

Mrs Lomas said: 'Yes, Miss Godwin would not have been happy anywhere else.' Mrs Lomas paused, then she said: 'I know it's not my place to say so but I am a bit surprised at Mr Godwin thinking of putting a tenant in because he kept telling Miss Godwin how much he admired the house and how proud he was to think he would be able to live here one day and continue the family tradition.'

'Mr Hedley Godwin was here? I had the impression that he hadn't visited Godwin Hall until the funeral.'

'Oh, no. He came with a letter of introduction a couple of

months or so into the new year. He went out of his way to be charming towards Miss Godwin and she was delighted to have another member of the family here, all her family having passed away.'

Eleanor sensed that Mrs Lomas had not been swayed by Mr Godwin's charm. 'Did he come often?'

'Only a few times, mainly to ride the horses, although when he was in the stable yard he was fond of coming to the back door and chatting to young Alice, the kitchen maid. Holding her up from her work. I warned her about it but she paid no attention. She'd rather listen to Mr Godwin and his sweet talk.'

Eleanor laughed. 'Yes, I had heard that he was a bit of a ladies' man.'

Mrs Lomas rolled her eyes and said: 'I've had to chase him out of the kitchen several times. Distracting her and putting silly ideas into her head but it's not my place to comment. He did stop to have lunch with Miss Godwin a couple of times. In fact, he'd been here the day she died and Miss Godwin had asked him to stay to lunch.'

'And was he still her when you found Miss Godwin?' asked Eleanor in surprise.

'No, he said he couldn't stop. He had an appointment in Buxton and he left before lunch.' Mrs Lomas paused. 'I've thought several times since then that it was a shame he didn't stop for lunch because he might still have been here with Miss Godwin when she was taken poorly. We would have known straightaway and there might have been something we could have done to save her.'

'Yes, that was unfortunate but even so there might not have been anything anyone could have done.'

'Perhaps you're right, Miss Harriman, but I can't help wishing that someone had been with her. I don't like to think of her being alone when it happened.'

'I know what you mean,' said Eleanor.

Mrs Lomas sighed. 'Still, there's nothing to be done about it.'

'I believe that on that last day, Miss Godwin had been to a meeting at St Peter's for the Girls' Friendly Society.'

'Yes, she had. She drove herself down to the church in the motor car. Right as rain she was and full of the idea of holding a fête here at the Hall. She said how nice it would be to see the old place alive again. What will happen to that idea now I wonder.'

'Well, the Misses Pymble are still hoping that it will be possible,' said Eleanor.

'Oh, Miss Godwin would like that, I'm sure.'

Eleanor and Mrs Lomas reminisced for a little while longer about Godwin Hall and its past and then Eleanor left to return to Hall Bank. She noticed as she went out to her motor car that the Crossley had gone and she was relieved that she had not encountered Hedley Godwin. She had no desire to meet him.

O O O

When Eleanor returned to the office from Godwin Hall she left the motor car parked on Hall Bank. She was greeted by Napoleon and then by James who said:

'Shall you be wanting the motor car again today, Miss Eleanor?'

'No, thank you, James. I'll be here for the rest of the day.'

'Then I shall have it taken back to the garage directly. While you were away, Dr Balderstone telephoned and left this message. She asked me to say that she would like to speak to you as soon as possible and she wonders if you will be free tomorrow after the office closes. She has surgery until two o'clock today and then house calls so she will not be able to take telephone calls and asks if you would leave a message with Mrs Ardern to say whether or not you will be available. She suggested one o'clock tomorrow and will come here if that is suitable.'

'Thank you, James. Would you telephone Mrs Ardern please and ask her to let Dr Balderstone know that one o'clock tomorrow will be convenient and I shall arrange some lunch.'

CHAPTER SEVENTEEN

'Here you are, Mr Harriman. I'm sure you're in need of this.' Mrs Clayton was carrying a laden tea tray. 'It's thirsty weather at the moment.'

'Ah, tea,' said Mr Harriman. 'Thank you, Mrs Clayton, perfect timing.'

Mr Harriman had just returned from opening the inquest into the death of Lily Penlington.

'I thought you might fancy one or two biscuits as well,' added Mrs Clayton, as she put a plate on the desk. 'Just to get you in the right mood again. Inquests are a nasty business.'

'You're quite right, Mrs Clayton. Excellent, I can see they are your own biscuits.'

'Hello, Father, how was it?' said Eleanor, coming into Mr Harriman's office. Napoleon wandered in and made himself comfortable on the rug in front of Mr Harriman's desk. 'I heard you were back. Ooh, are those your biscuits Mrs Clayton?' she added as she took one from the plate and bit into it.

'It's just as well I piled the plate full,' said Mrs Clayton, smiling. 'Would you like a cup of tea as well, Miss Harriman?'

'Yes, please. It's your fault, Mrs Clayton, you shouldn't make such tempting biscuits.'

'And now, here's Mr Talbot,' said Mrs Clayton, turning to Edwin. 'Tea?'

'Please, Mrs Clayton. And don't eat all those biscuits,

Eleanor. Leave some for me.'

Mrs Clayton handed Edwin a cup of tea and she turned to go, saying over her shoulder. 'No squabbling now. You're as bad as my boys.'

As Edwin sat down, Napoleon got up and brushed past him on his way out of the door of Mr Harriman's office.

'Where's he off to?' asked Edwin.

'He's coming with me, aren't you, Napoleon,' said Mrs Clayton as she headed for the stairs.

Eleanor said to Edwin: 'He saw Mrs Clayton preparing a leg of lamb earlier on, a particular favourite of his, and as soon as it goes into the oven, he will be sitting in the hall outside the kitchen door, savouring the aroma, and hoping to share more than just that. We won't see him again for a while. Now, back to the inquest.'

'Yes, Harriman, what did you decide?'

Mr Harriman said: 'I've adjourned as planned. I've taken evidence from Dr Patterson and Mr Gregory, the manager of the hotel, but that's all. Superintendent Johnson did request the adjournment but I got the feeling he was still sceptical about the need for further investigation. I'm sure he would prefer an open verdict or perhaps a finding of accidental death. I almost felt as if he were humouring me but there is definitely something about this case that troubles me. I am persuaded that further investigation is justified, in fact, essential. As to the nature of that investigation, I am still uncertain. So perhaps we should start by looking at the statements taken at the hotel. Here you are, Eleanor, let's see what we can make of them. I think if you read them out, we shall get a better feel for the evidence.'

'Yes,' said Edwin. 'It's easy to miss something when one just reads through a statement to oneself.'

Eleanor took the bundle of paper, flipped through to see who the statements were from, and assembled the pages in the proper order.

'Right, the first statement is by Mr Barnsley of the St Anne's Hotel. This is what he says:

"You are the maître d'hotel of the St Anne's Hotel and in charge of the staff in both dining rooms?
That is correct.
Lily Penlington was one of the waitresses on your staff.
Yes. She worked in the main dining room.
What can you tell us about her?
Lily, she was one of my best waitresses. She came to us at the beginning of the summer last year. Not very experienced but easy to train. A quick learner. But lately, I don't know what got into her. She was not happy. And then on those last two days, not paying attention to customers, mixing up dishes. She was a different person. I had to have words with her after she finished work that night.
What sort of words?
I had to tell her to mend her ways. I told her I was disappointed with her work and that I expected improvement otherwise I would have to give her warning.
How did she react?
She was not there.
What do you mean, not there? You just said you had words with her.
I mean it was as though she was not there. I can't explain. She said she was sorry and it would not happen again but she puzzled me.
You said that lately she wasn't happy. When did you notice her behaviour change?
Maybe a couple of weeks, perhaps a bit longer.

I'm not sure. The days pass. One is much the same as another in the hotel.

And you have no idea what the trouble was?

No idea. The girls, they don't confide in me. You need to talk to the girls.

Who would you suggest? Did she have any particular friend?

I don't know. Nellie Joule, maybe. They usually work together on the same shift.

When can I talk to her? When will she be on duty?

She is on leave at the moment. She won't be back until next week.

What time did Lily finish that night?

All the girls they finish at nine-thirty.

You said that you had to have words with Lily after she finished her shift. What time did Lily leave the hotel?

I don't know.

All right, what time did you finish having words with her?

Ten o'clock maybe, perhaps a bit before that.

So what was she doing between nine-thirty and ten o'clock?

She had to wait for me. At the office because I was held up when the shift finished.

What held you up?

Mr Gregory, he's the manager. There was a problem with a customer's bill and then with the supplies for the next day's menu. I had to sort those things out before I could see Lily.

Do you recall what was she wearing?

She had on her uniform still. Of course.

And would she have left to go home still

wearing her uniform?

No, not at all. The girls are required to change out of their uniform straight after the shift. They cannot be allowed to walk about in the street in their uniforms.

So she would have had to change into street clothes before she left the hotel. Do you recall what her street clothes were?

No. I did not see her again after she left my office."

'This second one is from Jessie Hobson a waitress at the St Anne's Hotel. She says:

"You work as a waitress at the St Anne's Hotel?

Yes.

How long have you worked there?

Since Christmas before last.

About eighteen months?

I suppose.

And you worked with Lily Penlington.

Yes.

When did you last see her?

Tuesday. We was both serving at dinner.

Tell me about that evening. Was it just as usual?

No. Something were different. She were right slow doing things.

What sort of things?

Laying the tables. Getting things off the shelves. The cruets, the serving spoons. It were like she were in a fog. She kept forgetting where things are kept. And she took some plates to the wrong table. Mr Barnsley

gave her a right ticking off.
Who is Mr Barnsley?
The *maître d'*.
Did she usually make mistakes?
No. She wouldn't have kept her job if she did.
Mr Barnsley's very particular, very strict.
So this was out of character?
What do you mean?
Different from usual. Did she seem any
different to you in the days before last
Tuesday?
Yes. I thought maybe she were worried about
something. But she never said.
So you have no idea what that might have been?
No, she just seemed a bit quiet. Not her usual
self, like, but she never said anything about
being in trouble or anything.
And how was she usually?
Always cheerful. Really happy. I thought she
might have been walking out with someone. But
she weren't so happy lately.
And you don't know why?
No."

'And the last one is a statement by Annie Weston also a
waitress at the St Anne's Hotel.

"You work as a waitress at the St Anne's
Hotel?
Yes.
How long have you worked there?
Three years come August Bank Holiday.
And you worked with Lily Penlington.
Yes.
When did you last see her?

Tuesday evening. We was both serving at dinner.

Did you know her well?

Quite well. Not as friends like, but when you work with someone you get to know them. She were often on the same shift as me.

How did she seem on Tuesday?

Sort of different.

Different in what way?

I don't know. She didn't talk much. Hardly said anything. And kind of muddled. I don't think her mind were on her job. But now I come to think of it, it were more like she'd forgotten things she should know. My gran's a bit like that.

Can you give me an example?

A couple of times I said things and she didn't seem to know what I were talking about.

What sort of things?

I were telling her something that had happened to one of the waitresses a couple of nights before and it were like she didn't know who I meant. But she must have done. And one of our regulars came in, he always has a joke with us, and Lily couldn't remember his name.

Had she been worried about anything, do you think?

I think she must have been but I don't know what.

When you finished your shift at the hotel that night, did you see her after that?

No, she should have been with us but she weren't.

What do you mean?

Mary, one of the chambermaids, turned twenty-

one that day. She's walking out with one of
the sous-chefs and he'd made her a cake so
after us'd got changed out of our uniforms me
and a couple of the other waitresses went down
to the kitchens for the cake and then us all
went up to the King's Head for a drink. Lily
should've come with us but Mr Barnsley sent
for her. I suppose he wanted to give her a
telling her off.
Did she come down to the kitchens?
No.
And she didn't join you later?
No. I thought she must have decided to go home
instead. I were a bit worried that Mr Barnsley
might have given her the sack, to be honest.
At what time did you last see her?
About nine thirty, I should think, or just a
bit after. The shift finishes at nine thirty.
And you didn't see her after that?
No.
Was she still in her uniform when you last
saw her?
Yes."

'And that's it,' concluded Eleanor as she put the statements
down on Mr Harriman's desk.

'Well, it is clear that there was something troubling her,'
said Mr Harriman. 'She seems to have been trying to behave
normally whilst, at times, being in a state of confusion.'

'It's almost beginning to sound like "whilst of unsound
mind" isn't it?' said Edwin.

'Yes, except that it's clearly not a case of suicide and we
still have no evidence of any action or omission by the
deceased that brought about her death.'

'Except taking off her shoes,' said Eleanor. 'Sorry to harp

on them.'

'Ah, now, you've reminded me. Superintendent Johnson told me this afternoon that a shoe has been found. At the edge of the cascade.'

The main arm of the river Wye flowed along the western side of the Gardens until it reached the northern boundary. It then raced dramatically and noisily down a steep, rocky cascade and disappeared into a culvert under The Square. From there it continued underground until it reached the flat plain behind Spring Gardens where it became a river again.

'Superintendent Johnson thought there had been an attempt to throw the shoes into the river intending that they would be swept away downstream. The flow of water is particularly strong there. A very astute young constable noticed that there was a shoe caught on a branch protruding from the water, low down near the mouth of the culvert and difficult to see. That same very astute young constable also had the wit to realise that the other shoe might be further downstream. He followed the river down to the back of the properties in Spring Gardens but without any luck. The other shoe is probably well on its way to Bakewell by now. The shoe had been in the water for some time but it is just possible that there may still be fingerprints. It was a woman's shoe, black with a small heel. No strap across the top though so it could easily have come off. On the inside of the shoe the letter R had been written in what looked like paint.'

'I expect the other one has the letter L for left,' said Edwin. 'Helen had to do that with the boys when they were learning to put their shoes on. But given the age of the young woman, that would seem rather odd, wouldn't it?'

'Yes, but also it was a left-hand shoe,' said Mr Harriman, 'so that explanation won't do.'

'When Cicely and I were at school, we had our initials inside our shoes so they didn't get mixed up.'

'That's a good thought, but why R and not L for Lily?' said Mr Harriman.

Eleanor shrugged. 'So, it might not even be the dead woman's shoe.'

'So where do we go from here?' asked Mr Harriman.

'I think we should try to find out more about Lily's state of mind,' said Edwin. 'According to the statement by Annie Weston, Lily was preparing to go out with them for their celebration which suggests she was all right by the end of her shift. The confusion seems to have been during the shift. Forgetting where things were or not recognising a customer. It's as though whatever was wrong was coming in waves rather than being there all the time, as though something was preying on her mind, something she managed to put out of her mind for a bit and then remembered again. Rather like a bereavement. Concentrating on everyday activity causes you to forget momentarily and then it all suddenly comes back.'

'I see what you mean,' said Mr Harriman, 'except that this seems to be the opposite. She seems to be forgetting the everyday things rather than the loss, or whatever the larger cause of the problem might have been.'

'Perhaps she was experiencing the early symptoms of some disease that affects the mind,' suggested Edwin.

'That's possible, I suppose, and at an early stage the disease might not have been detectable and, therefore, not come to the notice of Dr Patterson when he conducted the post mortem,' said Mr Harriman. 'It might even be the cause of the unconsciousness that caused her to drown.'

'I wonder if she had consulted a doctor,' said Edwin. 'Perhaps Superintendent Johnson should contact the local surgeries and see if she was a patient there.'

When Edwin suggested this, Eleanor recalled her conversation with Catherine about the patient who had consulted her and Catherine's concern about patient confidentiality. She decided not to say anything about that for the moment, but said: 'I believe that the surgeries have already been contacted when Superintendent Johnson was trying to identify Lily. He may already know if Lily was being treated by a doctor.'

'I see,' said Mr Harriman. 'I think that is all we can do for the moment. We have already spent a great deal of time on this so we had better get back to some of the other work that needs to be done.'

'Yes, I have an affidavit to prepare which must be done today.' Edwin picked up his teacup, saucer, and plate and put them on the tray that Mrs Clayton had left on the desk. Eleanor collected up her and Mr Harriman's cup, saucer, and plate together with the empty biscuit plate and put them on the tray. She picked up the tray and said: 'I'll take these up to Mrs Clayton. I've got to go and retrieve Leon.'

o o o

Napoleon was lying in the hall outside the kitchen door in a mood of anticipation. He got up and greeted Eleanor and then looked pointedly in the direction of the oven. Mrs Clayton noticed this and said to him: 'It's still cooking.'

'Ah, so the leg of lamb has now made it into the oven.'

'Yes. He's partial to a bit of lamb, isn't he?' said Mrs Clayton.

Mrs Clayton was standing at the kitchen table making an egg and bacon pie. There was a piece of bacon on the chopping board in front of her and she half turned to reach for a knife from the knife holder on the bench behind her, a movement she had made thousands of times before. Her hand did not connect with the handle of the knife as she expected. She was surprised, turned fully towards the bench, and then said: 'Oh, there it is? Someone's changed the knives around.'

'Oh, I'm sorry, Mrs Clayton. That's my fault. I borrowed

a knife last night. There was some coloured paper that Richard needed to be cut up into squares and they had to be exactly the same size so it was easier to use a knife than the scissors. I'm sorry. I must have put it back in the wrong place.'

'It's not important, Miss Harriman. Don't worry. It's just that I'm used to things being in the same place and I reach for things without thinking. It's just habit.'

'Yes, I suppose in the kitchen you do many of the same tasks in the same way every day and you get into a routine.'

'That's true. You can do some things without paying much attention because you're so used to doing them. If my mind's on something else I can be doing a job, slicing bread or peeling potatoes, without even realising that I'm doing it and then I'll reach for a cloth or a basin or something and if it's not where I expect it to be, that's when I come to. It doesn't happen here very often because I know where everything is, but if I'm in the kitchen at home I get confused. My sister-in-law has a different way of doing things and she has her utensils in different places. She's left handed as well, you see.'

Eleanor nodded and then she smiled. 'You've just given me an idea, Mrs Clayton. Thank you.'

Mrs Clayton looked puzzled and said: 'You're welcome, I'm sure, Miss Harriman, whatever it is.'

'Come on Leon, we have work to do.'

Napoleon did not move and suddenly became deaf. He averted his gaze from Eleanor and stared into space.

Mrs Clayton laughed at him. 'You can leave him there if you like. He's not in the way and I doubt if he's going to move.'

'If you're sure.'

'He's no trouble. He knows to stay out in the hall. He's afraid I'll forget him when the meat comes out of the oven.'

Eleanor looked at Napoleon and he studiously ignored

her. 'You win,' she said to him, and went back to her office.

CHAPTER EIGHTEEN

On Friday evening, Mr Harriman, Richard and Napoleon were keeping each other company while Cicely, Eleanor and Philip went with a group of their friends to a dinner dance at the Palace Hotel. It boasted a newly installed sprung dance floor and the Saxophonia Syncopated Orchestra, playing jazz, a style of music introduced with great success into England four years ago by the Southern Syncopated Orchestra, a group of touring American musicians which included Sidney Bechet and which had been invited to play at Buckingham Palace.

The evening was mild and Eleanor, Cicely and Philip decided that, after their exertions on the dance floor, walking home would be refreshing. They were strolling along Broad Walk and they had passed Derby House and were almost to the Stanley Hotel, when Eleanor noticed a man standing by the side of the building, not far from the entrance. After they had walked on a little further, Eleanor stopped.

'That man,' she said, quietly.

'What man?' asked Cicely.

'Did you not notice him? We just walked past him, standing beside the Stanley Hotel. He's wearing a trilby and a long overcoat, both of a dark colour. Do you think that could be Richard's mysterious stranger?'

Cicely looked back and said: 'He does fit the description, doesn't he?'

'Would someone tell me what this is about?' asked Philip, plaintively. 'If there are mysterious strangers about, I should like to know. I don't want to be left out.'

'Richard has seen someone walking up and down Broad Walk late at night,' said Eleanor. 'He thinks it's something to do with pirates. He's keeping a lookout for the seafaring man with one leg, on behalf of Billy Bones.'

'He's been reading *Treasure Island*.' added Cicely.

Philip roared laughing and said: 'Oh, *Treasure Island* was one of my favourites, too. I longed to meet a pirate. I'm not sure what I would have done if I had had my wish, mind.'

'Charmed him into giving you all his treasure, probably,' said Eleanor, laughing.

'I don't recollect a fellow in an overcoat and trilby in *Treasure Island*,' said Philip. 'I don't think the trilby had been invented then. What does this mysterious stranger do exactly?'

'Just walks up and down Broad Walk, as far as we know,' said Cicely.

'And why would someone be wearing a heavy overcoat on a night like this?' asked Philip.

'We don't know,' said Cicely. 'To be mysterious, I suppose.'

'Something has just occurred to me,' said Eleanor. 'Richard first mentioned seeing his mysterious stranger just before Lily Penlington died. If he is in the habit of walking up and down Broad Walk, it's possible that he saw Lily on the night she died. He just might know something that would help us piece together her story. Philip, do you think you could persuade him to come to Oxford House so that we can ask him some questions?'

'Good grief! What have I got myself into this time?' said Philip. He frowned at Eleanor. 'Is this one of your investigations?'

'No, more in the line of meddling in father's inquest,' said Eleanor.

'Oh, that's different is it?' said Philip.

'I don't think that is a very good idea,' said Cicely, cautiously. 'We don't know anything about him and for all we know he might have had something to do with her death.'

'But if that was the case why would he continue to walk up and down Broad Walk and why would he be lurking outside the Stanley Hotel?' said Eleanor. 'A guilty person would keep well out of sight, surely.'

'I still don't think it is a good idea. He might be dangerous,' said Cicely.

'Well, Philip will be with us and Father is at Oxford House. And, anyway, if he does agree to come, doesn't that suggest that he has nothing to hide?'

'Very well then,' said Cicely. 'I can never win an argument with you.'

'Look, if you're worried, Cicely, why don't you and Eleanor go on home and I'll go and speak to this mysterious stranger fellow and if I don't like the look of him, I won't bring him back. I'll leave him where he is. How does that sound?'

'Thank you, Philip,' said Cicely. 'I am glad someone is sensible and not carried away with wild ideas.'

Philip turned to Eleanor. 'Am I to offer this chap a bribe, as in a whisky and soda, or perhaps a beer?'

'You can offer whatever it takes to persuade him,' said Eleanor.

'Right then. Here goes.'

O O O

Eleanor and Cicely walked on until they came to Oxford House. Cicely let herself in with her latch key and she and Eleanor went into the sitting room. Napoleon gave them both an enthusiastic greeting and then retired to the hearth rug.

Mr Harriman said: 'Hello, you two. Had a nice time?'

'Yes, thank you, Father. A lovely time,' said Cicely. 'And thank you for looking after Richard.'

'He's safely tucked up and asleep. I checked only a few minutes ago. No watching for pirates or mysterious strangers tonight.'

'Ah,' said Eleanor, 'but we think we may have found the mysterious stranger.'

'One leg or two?' asked Mr Harriman.

'Definitely two. We saw him outside the Stanley Hotel and Philip is bringing him here, I hope. I thought that as he may have been on Broad Walk the night Lily Penlington died, he might have seen her and might be able to help with the investigation.'

Before Mr Harriman could comment, the doorbell rang. Napoleon got up from the hearth rug ready to defend everyone if necessary. Cicely went to answer the door. There was a pause and then Mr Harriman and Eleanor heard Cicely say: 'Oh, goodness. Oh, yes. Let me take those and hang them up for you.'

Eleanor assumed that the overcoat and trilby were being hung up on the stand in the hall. She put her hand on Napoleon's collar to restrain him.

Philip came into the sitting room accompanied by a woman of about forty, dressed in a light brown tweed suit, her hair tied neatly in a bun at the nape of her neck. Mr Harriman stood up.

'Good evening, Mr Harriman,' said Philip. 'Miss Clitheroe, may I present Mr Harriman.'

Mr Harriman said: 'Good evening, Miss Clitheroe.'

Miss Clitheroe extended her hand to Mr Harriman and said: 'How do you do.'

Eleanor looked at Philip, speechless. Philip was thoroughly enjoying himself at Eleanor's expense. He said: 'And may I present Mr Harriman's other daughter, Miss Eleanor Harriman. Miss Clitheroe is a private detective,

Lella.'

Eleanor came forward. 'How do you do,' she said, smiling and hiding her surprise well. Then she frowned and glared at Philip who was trying not to laugh.

Miss Clitheroe looked at Napoleon and held out her hand towards him. Philip said: 'And this is Napoleon.'

'Please do sit down, Miss Clitheroe,' said Mr Harriman.

When everyone was seated and Napoleon had returned to the hearth rug, Philip said: 'Miss Clitheroe, I'm much obliged to you for agreeing to accompany me here. Miss Harriman has some questions she would like to ask you, if you don't mind.'

Philip looked at Eleanor, his face a solemn mask, but Eleanor could see that his eyes and eyebrows were expressing repressed laughter as well as triumph. Eleanor ignored the challenge and concentrated on the task in hand. Mr Harriman watched the exchange between Eleanor and Philip with amusement.

Eleanor said: 'Miss Clitheroe, it's awfully good of you to agree to come here and talk to us, I should explain that my father, Mr Harriman, is a partner in a local firm of solicitors, Harriman & Talbot.'

'On Hall Bank,' interrupted Miss Clitheroe. 'Yes, I have noticed your brass plate.'

'I asked Mr Danebridge to approach you because I believe that you may have been on Broad Walk recently late at night.' Miss Clitheroe looked surprised but said nothing. Eleanor continued: 'I am sure that you will be aware that a young woman was found a few days ago in the Gardens and that she is believed to have drowned. While you have been on Broad Walk you may have seen or heard something which would be helpful to the enquiry into the young woman's death.' Eleanor looked at Mr Harriman. 'Father, I think perhaps you had better ask the questions.'

'Miss Clitheroe,' said Mr Harriman, 'I should explain first

of all that I have been appointed as Coroner and as such, I have the power to make enquiries regarding the death of the young woman. I should like to ask you a few questions, if I may, in case you do have any information relevant to the enquiry. If not, I am sorry to have taken up your time. If you are able to help us, I shall ask you to make a formal statement to the police in the usual way and, of course, you may have to be called as a witness at the inquest.'

'Mr Harriman, may I interrupt you there. If I were required to appear at an inquest, my identity and my presence in Buxton would be made public. I would prefer that not to happen. Not at this stage, at least. You see, as Mr Danebridge explained, I am a private detective and I am engaged at the moment in gathering evidence for a client on a rather delicate matter. I must remain in the shadows for a few more days in order to complete my assignment. If I explain the nature of my commission, I think you will understand my position. However, before I explain further, may I have your assurance and the assurance of everyone in this room that what I am about to tell you about my assignment will go no further. I am aware of the death of the young woman and I can assure you that my investigation is in no way connected with her death.'

Mr Harriman said: 'I am certain that I can assure you on that point, Miss Clitheroe. My daughter Eleanor is also a solicitor in my practice, and my daughter Cicely has grown up with the law. They both understand the concept of confidentiality. And Mr Danebridge I can certainly vouch for. I know that I can rely on everyone here to treat what you say as being given in the strictest confidence. If you have not witnessed anything relevant to my enquiry, we need trouble you no further. If you have, then I am sure I can make some accommodation that will prevent you from breaching the terms of your engagement.'

'Thank you, Mr Harriman. My assignment involves a

married man, a man of some consequence in his home town. As a solicitor you will be aware that the private member's *Matrimonial Causes Bill* passed from the House of Commons last Tuesday to the House of Lords and is due for its second reading on the twenty-sixth of this month.'

'Yes,' said Mr Harriman. 'I think it is generally accepted that it will become the law. The report I read suggested that it is expected to receive Royal Assent next month.'

'I believe so. And you will also be aware that this legislation will, for the first time, grant to a wife the right to petition for divorce on the grounds of her husband's adultery, that right being currently restricted to the husband. My client is the wife of a serial adulterer and he is the reason for my presence on Broad Walk. My client wishes to file a petition at the earliest possible moment and she has engaged me to obtain the relevant evidence. The husband is particularly active during the summer months and my client informed me that he was coming to Buxton. She believed that he had arranged to meet his latest conquest here, although she did not know where he intended to stay.

'I located the other party in Manchester and travelled on the same train with her as far as Chapel-en-le-Frith. There, by a lucky chance, or rather because of the rude manners of my quarry, I was able to ascertain which hotel they intended to stay at and I have been watching them since then. Also, thanks to the rudeness of my quarry, the manager at the Stanley Hotel has taken a dislike to him and that has made my task very much easier. I have been provided with information and the sort of evidence I would not normally have access to. I am confident that my client will be successful and I do not want to jeopardise this enquiry. I cannot provide any information about the parties in question but I can tell you that my surveillance has required me to be on Broad Walk late at night.'

'That is all we wanted to ask you about, Miss Clitheroe,'

said Mr Harriman. 'You may find this amusing but we have been alerted to your presence on Broad Walk by my young grandson, Richard, who mistook you, first of all, for a pirate and then for a gentleman.'

Miss Clitheroe did find this very amusing. She laughed and said: 'Then I am pleased to know that my disguise is very convincing. I find that to carry out my surveillance I sometimes have to remain on a street corner or in the vicinity of a particular establishment for quite a time. You will appreciate, I'm sure, that a lone woman loitering about late in the evening would be remarked upon and can attract attention of an unwanted kind whereas a gentleman is free to go where he pleases and is not so carefully scrutinised. Hence, the disguise. And I have found that it serves its purpose admirably.'

Mr Harriman smiled and Eleanor nodded in agreement, studiously avoiding looking at Philip.

'Ah, I see,' said Mr Harriman. 'Now, I must take you into my confidence, Miss Clitheroe, and I am sure you will not repeat what I have to tell you or discuss with anyone the questions I ask. At present, the death of the young woman is unexplained and the circumstances are rather odd. So far, we have no evidence as to why she was in the Gardens or whether anyone was with her. The police have not been able to find any witnesses. There may have been nothing untoward about her death but there are certain unanswered questions, matters which still need to be clarified before I can be certain of the verdict. I need not go into those, but I feel sure that someone must have seen the young woman at some point during the evening on which she died. It is possible that you know nothing of this matter and therefore we need not trouble you further. However, if you are willing to answer a few preliminary questions, without compromising your investigation, we can decide whether or not you do have any relevant information and, if you do, we can agree on the best course of action.'

'Certainly, Mr Harriman.'

'Thank you. Then what I should like to know is whether you were on Broad Walk that evening, Tuesday the fifth of June, and, if so, whether you saw anyone fitting the description of the young woman, particularly anyone going into the Gardens. We have very little to go on as far as a description goes. She was about eighteen or nineteen, had brown hair, no hat, and was wearing a pink frock with red flowers.'

'Ah, it is possible that I may have seen something but I am not sure whether it will be of any help. I did not realise it at the time, but I may have seen the young woman earlier in the evening, that is, on the night she died. Not in the Gardens but on Broad Walk.'

'And roughly what time would that have been?' asked Mr Harriman.

'I'm afraid I can't be sure. At about ten o'clock, I should think. The person in whom I am interested and his companion were dining at the Old Hall and I was on Broad Walk a little distance from the end of Fountain Street where the entrance to the Gardens is. I was under some trees and close to the railings of the Gardens so as not to be conspicuous. It had been raining rather heavily during the earlier part of the evening and there were very few people about.

'I noticed a young woman walking towards me coming from the direction of the Old Hall. She was some distance away and it was dark and I thought that it was the companion of the man in whom I am interested, returning alone to the hotel. Then I realised that the young woman was being followed. As she got closer, I realised it was not who I had imagined. The man who was following her caught up with her, took her arm, and steered her towards the entrance to the Gardens. It happened rather quickly but I had the impression that the young woman was taken by surprise at the arrival of the man. I turned my attention back to Broad Walk to continue my surveillance and didn't think any more about it. Later, of course, I thought it might have been the young woman who died but to go to the police would have meant revealing my identity and compromising my work. I wasn't sure that my information had any relevance so I felt justified in taking no action.'

'I quite understand, Miss Clitheroe. Thank you for being so open about your observations. You have been most helpful.' said Mr Harriman. 'Can you recall what the young woman was wearing?'

'Yes, it was a pink dress with a red pattern. It was similar to a frock worn by the companion of my quarry. That is what attracted my attention to the young woman in the first place.'

'And are you able to be certain that this incident occurred on the fifth of this month?' asked Mr Harriman.

'Certainly,' said Miss Clitheroe, reaching into the pocket of her jacket and taking out a small notebook. She found the page she wanted and said: 'Yes, the fifth. My quarry left Buxton the following day as did I. I sought further instructions from my client and then returned here to continue my surveillance.'

'And the young woman who was with the person in whom you are interested did she also leave the following day?'

'I'm afraid I have no idea,' said Miss Clitheroe. 'My quarry left the hotel alone. I did not see the young woman again.'

'Then, am I to understand that when you returned to Buxton to continue your surveillance, your quarry was with a different woman?'

'That is correct.'

'I see. Could you describe the man whom you saw following the young woman along Broad Walk?' asked Mr Harriman.

'I did only catch a fleeting glimpse of him and I didn't

pay particular attention to him. He was dressed in a suit and my impression is that he was tall and thin. I don't remember anything remarkable about him.'

Mr Harriman looked at Eleanor, one eyebrow raised, inviting her to comment.

'Miss Clitheroe,' said Eleanor, 'this may seem an odd question but I assume that the young woman was wearing shoes when you saw her. Can you remember anything about them?'

Miss Clitheroe looked a little surprised by the question. She looked down at the carpet, frowning in concentration, then she looked up: 'If she had not been wearing shoes, that certainly would have been extraordinary and I am certain I would have noticed. I don't believe they were remarkable in any way just the sort of shoe that all the young woman where these days, with a small heel. There may have been a leather strap across the top of the foot. However, my recollection is not clear and I may be confusing it with an image I have of the shoes worn by the companion of the person I am interested in.'

Mr Harriman resumed: 'Can you recall anything else about this couple, at all?'

Miss Clitheroe nodded: 'Yes, there was one thing which, at the time, I thought was rather peculiar. I had the impression that the young woman was rather startled at the approach of the man, it was almost as though she didn't recognise him but, because of the way the man spoke to her, I think she may have known him. I heard the man say, as best I can recall, something like: "What are you doing here? I told you to get rid of him" or something like that. I'm not sure. I was anxious not to attract attention so by then I had turned away and I did not see where they went. I assume that they went through the entrance to the Gardens but I did not see them do so.'

Mr Harriman said: 'Miss Clitheroe, I very much

appreciate your giving up your time to answer my questions. What you have told me is very helpful indeed. I don't think that I need trouble you further at this stage so I shall not get in the way of your work but would you be good enough to let me have your card so that I can contact you in future should it become necessary?'

'Certainly,' said Miss Clitheroe.

'May we offer you some refreshment before you go, Miss Clitheroe. I think that is the least we can do to thank you for your trouble,' said Cicely, standing up.

'That is very kind of you, but I really should be returning to my post,' said Miss Clitheroe. She stood up and Mr Harriman and Philip followed suit. Miss Clitheroe pulled a card holder out of her pocket, took out a card and, handing it to Mr Harriman said: 'Good evening, Mr Harriman, Miss Harriman, Mr Danebridge.'

Cicely had moved to the sitting room door to show Miss Clitheroe out and as Miss Clitheroe reached the door, she smiled at Cicely and said: 'Perhaps I can accept your hospitality on another occasion and reassure your young Richard that I am not a pirate.'

Everyone laughed and then resumed their seats. Napoleon accompanied Cicely as she went into the hall with Miss Clitheroe.

O O O

Mr Harriman said: 'Well, Eleanor, what do you make of your mysterious stranger?'

'So mysterious she wasn't even a man,' teased Philip.

'I like Miss Clitheroe,' said Eleanor, 'and I am ignoring you, Philip. She described only what she could remember and she didn't speculate. She would make an excellent witness.'

'No doubt, given her profession, she has had plenty of

practice,' said Mr Harriman.

'It must be jolly interesting,' said Philip, 'I mean, going about prying into other people's business like that, and getting paid to do it.'

'Not if it requires standing for ages in the rain or a howling gale,' said Cicely, coming back into the sitting room with Napoleon.

'No, I suppose not,' agreed Philip. 'I think I'll stick to what I know.'

'Anyway,' pointed out Eleanor, 'you already do a bit of that sort of thing yourself. You look into people's lives and the lives of their ancestors when you appraise their furniture and check the provenance of their family heirlooms. And you sometimes have to ask awkward questions.'

'Hmm,' said Philip, 'Yes, I suppose I do. Hadn't thought of it like that.'

'I don't know that any of this takes us much further though,' said Mr Harriman.

'We have solved one little mystery though, haven't we,' said Eleanor.

'And what's that?' asked Mr Harriman.

'Miss Clitheroe has given the game away. She wasn't to know that we had met that couple on Broad Walk, the young woman who stopped to make a fuss of Leon. Those two people were clearly the ones she was watching. The woman was quite young and attractive and the man was considerably older. I even thought he was her father but she called him Robert. The woman said they were staying at the Stanley Hotel. I think that older man must be Miss Clitheroe's quarry. And now it seems that he is with someone else.'

'Well, Robert's in for a nasty surprise,' said Philip.

'I think it might serve him right. He was very rude to the young woman,' said Eleanor. 'Perhaps his case will be the first one under the new law. It's bound to get publicity and we'll be able to read all about it. But, in the meantime, we mustn't say anything to anyone and if we see Miss Clitheroe when she is being the mysterious stranger, we must be careful not to notice her. Miss Clitheroe has been very helpful and she need not have told us anything at all.'

'Now, to return to the young woman,' said Mr Harriman, patiently. 'When we heard that the person found in the lake was quite young and was wearing a pink frock with red flowers printed on it, we told Superintendent Johnson about the woman and suggested that he check at the Stanley Hotel and when he found that she was no longer there, we thought she might be the person in the lake.'

Eleanor interrupted: 'You don't suppose the young woman we met on Broad Walk was Lily, do you? The companion of Miss Clitheroe's quarry. The young woman we met on Broad Walk was certainly very pretty.'

'It's possible, I suppose,' said Mr Harriman, cautiously, 'but Miss Clitheroe did say that they were dining at the Old Hall Hotel that night and Lily was on duty at St Anne's Hotel.'

'She might have gone there with the older man after she finished her shift,' said Cicely.

'And Miss Clitheroe did say her quarry left Buxton the next day alone. So where was the young woman? And if the young woman was Lily, she couldn't leave because she was in the lake,' said Eleanor.

'Are you suggesting that Miss Clitheroe's quarry is responsible for Lily's death?' said Mr Harriman. 'I think we may be jumping to conclusions and it doesn't account for the other man who was seen going into the Gardens.'

'But Miss Clitheroe didn't see him go into the Gardens. He may be entirely irrelevant,' said Eleanor.

'If that was Lily whom Miss Clitheroe saw on Broad Walk and not anything to do with Robert, why would Lily be on Broad Walk if she worked at the St Anne's Hotel? Where would she be going?' asked Philip.

'If I recall correctly,' said Mr Harriman, 'the address that the manager of St Anne's Hotel had for her was at Burbage. On Macclesfield Road, so perhaps she was on her way home.'

'I see. Yes, she could have been cutting through from the hotel,' said Philip. 'So, perhaps we should get back to the facts and stop speculating.'

Eleanor said: 'I was interested in what Miss Clitheroe said about the shoes because, if her recollection is correct, perhaps we can assume that the shoes were the type to fall off easily. But the information about the shoes is nowhere near as important as the other information from Miss Clitheroe. We now know roughly what time Lily entered the Gardens and also that Lily probably didn't enter them alone.'

'And it sounds as though it might not have been by choice,' said Mr Harriman.

'It did seem a bit contradictory though,' said Philip. 'Miss Clitheroe seemed to think the young woman didn't recognise him and, if her memory of what he said is accurate, that doesn't tally. One wouldn't say those words to someone that one doesn't know.'

'And how could Miss Clitheroe remember in such detail when they weren't even the people she was interested in,' said Cicely.

'Someone in Miss Clitheroe's occupation needs a good memory and a keen eye for detail to be successful and I suspect Miss Clitheroe has developed both of those skills,' said Mr Harriman. 'I think it may be safe to assume that it was Lily that she saw.'

'Aren't we assuming though that when they got through the entrance gate at the Gardens the two people stayed together,' said Eleanor. 'Or even that they did both go through the entrance gate into the Gardens. It's possible that the man mistook Lily for someone else and then apologised for his mistake and parted company.'

'That's true,' said Mr Harriman, 'but now I think it is time for us to part company. We now have some very valuable information, thanks to your initiative, Eleanor, and your power of persuasion, Philip, in getting Miss Clitheroe here. She will be back at her post now so as we pass on our way home, we shall have to pretend that she is invisible.'

'I suspect like a true professional she will look right through us,' said Eleanor.

CHAPTER NINETEEN

On Saturday morning, Eleanor had some shopping to do so she left Napoleon supervising Mrs Clayton from the hall outside the kitchen door. She went out early before the office opened. Walking along Spring Gardens and The Quadrant was always a pleasure. Many of the shopfronts had been brought up to date at the end of the previous century and there was a uniformity of building style with cast iron posts, decorative work, and glass canopies. The shopkeepers added to the elegance of the buildings by always displaying their goods in the most attractive way possible, making window shopping a popular pastime. Eleanor went first to Milligans the drapers to choose some dress fabric to send to her dress-maker and then to buy some coloured pencils she had promised for Richard. Her last stop was Collinsons for a selection of pastries to take to Cicely's for tea on Sunday afternoon.

When Eleanor returned to the office, she retrieved Napoleon and settled down at her desk to work. Catherine was due to arrive when the office closed and there were several files that needed her attention before then, so she worked methodically through a large pile of papers, including two letters that had to be written for the Godwin file. Napoleon spent most of the time sitting at the window to watch the passers-by on Hall Bank and the people strolling on The Slopes, a popular place for visitors and residents alike. Mrs Clayton had prepared a basket of food so that Catherine and Eleanor could have a picnic on The

Slopes while they discussed Catherine's need for advice.

○ ○ ○

The Slopes had come into existence because of a dispute over land. When the fifth Duke of Devonshire had decided to have The Crescent built, he had not been able to secure the site for the building that his architect preferred. This ideal site was on Devonshire land except for a small parcel which belonged to a local landowner. Allegedly motivated by greed, the landowner kept refusing the offers made to him for the land in the belief that the Duke would eventually pay whatever it took to get what he wanted for his new building. It was a case of spectacular misjudgement and an often-repeated story, told with sympathy by some and with triumph by others depending on their class and political persuasion. The Duke, instead of paying more than the land was worth, changed the location of The Crescent, and instead of having a sweeping vista across the river valley, it looked out onto a steep and craggy outcrop about fifty yards away.

That seventy feet high outcrop was known as St Anne's Cliff and consisted of very hard limestone which had resisted erosion by the river Wye. The Slopes had been created in about 1818 for the sixth Duke by smoothing and levelling the cliff to a design by Sir Jeffry Wyatville and later remodelled by Sir Joseph Paxton. It was now a park of nearly eight acres, planted with shrubs and trees, dotted with park benches, and criss-crossed by a clever network of paths of varying gradients and flights of steps which gave access to the various levels. From the top of The Slopes visitors could get an excellent view of The Crescent, the Thermal Baths and other interesting buildings of the lower town as well as the domes and towers of the Devonshire Hospital.

When Catherine Balderstone arrived at Hall Bank.

Eleanor and Napoleon met her in the hall. Eleanor said: 'It was so lovely this morning, I thought we could have a picnic on The Slopes. I think we shall be all right but I shouldn't be surprised if it rained later on.'

'Excellent idea, we might as well enjoy the sunshine while we can, especially with one of Mrs Clayton's picnics.'

Napoleon accompanied Eleanor and Catherine across Hall Bank to the flight of steps which went up to The Slopes. Eleanor was concerned because Catherine did not seem her usual animated self and she looked tired. Eleanor wondered if she was still worrying about the problem of patient confidentiality that they had discussed earlier. They chose a bench towards the top of the park from which they could look down towards the Grove Hotel. Napoleon sprawled on the grass and Eleanor unpacked the basket.

'Here we are. A selection of sandwiches, Mrs Clayton's cake and some of her Elderflower cordial.' said Eleanor as she handed Catherine a plate and a table napkin.

'Perfect,' said Catherine.

'Please, help yourself.'

Eleanor said: 'Catherine, I'm sorry I haven't seen you before this. When we spoke last Sunday you thought that the dead young woman might have been a patient of yours and you were worried about breaching your duty of confidentiality by disclosing information about her. I said that I would let you know if I thought your information was relevant so that we could decide what to do. I've been meaning to call in and let you know but I've been too busy to come in person and it's not the sort of conversation one can have over the telephone. One never knows who is listening at the exchange. The information about your patient that you thought might be relevant turns out not to be so you don't need to worry any further. A few days after we'd had our discussion, the post mortem report came in and, as I said, I'm sorry I didn't come sooner but I can assure you that your patient is not Lily Penlington.'

Catherine was about to take a bite out of a sandwich and paused, the sandwich in mid-air. She looked startled. 'But how did you know she isn't Lily Penlington? That's what I wanted to talk to you about.'

'Well, the post mortem report was quite clear. Lily was a virgin and your patient clearly was not,' said Eleanor, 'considering the reason that she came to see you.'

'Ah,' said Catherine, 'that confirms what I have been told.'

'What did you mean? Confirms what? What have you been told?'

'You are quite right but you are also wrong,' said Catherine. 'The young woman who drowned was not my patient. But Lily Penlington is.'

Eleanor looked puzzled: 'You're confusing me. The young woman who drowned was Lily Penlington and she has been formally identified. My father opened the inquest yesterday and took evidence of identity from the hotel manager, Mr Gregory.'

'Mr Gregory was mistaken,' said Catherine, her voice sounding dull.

'I don't understand,' said Eleanor.

'Eleanor, if I tell you what I know I shall burden you with a responsibility you won't want. I asked you for advice about my duty of confidentiality to my patient but now I need advice as to my duty to report a crime. You're the only person I can trust but I don't want to implicate you and I have been battling since Wednesday trying to decide what to do for the best.'

'There have been a lot of ups and downs in our lives, Catherine, and we have always shared them, so why should this be any different. I have relied on your professional advice many times and now, if it is my turn to help you, please do not hesitate. I can see that something is troubling you and I am quite prepared to share the burden, whatever it is.'

'I won't deny that it would be a great relief, Eleanor, not only to share the burden but to have your opinion. With your ability to think clearly perhaps you will see a way forward.'

'So, begin by telling me why you think Mr Gregory was mistaken.'

'I don't just think he was mistaken. I know he was. But that concerns the end of this story so, if you don't mind, I shall start at the beginning of it. It will be easier to understand. Lily Penlington is my patient and she may still be alive.'

Eleanor interrupted: 'Then who is the young woman who drowned?'

'I'm coming to that. On Wednesday someone came to see me. Let's call her Mary for the moment although that is not her real name. She also is a waitress at St Anne's Hotel and a friend of Lily's. A very close friend, in fact. Lily came from Sheffield, not one of Lady C.'s protegés, just someone with initiative who came via Mrs Wright's servants' registry in Spring Gardens. When she arrived, she didn't have any accommodation and Mary's mother was looking for a lodger to help pay the rent. She's a war widow so they offered Lily a room in their cottage at Burbage.

'Some months ago, Lily met a man, well, a gentleman according to Mary, who paid her a lot of attention and made all the usual promises which, inevitably were not met and which lead to Lily coming to see me. That is the visit I told you about when we were walking. Lily had given me a false name and address and had said that she was married when she was not. The reason she did not come back to see me was that she didn't need me to confirm her pregnancy. She confided in her friend Mary and Mary covered for her when she started to be nauseous in the mornings. The so-called gentleman did not want to know and gave Lily forty pounds and an address in Manchester and told her to get someone to, as he put it, "help her with her problem" and made it clear he wanted nothing more to do with her.'

'I'm guessing this doesn't have a happy ending.' They looked at each other, shaking their heads, in despair. Eleanor said: 'So, did Lily take the money?'

'Yes, and she went to Manchester intending to visit the address.'

'I have no idea how much money she would have needed but forty pounds, even taking into account the train fare, seems like a lot of money. Probably more than half of what she earns in a year.'

'You are quite right. From what I have heard ten pounds would be the more usual charge, certainly no more than twenty. Forty pounds seems to be an attempt to buy her off.'

'Have you spoken to Lily? How do you know all of this?' asked Eleanor.

'No, I haven't spoken to her. And, don't worry, I know enough about the law to know that she may have committed a crime.'

'Yes, she may have, depending on the method used. And then you may have an obligation to report it.'

'I know that too. My information is all third hand through Mary'

'So, how does Mary know? And if she works at St Anne's Hotel, how is it that she didn't provide information to the police when they were trying to identify the young woman in the pond, whom you now believe is not Lily Penlington?'

'Mary wasn't there at the time. She had a few days' leave. On the day before the young woman was found, Mary had gone to Chesterfield to join her mother there. Mary's elder sister was having her first baby and they were going there to help her. By the time Mary came back to work, the young woman had been identified as Lily Penlington. Mary was confused because she knew Lily had gone to Manchester.

She assumed that Lily had changed her mind, had decided not to have the abortion, and had come back earlier than planned. Then she thought maybe Lily had killed herself. Mary couldn't say anything because she didn't want to give Lily away. Also, she was afraid that she would be in trouble herself because of what she had done to help Lily. So the day after she came back to work Mary went to Manchester to look for Lily.'

'But why? If she thought Lily was the young woman who drowned?'

'Because she realised that there might have been another explanation. She realised that Lily might still be alive. You see, the young woman who drowned in the lake was not Lily. It was Lily's sister. Mrs Ardern was mistaken when she looked at the photograph the police sergeant showed her. The person in the photograph that she thought she recognised was not my patient nor was she Lily.'

Eleanor stared at Catherine and then frowned as she tried to take this new information in and make sense of it. Eventually, she said: 'But, I still don't understand. How did all this confusion arise?'

CHAPTER TWENTY

'Let me explain in a little more detail,' said Catherine. 'Mary and Lily have been close friends for some time and Mary seems to know a lot about Lily and her history. The story of Lily and her sister, Rose, is incredibly sad even before this latest tragedy. Their father was killed in France during the War and their mother couldn't cope. She took her own life with an overdose of sleeping pills. The girls were sixteen at the time but they had no income so they had to find work. They were reasonably well educated but weren't trained for anything and they looked for jobs as waitresses. The trouble was that they are identical twins. Lily got a job in one of the large hotels in Sheffield but the manager wouldn't employ Rose as well because he said it was too confusing employing two people he couldn't tell apart, confusing both for the customers as well as for him. So Rose went to Manchester and got a job in one of the big hotels there. Then Lily got the job in Buxton and they used to co-ordinate their days off, get the train to Stockport and meet up there. Rose knew all about the trouble Lily was in and the attitude of Lily's so-called gentleman friend. Lily decided that there was only one way out but she didn't want anyone to know that she was having a child, or worse, that she had had an abortion. You know what it would have been like for her to make that public. So between them, when they met up at Stockport, they hatched a plan.

'They decided to make it appear that Lily had never left Buxton by simply swapping places for a few days.

Apparently, they used to do that all the time at school and no-one ever guessed and even their own mother used to get confused. Of course, they needed Mary's help to make it work and she agreed. Mary has seen both sisters and she says she could not tell them apart. So, on the Saturday before Rose died, Lily packed a bag with her clothes and her uniform from St Anne's Hotel and Rose did the same with her things. They planned to meet on the platform at Stockport, go to the ladies' cloakroom, swap bags, change into each other's clothes and then leave the station as each other. Lily was to go on to Manchester and pretend to be Rose. Apparently, Rose had an attic room at the hotel where she worked and Lily was able to stay there. Rose was to come back to Buxton. This swap went as planned and Mary said she met Rose at the station here and took her back home. Mary's mother had already gone to Chesterfield. So, on the Monday, Mary took Rose to work and Rose pretended to be Lily. Mary showed her as much as she could and then on that night left for Chesterfield and Rose continued to pretend that she was Lily.'

'Ah, things are starting to fall into place. I've read the witness statements of the other waitresses at St Anne's and they said that Lily, or rather the person they thought was Lily, didn't seem to be herself on the day she died and, of course, she wasn't. She was someone else. Mary wouldn't have been there to help her that second day and, apparently, she got a telling off because she failed to recognise a regular customer.'

'Oh dear, that was obviously something they couldn't plan for.'

'Have another sandwich,' said Eleanor as she took one.

'Thank you.' Catherine helped herself to another sandwich. 'Mary only found out about the drowning when she came back to work on the Friday. It must have been quite a shock and, of course, everyone thought it was Lily who had died. The plan had been for Lily and Rose to meet up again at the station at Stockport and swap identities back again and that should have happened before Mary got back from Chesterfield. So Mary was expecting Lily to be back at work when she got back to work herself. When she first heard about the drowning, Mary thought it was Lily but then she found out that the drowning was on Tuesday night and she knew that it must have been Rose who died. Then she thought perhaps Lily had changed her mind and come back from Manchester early. Mary started to panic and didn't want to say anything about the swap or the abortion because she didn't want to give her friends away. Also she was afraid that by helping Lily to have an abortion she might have done something illegal and would be arrested. Then she realised that, if Lily hadn't come back early and it was Rose in the lake, Lily wouldn't know that Rose was dead.'

'I've just remembered something else that now falls into place. The young woman's shoes were missing and one thought to be hers was later found. We were puzzled because it had the letter R marked inside and that seemed a bit odd as it was the left shoe. But now that makes sense. The R was for Rose.'

Catherine nodded. 'Yes, that does make sense. Obviously although they were identical twins there would be slight differences and the size or shape of their feet might be one such variation. If so, when they swapped clothes, they would probably still prefer to keep their own shoes.'

'So when did Mary realise what had happened?'

'On Saturday, Mary went to Manchester. She knew which hotel to go to and when she asked to see Rose, that is Lily, she was told that Lily wasn't there. The restaurant manager said that Lily finished work on the Wednesday and hadn't been seen since. He introduced Mary to one of the waitresses and she told Mary that, on Wednesday evening, Lily went out saying she was going to meet a friend. The waitress said

Lily hadn't been very well that day and thought she must be getting a cold. Lily didn't turn up for work on the next day and the manager sent someone to check on her room and Lily wasn't there but her things were still there so they put it down to "women's troubles" and assumed she would turn up. Mary knew that the plan had been for Rose and Lily to meet at Stockport station on Wednesday evening, go to a café and have tea together, and then swap bags and return to their respective towns. Mary seems a pretty level-headed person and she asked to see Lily's room and realised that some things were missing. Lily's purse and her bag that she had her clothes in were gone. So Mary concluded that Lily had left for Stockport on Wednesday as planned and, as you can imagine, by now she was really worried. And when Mary told me this, so was I.'

'I can well understand that,' said Eleanor, 'because if Lily was not well on the Wednesday it suggests that she had had the abortion.'

'Exactly and, as we all know how dangerous that can be, I immediately feared the worst.'

'If she did get the train to Stockport and was taken ill, why did she not just go back to Manchester?' asked Eleanor.

'According to Mary, they had checked Bradshaw beforehand and Rose was to get the train from Buxton at ten past six in the evening so Lily would have been planning to get to Stockport to meet that train,' said Catherine. 'If she wasn't well, she probably was hoping Rose would be able to take care of her. She may not have been in any fit state to make it back again to Manchester.'

'And Rose would not have been on the train, of course, so I suppose Lily might have waited on the platform for the next train thinking that Rose had missed the one she had planned to catch.'

'Possibly.'

'I've just remembered something, something Philip said.

It was at Lady Carleton-West's reception, don't you remember. When you asked if the waitress had been identified.'

'Yes,' interrupted Catherine. 'Now that you mention it, I do remember. Philip said he thought he knew the waitress concerned because he sometimes goes to St Anne's Hotel with clients and he said she was very attractive. I thought it might be my patient because she had said she was a waitress and she was certainly very attractive. I was anxious to know who the woman was but we never finished the conversation.'

'Philip said he thought he had seen her on the platform at Stockport when he was on the way to Manchester but then he realised it couldn't have been her because that was in the evening and the woman had been found in the lake that morning. It must have been Lily he saw. So what do you think has happened to Lily?' asked Eleanor.

'Well, as I said, when I heard that Lily was not feeling well, I feared the worst. Back street abortionists are renowned for their dangerous practices and there are several complications which can develop, the most common being haemorrhage and puerperal fever. I think I can safely rule out haemorrhage in Lily's case because it is not something she could have hidden but, if she was feeling unwell it suggests that she may have developed puerperal fever caused by infection.'

'Which can be fatal. Isn't that what Jane Seymour is thought to have died of? Henry the Eight's Third.'

'Possibly. I don't think anyone is sure,' said Catherine. 'But it was a pretty common hazard then and it still is. The condition can progress very rapidly. In Lily's case, the timing seems right given the symptoms.'

'Would you like some of Mrs Clayton's cake?'

'Yes, please, her cakes are delicious,' said Catherine.

'So, what do we do now?'

'That's what I want to ask you. Mary wants to know what has happened to her friend. She is afraid to go to the police because she is frightened that there may be consequences for her because of her involvement. She came to me because she knew that Lily had consulted me and she thought that, as I already knew part of the story, I would be more likely to believe her than anyone else would. And I must admit it is an unlikely story.'

'So, clearly, the first thing we need to do is to find Lily. The second thing is to clear up the mistake over Rose's identity and the third thing we need to do is find out how Rose died. Do you have any ideas as to how to find Lily?'

'I thought the first place to start might be Stockport. If Lily did get the train to Stockport to meet Rose as arranged and was taken ill there, that seems to be the most likely explanation for her absence from the hotel the following day. If she did have puerperal fever as I suspect, she could have collapsed and lost consciousness, in which case she may have been taken to hospital. So, she may be in a hospital in Stockport or she may not have survived. As a doctor, I am the obvious person to make enquiries at the hospital but I do have to be cautious. A doctor enquiring about a patient who has puerperal fever may be mistaken for someone who has been involved in the abortion itself.'

'Yes, I see your point. I know that you would not have suggested an abortion but other people might imply that you did, and, after all, she was your patient and she went to Manchester after she had consulted you. They might imply that she went at your suggestion and possibly to an address provided by you.'

'Unfortunately, there are doctors who will provide an address for a patient. Sometimes the women are very desperate and it is obvious that they are intending to find someone who can help them, so giving them the address of someone reliable is the best way to protect them from worse harm. It is a far from satisfactory situation and certainly not a solution that I ever offer but I cannot prove that.'

'No, because there is no independent record of what you may or may not have said to your patient in the privacy of your consulting room. People are very willing to see a cause and effect between two unrelated facts if it suits their theory of how the world does or, according to them, ought to operate.'

'Exactly.'

'I think we do have to try and find Lily because she may need help and also she should be told about Rose.'

Catherine nodded. 'Although how will she ever live with that? Knowing that Rose would still be alive if she hadn't swapped with her.'

Eleanor looked at Catherine. 'You're right. Officially, the death is still unexplained but there are some facts that suggest that another person may have been involved in her death.'

'Unless that other person knew of the swap,' suggested Catherine.

'Which is unlikely if Mary is to be believed. So, we now have to identify someone who had a motive to kill Lily.'

'Well,' said Catherine, 'what about the person who gave Lily the forty pounds to go to Manchester. Who would have done that apart from the person Lily believed to be the father?'

'And if he did pay it suggests that he too thought he was responsible. Surely he wouldn't pay otherwise.'

'And clearly he had no intention of marrying Lily,' said Catherine, 'although, according to Mary, that is what Lily believed he intended, otherwise she would never have allowed herself to give in to his demands. Sadly, this is a story I hear all too often.'

'Women never learn,' said Eleanor.

'But why would he kill Rose?' said Catherine. 'Oh, of course, because he didn't know it was Rose.'

'I have a witness who saw two people, one of whom may

well have been Rose, on Broad Walk the night Rose died. The other person, a man, said to her: "What are you doing here?" which suggests that the man recognised the woman he was talking to and his comment would make sense if he thought he was speaking to Lily and expected her to be in Manchester.'

'And this witness is reliable?'

'Very,' said Eleanor. 'And she also recalled that the man said: "I told you to get rid of him" or something like that, she wasn't sure. And, another thing. She said that the young woman looked surprised when the man spoke to her. If that was Rose and not Lily, that would make sense because Rose would not have known who the man was who spoke to her.'

'It does seem to fit, doesn't it? And the young woman that your witness saw was on Broad Walk?'

'Yes,' said Eleanor, 'some time around ten o'clock on the night before the woman was found in the pond. According to the witness statements, Lily, in other words Rose, left St Anne's Hotel around ten o'clock and, if Lily was lodging with Mary's mother at Burbage she was probably walking home when she met the man on Broad Walk. I've just realised that there are some details from the witness statements that help to fill in the picture. That night, it was the birthday of one of the waitresses and she and her friends had arranged to go down to the kitchens at the end of their shift for birthday cake, and then they were going to the King's Head for a drink to celebrate. They invited Lily, that is, Rose, to join them but she had been told to go and see the *maître d'* at the end of her shift because he was displeased with her and she had to wait for him. She didn't get away from the hotel until about ten o'clock. The other waitresses would have left by then and Rose may not have known where the King's Head is. So, no doubt, she decided to go straight home, which puts her on Broad Walk at some time around ten o'clock.'

'So was the encounter with the man just bad luck?' said Catherine. 'How did he know she was there?'

'The witness said that she thought the man had been following the young woman along Broad Walk. She would have been coming from St Anne's Hotel so perhaps he had been somewhere near there himself and spotted her. We definitely need to find the man and Lily is the obvious person who can lead us to him. Failing that, we shall have to rely on Mary. Does Mary know who Lily was seeing, do you think?'

'I did ask Mary but she doesn't know his name. He's a customer at the hotel that is how Lily met him. Lily used to meet him sometimes after she had finished her shift. According to Mary, he would go to the bar and have a message sent to Lily to say that he was there. It all had to be kept secret because the staff are forbidden to fraternise with the hotel's clients. She would have been dismissed if the manager had found out. I suppose all the secrecy made it seem romantic to Lily but it sounds rather sordid. She was clearly being taken advantage of.'

'And I suppose she thought that she wasn't taking much of a risk. If she was found out and lost her job it wouldn't matter because the man was going to marry her.'

'Probably. Mary said that when Lily asked her to help with the plan to go to Manchester, all thought of marriage had gone, and Lily told Mary that she felt a fool for trusting the man and she never wanted either to see him or mention his name ever again.'

'A hard lesson to have to learn.' said Eleanor. 'So, back to our first task. How are we going to find Lily? You can't do it, and I have no authority, so the only person who can make the appropriate enquiries is my father. As Coroner he certainly has the authority to do so and that includes contacting a hospital to ask about one of their patients.'

'Does that mean he has to know all the facts? I did

promise Mary that I would keep her out of it.'

'I don't have to tell him about Mary at this stage but he is entitled to know the identity of the person whose death is being investigated. And he will have to tell Superintendent Johnson. I am sure he will be prepared to try to find Lily first before he has to take any further action.'

'All right. I would suggest that the first place to enquire is the Stockport Infirmary. If, as I suspect, Lily didn't get back to Manchester, that would be where she would have been taken. It is only a short distance from the station. Almost next to it, in fact.' Catherine paused. 'Since Mary came to see me, I have been wondering what I could have done to prevent this. Perhaps I should have been more help to Lily when she was so clearly distressed. I feel that, in a way, I have let her down.'

'But that's nonsense. You weren't going to help her get rid of her problem or even recommend someone who would. What could you possibly have done?'

'Oh, I don't know. Been more sympathetic. Found somewhere for her to go until she had had the baby.'

'And just where would you have found such a place? We all know that there is nowhere for single women in that condition to go. Except the workhouse or an institution for fallen women. That is why they so often end up seeking an abortion or committing suicide. You know that. As a doctor you've seen the figures. I don't think you should be blaming yourself.'

'I know. I know. But all the same, I do wish I had been able to do something.' Catherine stood up. 'And now I must go. I have a heap of paperwork to do.'

Eleanor said: 'You may still be able to help Lily if she is alive because not only has she lost a baby, she has lost a sister, and if anyone has reason to blame herself it will be Lily having inadvertently brought about Rose's death. In the meantime, there is Mary to be concerned about. She has been dragged into this and probably was just trying to help a friend who may now be dead.'

'Yes, you're right. Practical as ever, Eleanor,' said Catherine. 'I cannot thank you enough for your clear-sightedness.'

'I am very glad that you asked for help and shared this information with me because it has confirmed my suspicions about Rose's death and I intend to find the person responsible.' Eleanor picked up the picnic basket and re-packed it. 'My father was planning to play golf this afternoon but he may not have left yet. I shall ask him to telephone the matron at the Stockport Infirmary and I shall telephone you to let you know the result.'

'Thank you again, Eleanor, and thank you for lunch. Tell Mrs Clayton I enjoyed it.'

Catherine gave Napoleon a farewell pat and headed towards the short cut to Hardwick Square. Eleanor and Napoleon returned to Hall Bank.

CHAPTER TWENTY-ONE

M r Harriman had already left for the golf course when
Eleanor and Napoleon returned to Hall Bank so
Eleanor took Napoleon for a walk. He trotted happily along
oblivious to Eleanor's sombre mood. Eleanor replayed in
her head the conversation she had just had with Catherine.
By the time they returned to Hall Bank half an hour later,
Eleanor was sure that Rose's death was no accident. They
went up to Eleanor's office, Napoleon to snooze and Eleanor
to think. While she waited for Mr Harriman to return,
Eleanor decided to review the evidence. She took a large
sheet of paper, drew up a chart headed: Means Motive
Opportunity. Then she set herself the task of filling in all the
facts that she had under these three headings.

Eleanor decided to skip the first two headings for the
moment and tackle Opportunity. Rose had no connection
with Buxton apart from her swap with Lily and that absence
of connection seemed to argue against Rose being known to
her killer. On the other hand, the words overheard by Miss
Clitheroe on Broad Walk suggested that the killer knew, or
thought he knew, the person to whom he was speaking. The
words also indicated that he had not expected to see that
person in Buxton on that night. Eleanor noted these facts on
her paper and considered the next heading. If, as it seemed,
the opportunity had presented itself unexpectedly giving the
assailant no time to plan, the choice of means was limited.
With no weapon available, the only means were the killer's
hands and probably his superior strength. Eleanor wrote the

words "half-strangled and carried to lake" followed by a question mark. Then she wrote "half-strangled, victim staggered into lake, and passed out" and added several question marks. "Minus shoes. Removed by killer??"

Finally, Eleanor looked at the heading: Motive. As she stared at the paper, she recalled Philip's words when they had been down to the lake and tried to reconstruct the scene. He had said: "Now all you have to do is work out what made me angry enough to half-strangle you." Only one motive had suggested itself so far. The man seen by Miss Clitheroe had said: "What are you doing here?" Mary had told Catherine that Lily had been given money and told to go to Manchester. The killer, seeing "Lily" on Broad Walk, thought she had disobeyed him. Perhaps that had made him angry enough to take matters into his own hands, literally, and dispose of both mother and child.

Eleanor turned then to the evidence and had to admit that it seemed fairly thin. A body found in the ornamental lake in the Gardens, mistakenly identified as Lily Penlington. An unexplained death. Two missing shoes, one retrieved from the river about two hundred yards away. A man who followed a young woman, who may or may not have been Rose Penlington, along Broad Walk, who spoke to the young woman, and then may or may not have gone into the Gardens. The only certainty was that a private detective witnessed the events on Broad Walk at some time around ten o'clock on the night before Rose Penlington was found dead. Eleanor chose to believe that this was not co-incidence but she also admitted to herself that it could well be.

It was clear that the only way forward was to establish the identity of the man whom Lily had believed was going to marry her and establish a link between him and the man on Broad Walk. Eleanor thought back to her conversation with Catherine and remembered that although Mary did not know the name of the man Lily was meeting, she did know that he was a customer at the hotel. That reminded Eleanor of something Philip had told her.

Eleanor had been so absorbed with her thoughts and her notes that she had not noticed that it had started to rain quite heavily. Mr Harriman and his partners had decided that it was too wet to continue. They declared their round to be nine holes instead of eighteen, and Mr Harriman came home earlier than expected. Eleanor said that she needed to talk to him. She made them a cup of tea and then went into the sitting room, taking with her the sheet of paper on which she had jotted down her thoughts. She told Mr Harriman of her conversation with Catherine and he agreed that the priority was to find what had happened to Lily. He agreed to telephone the Stockport Infirmary.

Eleanor said: 'If Lily is there, she may have no identification. In the same way that Rose was without any. So if they do have a patient there that might be Lily I was thinking about how we could be sure it was her. Could we ask if the patient has shoes with an L inside?'

They went down into Mr Harriman's office and he telephoned the Stockport Infirmary. The Matron was doing her rounds and it was going to be some time before she would be available. Mr Harriman left a message asking her to call him back. While they waited, Mr Harriman looked at Eleanor's notes.

'I agree with your summary, Eleanor, and I think it covers everything that we know so far,' said Mr Harriman. 'I also agree that the inquest verdict is looking less and less like accident or misadventure. I should certainly like to know more about the man that Lily met at St Anne's Hotel. Do you have any thoughts on that?'

'Something has occurred to me and I need to speak to Philip. He's been doing a little research for me already.'

Before Mr Harriman could enquire further, the telephone call from the hospital came through. Mr Harriman explained who he was and what he needed to know. Eleanor then listened to a one-sided conversation which mostly consisted of 'I see' and 'When was this?' all said in a grave tone. Finally, Mr Harriman said: 'I may be able to help you. Can you tell me what she had with her?' He listened and then said 'I can do that but I shall need to make a formal arrangement first. I shall telephone you again as soon as I can.' Mr Harriman said goodbye to the matron, replaced the listening device, and put the telephone stand back on his desk.

'It's not good news, is it?' said Eleanor.

'I'm afraid not. The matron said that a young woman of about eighteen was brought in by ambulance from Stockport station on the Wednesday before last, that is, the sixth. The hospital has not been able to identify her. The Matron will ask someone to telephone us with a description of the things she had with her. I shall ask about the shoes. The patient was brought in from Stockport station. She had collapsed on the platform and was initially diagnosed as having a fever accompanied by abdominal pain. The woman was barely conscious when she was brought in and only able to say a few incoherent words to the doctor who examined her and she died twenty-four hours later without regaining consciousness. The matron said that she had no proof but she suspected that, as she put it, "the woman had recently undergone an illegal procedure." I am sure she has seen enough of those to be able to recognise the signs.'

The telephone rang again and Mr Harriman picked up the telephone stand again. Mr Harriman identified himself. 'Yes, thank you, I've got all that. Now would you just look at the patient's shoes for me and tell me if there is a letter marked on the inside of the shoe.' There was a pause. 'Ah, yes. Thank you. Good-bye.'

As he replaced the telephone stand, Mr Harriman said: 'That was a good idea of yours, Eleanor. Both shoes have the letter L inside them. These are the other items she had with her. A bag containing clothes, including a uniform, a purse which contained a pound note and some coins, a return train ticket for Manchester, I suppose they were going to swap train tickets, a platform ticket for Stockport, and a key with a tag on which has the numbers one-seven-one, presumably a room number. There will have to be a formal identification, of course but, from what you have told me, it does not seem as though there is much doubt. The matron sounded relieved by my telephone call because she is keen to identify the patient and any next of kin. I shall get Superintendent Johnson to organise that as soon as possible.'

'The shoes, the bag of clothes and the items in the purse really leave very little room for doubt as to their patient's identity,' said Eleanor. 'Also, it means that the shoe that was found in the river does belonged to Rose.' She sighed. 'All I can think is that, if it is Lily, at least she won't have to spend the rest of her life blaming herself for her sister's death. I know how I'd feel if I had put Cicely in that situation. And it would be so much worse for Lily because she would have been left alone without her twin and twins are known to be very close.'

'Yes,' said Mr Harriman, 'she was not to know that she was putting her sister in danger but, nevertheless, it would be something she would certainly regret. Thanks to Catherine, we are getting a much clearer picture of what happened. I shall speak to Superintendent Johnson so that we can have both of the young women correctly identified and then we shall concentrate on identifying the man involved with Lily. It looks as though Miss Clitheroe's information may be important after all and, if so, I hope she will have finished her investigation by the time it becomes necessary to call her as a witness.'

'Yes, her information has been vital in allowing us to piece together this sequence of events. Now, I must go and telephone Catherine. I promised to let her know if we managed to find Lily.'

O O O

Eleanor and Philip had agreed to play tennis at five o'clock that afternoon. When Philip arrived at Hall Bank, the rain had stopped but they knew the courts would still be wet so they decided to go for a walk instead. Although Napoleon was always willing to sit and watch Eleanor play tennis, he much preferred walking and wholeheartedly approved of this decision.

'Let's go up Macclesfield Road and then back via Green Lane,' said Eleanor.

'Good idea,' said Philip. 'We haven't been that way for a while.'

Eleanor said: 'I should warn you though, I do have a favour to ask.'

'Hmm. What sort of favour? Is this more of the snooping on Hedley Godwin kind of favour?'

'I really am grateful for your help, Philip, and this is another one of those tasks that I can't do myself. If I thought I could disguise myself as a chap I would certainly do my own snooping.'

Philip snorted with mirth. 'Oh yes, I can just picture you in a false moustache and beard and one of your father's suits, the trousers baggy and too long, flopping over your shoes. You'd look very convincing, I'm sure.'

'Don't be unkind,' said Eleanor, laughing. 'I was not suggesting that I should do that, I was just expressing my regret that I could not. I rather fancy a false moustache and beard.'

'Then you can dress up as Father Christmas at the Tennis Club's children's party this year. We're always short of volunteers. So, what is this favour?'

'I need to find a friendly and preferably gossipy barman at the St Anne's Hotel who will provide information about a regular customer. In particular, one who may have had a particular interest in a waitress there.'

'And this has something to do with Lily Penlington, I suppose.'

'Yes. I can't tell you the whole story at the moment but I'll tell you as much as I can so that you know how best to get the information. I believe that, strictly against the hotel's policy, Lily was friendly with, well more than friendly with, one of the customers who was regularly in the bar. You might find it difficult to get anyone to talk, given that such a relationship is a breach of the rules, but any information you can gather will be of help. It would be best to find a barman who was on duty in the evenings. That's when the customer in question was usually there.'

'I shall certainly do my best,' said Philip. 'I have been persevering with my assignment at the Club and I'm almost ready to report so I can swap my evenings at the Club with evenings at St Anne's instead.' Philip laughed. 'Some people would envy my job. And now, we had better get going. I can see that, having heard the word walk, Napoleon is champing at the bit.'

They set off down Hall Bank and turned on to Broad Walk which was busy with visitors who had come out of their hotels and lodging houses now that the rain had stopped.

CHAPTER TWENTY-TWO

On Sunday afternoon, when Eleanor and Napoleon reached Oxford House, Philip had already arrived. Ellen, Cicely's maid answered the door and Eleanor handed her the box of pastries from Collinsons and went into the sitting room.

'Hello, both,' she said, as Napoleon checked to see who was present and then occupied the hearth rug.

'Where's Richard?' asked Eleanor. 'I've got some coloured pencils for him.'

'He's gone out with the family of a school friend to visit some relations who have a farm at Tideswell,' said Cicely. 'They invited him to lunch so he'll probably be back shortly. The friend lives on Temple Road and he's going to walk back from there.'

'It's a beautiful day for being out in the countryside,' said Eleanor. 'Except for yesterday, the weather recently has been exceptional. I'd much prefer to be outside rather than in the office.'

'I hope it's fine next week for the West Indies tour. It would be a shame to have it washed out,' said Philip. 'It's the first international cricket we have had since before the War.'

'Yes,' said Cicely, 'Richard's been asking if he can go. It's such a good thing for the town. First the National Liberal Federation conference and now the cricket.'

'The publicity will certainly be a boost to the town,' said Eleanor.

'And speaking of publicity,' said Philip, 'when I was in

town last week, I happened to go past a motor car showroom and as I had a few minutes to spare I went in to have a chat.'

'Oh, yes,' said Eleanor.

'I came away with this leaflet for the new model Bentley. What do you think?' Philip handed over the leaflet to Eleanor and before she could comment the front door-bell sounded.

Cicely said: 'That will be Richard.'

At the sound of the bell, Napoleon sat up and listened, head tilted to one side, in anticipation of a new arrival. Cicely got up and went towards the door of the sitting room at the same time as Ellen came along the hallway to open the front door.

Eleanor heard the front door open and then there was a shriek from Ellen followed by a high pitched: 'Nooo!!!'

Cicely rushed into the hallway to see what was happening and then heard Ellen, clearly upset, say: 'Oh, no, no, Master Richard. You mustn't bring that inside. Take it out. Quick!'

Napoleon went into the hall to investigate and Eleanor and Philip looked at each other with raised eyebrows, unaccustomed to such a forceful and decisive outburst from Ellen who was usually a very gentle soul bordering on timid. As they waited to hear the cause of the commotion, Eleanor said: 'It sounds as though he's brought home something from the farm.'

'A lamb or a piglet, perhaps?' joked Philip.

'Oh, goodness. I hope not.'

Napoleon returned to the sitting room, followed by Richard, who said: 'Hello, Aunt Lella. Hello Mr Danebridge.' He plomped himself down on the sofa next to Philip, looking very dissatisfied with life, folded his arms, and said, rather scornfully: 'I don't know what all the fuss is about. It was only flowers. And I picked them specially.'

Cicely returned to the sitting room, shaking her head, having restored calm in the hall. She said: 'Richard brought home some lovely daisies for me from the farm and there was some Cow Parsley mixed in with them. That's what Ellen was upset about. Richard didn't realise. He just thought he was bringing home some pretty flowers for me but as soon as Ellen saw the Cow Parsley she panicked.'

'And she doesn't even know the proper name for it,' said Richard, indignantly. From a young age, Richard had been interested in botany and could recognise and name all the local wild-flowers both by their common and their botanical names. 'It's called Anthriscus,' he said. 'Anthriscus silvestris, actually.' he added, for emphasis.

'I'm sure you're right, Richard,' said Cicely, 'but the local girls call it Mother Die and get quite anxious about it being brought inside.'

'Oh, I know,' said Eleanor. 'They are quite superstitious about it. They won't allow it at all.'

'I don't know why,' said Cicely, 'and it's quite irrational because, after all, it's just a common wild-flower. It's in all the grass verges.'

'Exactly,' said Richard, gloomily. 'And there was only one piece of it anyway. I had to throw it away to please Ellen.'

'Never mind,' said Cicely. 'It was very thoughtful of you to bring some flowers for me and the daisies still look lovely even without the Cow Parsley but Ellen was really upset so it was kinder to her not to bring that into the house.'

'Girls are so silly,' said Richard and sighed.

'Come and look at the photograph Mr Danebridge has brought,' said Cicely. 'It's the new Bentley.'

Philip held out the photograph to Richard and, as he took it, his eyes went wide and there was a long drawn out: 'Cor!'

Cicely frowned at this colloquial language which Richard had copied from school friends but refrained from comment, pleased that his attention had been distracted from his wounded pride.

Philip smiled. 'Yes, that's exactly what I thought when I saw it.'

'Are you going to get one?' asked Richard, eagerly.

'Well, I'm not sure. It's a three litre tourer. Tell me what you think of it?'

The two of them went into a huddle to discuss the merits of the new model and Eleanor said to Cicely: 'Is Ellen all right?'

'Yes, just a bit anxious. I tried to reassure her but these old country beliefs are deep-seated and she was really quite shaken.'

'I'm sure. We all know about the superstition, of course, but I've never bothered to enquire into its origins.'

'Ellen was quite worked up about it and you know how meek and mild she usually is. She was determined that Richard's bunch of flowers would not come into the house. Luckily, Richard didn't manage to get inside the hall with his offering before I got to the door and I managed to extract the Cow Parsley from the bunch before it came in so, strictly speaking, it didn't cross the threshold.'

'I suppose that helps to minimise the evil, whatever it is, but I can't see what damage Cow Parsley could do. I find it very attractive, at least, outside along the verges. Nevertheless, you don't want Ellen refusing to stay in the house because it has a curse on it.'

'Certainly not,' said Cicely, emphatically. 'We're fully booked for the whole of July and August, and I couldn't possibly manage without Ellen. I'll just go and check on her and ask her to bring in tea.'

Eleanor turned her attention to the conversation between Philip and Richard.

'You could race it at Brooklands,' said Richard, excitedly, his eyes alight at the prospect.

'Or even, Le Mans,' added Philip. 'Have you heard of that?' Richard shook his head. 'No,' continued Philip, 'not many people have but they will soon.' Philip pointed to the photograph on the leaflet that Richard was holding. 'And they will have heard of that motor car soon as well. Le Mans is a village in France and there was a motor car race there last month, for the first time ever. It started in the village and the cars drove in a circuit around the country roads and back to the village. That motor car, the three litre Bentley, was racing against Excelsiors and Bugattis. The Bentley didn't win but that was only because of a piece of bad luck. I think it would have won otherwise even though the Excelsiors have a much bigger engine. The King of Belgium has an Excelsior.'

'What bad luck did it have?' asked Richard, much more interested in cars than in royalty.

'Well, you know John Duff?'

Richard nodded. 'Rather! He races at Brooklands.'

'That's right. He was driving the Bentley. It had on some new long endurance tyres, specially made for it so they didn't need to carry a spare wheel and that made the motor car much lighter.'

'And faster,' added Richard.

'That's correct. When the race started at four o'clock in the afternoon, it was raining very hard and the roads were muddy and slippery. It was very difficult for the drivers to see through their windshields and they had to drive all through the night in very dangerous conditions. Some of the motor cars didn't even have headlamps and they had to follow the ones that did. Some of the motor cars crashed during the night and were out of the race. In the morning, the Bentley was only two laps behind the Excelsiors and then a stone hit the Bentley's fuel tank and all of the petrol drained out. So then the drivers had to repair the hole and go and fetch more petrol to refill the tank. That cost them two and a half hours.'

Richard groaned. 'Oh, no!'

'Yes,' continued Philip. 'It was jolly hard luck. One of the drivers had to walk all the way back to the pits to get the petrol and then I'll bet you can't guess how he got back to the motor car.'

'On a horse,' said Richard, confidently.

'No, he borrowed the bicycle of one of the gendarmes.'

'What's a gen…one of those that you said?'

'A gendarme. A French policeman.'

Richard giggled. 'An Englishman on a French policeman's bicycle?'

Philip continued: 'Yes, the poor chap had to cycle all the way back to the motor car carrying two tins of petrol strapped to his back. I bet he wobbled about a good bit.'

'Especially in all that mud,' added Eleanor, who had been watching with amusement the enjoyment of the two motoring enthusiasts.

Philip smiled at Eleanor and nodded in agreement.

'How did they repair the hole in the tank?' asked Eleanor.

Philip turned back to Richard: 'I'll bet you can't guess.'

Richard thought for a minute and said: 'Sticking plaster.'

'Good guess, but no, not sticking plaster.'

'Hmmm…a glove!' said Richard.

'Another good guess but no, not a glove. It was only a small hole and they used a cork.'

'Perhaps the French policeman had a bottle of French wine handy,' suggested Eleanor.

Richard and Philip both ignored this female levity and Philip continued: 'But, you see, the Bentley couldn't win the race because the rules said that the winner had to be the motor car which had driven the furthest distance in the time. And while the Bentley was stuck on the side of the road having its petrol tank repaired, the other motor cars that were left in the race were still driving and travelling more miles. So, the Bentley only came equal fourth, but I think it was the best motor car in the race and I'm confident that it will win next year. And even though it didn't win the race, it did win the competition for the fastest lap.'

'How fast did it go?' asked Richard.

'About seventy miles an hour. What do you think of that?'

'Gosh. And if you got one of those motor cars, you could go that fast too?'

'Of course,' said Philip.

'And then you could drive in that race.'

'I could. That is, as long as Aunt Lella wouldn't mind,' said Philip, casting a mischievous glance at Eleanor.

'Oh, she wouldn't mind,' said Richard, confidently, 'She's a real sport!' Then he added: 'And she'd let me come with you too.'

Philip saw that Eleanor was trying not to laugh. 'Your mother might have something to say about that though, so we would have to consult her first. That is, if I decide to buy a new car, of course.'

Eleanor rolled her eyes. 'And what is the chance of you refusing such an opportunity?'

'Well, I don't know. After the report I read last Saturday in the *Manchester Guardian*, if I do buy a new Bentley I shall have to move from Buxton or leave the motor car in the garage. Apparently, the Automobile Association has com-pared our local roads with the roads which serve the spa at Harrogate and found them wanting. So much so that the Association has black-listed three of our main roads.'

'That's not very encouraging,' said Eleanor. 'Which ones?'

'The roads to Leek, to Bakewell and to Whaley Bridge.'

'But that means all the main roads in and out of here,' said Eleanor.

'Yes,' said Philip, 'and it will come as no surprise to you I am sure that our local councillor, who made representations to the Derby Council for improvements, formed the opinion that the Derby Council had no intention of doing anything to improve the black-listed roads and didn't take the slightest bit of pride in having a spa in the county.'

'If we had a race in Buxton like the one in Lemons,' said Richard, 'then they would have to make the roads properly, wouldn't they?'

'That's a very good idea, Richard,' said Philip. 'Perhaps we should write to our local councillor and suggest a race. It's Le Mans, by the way, not lemons.'

Cicely came back into the room followed by Ellen, who was now restored and calm enough to carry the tray without rattling the tea things. The photograph of the Bentley was put to one side and Richard was momentarily distracted by the pastries, in particular, the cream puffs. Eleanor was distracted by a thought on an entirely different subject.

O O O

Next morning as Mrs Clayton was preparing breakfast, Napoleon had positioned himself in the hallway as usual so as to supervise proceedings. He was stretched full length on the hall floor, haunches square on, front legs extended as far as possible towards the kitchen doorway, with his chin on the ground between his front paws, eyes alert, and watching Mrs Clayton's every move.

Eleanor came to stand beside the kitchen door and said: 'Mrs Clayton, yesterday Richard brought home some Cow Parsley and Cicely's maid Ellen wouldn't have it in the house. Can you enlighten me as to the traditions associated with Cow Parsley? I've heard it called Mother Die, of course, but I haven't a clue as to why. All of the wild plants have rather odd local names so I've never really thought about it before. Have you any idea?'

Mrs Clayton was in the process of cracking an egg onto a saucer. She looked up and turned towards Eleanor, holding half an eggshell in each hand. 'Has someone died?' she asked, frowning.

'No, not at all,' said Eleanor, surprised by the look of concern Mrs Clayton had given her. 'It's just that Ellen was very upset when Richard tried to bring some into the house and that made me wonder about the reason behind her alarm.'

'I'm not surprised Ellen was upset,' said Mrs Clayton, discarding the eggshells, slipping the egg from the saucer into a bowl and cracking another egg. 'It's considered to be very bad luck.'

'But why? It seems harmless enough. In fact, it's rather attractive.'

'Well, it is, in the hedgerows,' said Mrs Clayton, 'but, if you bring Cow Parsley into the house your mother will die.'

'So I have heard. But, surely that's just a case of superstition.'

'Yes and no,' said Mrs Clayton, picking up some tongs and turning her attention to the bacon in the pan on the hob. 'The superstitious bit is thinking that your mother will die just because you brought the plant into the house but it seems that there's a good bit more to it than that.'

'There must be, surely, for it to create such fear,' agreed Eleanor.

Mrs Clayton nodded as she lightly whisked the eggs in the bowl. 'I know Alf's come up against the belief a few times when he's been doing a collection, especially if he's had to go to one of the outlying hamlets or the farms. The neighbours always come to pay their respects, of course, and if it's a woman who's died, they'll ask if Mother Die had been brought into the house.'

'So, obviously people think there is a connection of some sort?'

'Yes, and this is what Alf told me.' Mrs Clayton paused while she tipped the beaten eggs into a saucepan and began stirring them slowly. 'It was a good few years ago now, early on in his work. He was curious about it when he first heard people ask, so Alf being Alf, he went into it a bit. He read what he could and he asked around and eventually one old lady he met came up with an answer. She told Alf that when she was a child, and she was then in her nineties so she must have been speaking about early last century, the Quality, as she called them, meaning the gentry who owned the land, didn't pay very well and there wasn't farm work all year round so the common folk often didn't have enough to feed their families with. So they would gather what they could from the verges at the roadsides and along the riverbanks. A lot of the wild plants can be eaten, you know, and they can be used to help flavour a broth made of water and, if that's all you have, you're grateful for them. And if you don't have carrots or parsnips you can use the roots of the Cow Parsley in your broth. But,' added Mrs Clayton, turning her attention from the eggs to the bacon and waving the tongs to emphasise her point, 'if you don't know what you are looking for when you are out foraging, you can easily be deceived. If you gather something poisonous by mistake, you pay the price.'

'And are you saying that Cow Parsley can be poisonous?'

'No, no,' said Mrs Clayton, shaking her head and turning back to the hob. Expertly, she flipped the bacon cooking in the pan and Napoleon watched the manoeuvre attentively. 'Not the Cow Parsley, that's not poisonous. The trouble is though, it looks very like another plant that is poisonous. If you mistake Cow Parsley for that and use the roots by mistake, your goose is cooked.'

'That's very interesting. And what is that other plant?'

'Hemlock,' said Mrs Clayton, soberly. 'The leaves are very similar. Easily mistaken and they grow in the same places.'

'Ah,' said Eleanor. 'I see. Hmm, so, in gathering the Cow Parsley, one might easily mistake the leaves of the Hemlock plant for the leaves of the Cow Parsley plant and gather the two together.'

'And, if you don't have your mind on what you are doing, you could easily not notice and once you have cut the leaves off, the two roots look the same.'

'So, having discarded the leaves, one could easily end up eating the root of the Hemlock, thinking that it is Cow Parsley and a harmless substitute for parsnip or carrot.'

'That's it, exactly,' said Mrs Clayton. She picked up a spoon, tasted the scrambled egg, and added a pinch of salt.

'But, if that is the case, everyone's at risk of poisoning, not just the mother. Why Mother Die specifically?' Eleanor's logical mind was whirring, trying to make sense of the connection between the practical situation and the superstition. 'What about other members of the family?'

Mrs Clayton looked puzzled. 'I've no idea,' she said. 'Alf didn't think to ask that.' Mrs Clayton began putting the eggs and bacon into warmed dishes. 'I suppose it's just one of those superstitions that frighten people.'

'Hmmm.' said Eleanor, reflecting on the actions of Mrs Clayton that she had just witnessed with the eggs and the salt. 'I think you may have just supplied the answer to my question. The mother of the family is likely to be the one preparing the broth and no doubt will be the one who tastes the broth for seasoning. Therefore, she samples the broth before anyone else does and is the person most likely to be poisoned.'

'I suppose you may be right. It's certainly an explanation,' said Mrs Clayton as she assembled the warm dishes onto a tray ready to take them into the dining room and arrange them on the sideboard.

Eleanor laughed. 'The ancient Greek philosopher, Socrates, is supposed to have died from Hemlock poisoning. I wonder if someone brought the Hemlock in by mistake, thinking it was Cow Parsley.'

'Did they have Cow Parsley in those days?' asked Mrs Clayton.

'I don't know,' said Eleanor, as she looked distractedly at Mrs Clayton, not really seeing her. She frowned as she concentrated on three pieces of information which had just clicked together in her brain. Then she said: 'Thank you, Mrs Clayton. You've just given me an explanation for something that has been puzzling me.'

'You're welcome, Miss Harriman, I'm sure, though I don't know what that was,' said Mrs Clayton, unperturbed. 'Well, whatever it is you are thinking about, breakfast is ready.' She picked up the tray to carry it into the dining room. Napoleon sat to attention.

'I think it's my turn to ask Catherine for advice,' said Eleanor as she followed Mrs Clayton and Napoleon into the dining room.

CHAPTER TWENTY-THREE

Philip had completed the assignment of gathering information about Hedley Godwin and he had arranged to come
to Hall Bank that evening so that Mr Harriman could also
hear his report.

When they were all settled in the sitting room, Philip said:
'Well, old thing, I know you asked me to find out as much
gossip about Hedley Godwin as possible but I don't think I
can stand any more of these sessions. So, I hope to goodness
what I have to tell you is what you wanted to hear.'

'Oh, I'm sorry. Are they terribly exhausting?'

'Yes, unbelievably so. They are so enormously tedious
and so, so incredibly dull. You would not believe how dull.
Sitting around with a lot of chaps who have imbibed too
freely and are barely coherent is not my idea of a pleasant
evening. And they talk such gibberish when they are in their
cups. Not that they're intellectual giants when they're sober.'

'Poor you,' said Eleanor, 'but I do appreciate your sacrifice. We really do need as much information as possible.'

Mr Harriman smiled and said: 'Given my role in this
affair, I think it will be best if I just sit and listen without
commenting. So, you two go ahead.'

'Jolly good,' said Philip. 'Well, I didn't have much luck
the first two evenings because Hedley wasn't there. He and
some of his chums go down to the Milton's Head to play
cards and I didn't fancy that and, in any event, I thought it
would look a bit suspicious if I suddenly decided to join their
group. On the third night, I managed to get Hedley on his

own. He was there with a group and I had to listen to absolute drivel for a while, fishing stories mostly, and then eventually I found myself alone with Hedley. His chums all went off to the Milton's Head and Hedley stayed behind. I'm not sure why. I asked the barman to keep Hedley topped up with whisky and that made me his friend for life. We had a rather one-sided conversation and he poured out his heart to me. I felt a bit of a cad taking advantage of him like that so I kept reminding myself that it was in a good cause.

'Anyway, he started telling that he had come to Buxton because he knew Godwin Hall was rightfully his. His solicitor in Kent had told him Miss Godwin only had a life interest. I'm telling you the short version, by the way, because this all took a long time to come out. He kept losing the thread of the story and then repeating himself and I kept having to promise him more whisky in order to get his attention again and prompt him back on to the right track. He told me that before he came here, he thought that Miss Godwin was old and frail and would soon die and that he would inherit Godwin Hall the next day. It was obvious that he knew nothing about probate. He spent quite some time telling me that when he met Miss Godwin he was disappointed to find her healthy and he moaned on about how he had travelled all this way only to find that he had been tricked and how unfair it all was. I never did find out who he thought had tricked him. He kept assuring me that it was not his fault that things had gone wrong and kept asking me to agree with him that it wasn't his fault, and then he progressed to asking me, several times, to tell his creditors that he couldn't pay them just yet but that it wasn't his fault. I was his pal and he was relying on me to tell them.'

'This must have become rather monotonous,' said Eleanor.

'It did, I can tell you. Anyway, then there was another long meandering ramble, fuelled with more whisky, and eventually I understood what he meant. When he realised that he was not going to inherit Godwin Hall in the near future, he came up with a scheme to breed horses there. He said Miss Godwin had agreed to it and he telephoned to his solicitor and asked what he should do to get the funds he needed and was advised to go to a bank and ask for a loan on the strength of being the heir to Godwin Hall. He very stupidly promised his creditors that this plan was going to be successful and that he would be able to pay his debts. Of course, the bank was not keen on the proposal and refused the loan and that made him very angry. It was very hard to make sense of what he said.

'The narrative jumped backwards and forwards in time and it was difficult to understand the order in which these events took place but I think the sequence went like this: first of all, he approached the bank not long after he had met Miss Godwin and realised that he was not going to inherit Godwin Hall in the near future, then after Miss Godwin died he went back to the bank or to another bank and was again refused and then he approached you, Mr Harriman. He had a few unkind words to say about you, because I gather you refused to advance any money from the estate?'

'Yes, he came to the office,' said Mr Harriman.

'What did he say about Father?' asked Eleanor.

'Oh, I couldn't possibly repeat that in the presence of a lady!' said Philip and grinned. Eleanor pulled a face at him. 'Shorn of its uncomplimentary expressions, Hedley thinks Mr Harriman is deliberately taking a long time with the paperwork for the probate application and the trust deeds and that his only purpose in doing so is to annoy Hedley Godwin and he wouldn't be doing this if he realised that the delay is putting Hedley Godwin in deadly danger. He didn't put it as lucidly as that and most of his sentences were half finished or they were so long I lost the thread but that is the gist of his oration. You may be getting the impression by now that Hedley is a trifle self-centred.'

'And did he say why he was in danger?' asked Eleanor.

'Apparently, when Hedley was confronted by his creditors in Kent, he gave them an incorrect version of his prospects and they agreed to allow him time to pay and they also allowed him to leave town and come to Buxton, which I thought was rather gracious of them. They sound like thugs to me and his debts are gambling debts so I am sure these creditors are not your ordinary sort who use lawful means to recover their money and then present you with a receipt. Now Hedley is afraid they will find out the truth about his prospects and he will be punished. He kept begging me to tell them it was not his fault. His brain seemed to get stuck on this idea and he kept repeating himself, insisting that I promise to tell them, meaning his creditors. He was so pathetically worried that I kept reassuring him that I would tell everybody it wasn't his fault and I progressed from being his best pal to his only pal in the world and he wanted me to tell everybody that it wasn't his fault and he didn't mean to do it.'

'If his debts are gambling debts and are so enormous that he is in fear of his life, it is hard to see whose fault it is except his own,' said Eleanor.

'Well, quite. I was about to give up and he started on another grievance and there was a monologue about women: women are unreliable especially the good looking ones and they lead a fellow on and then blame the fellow when they change their minds. And then they come back and complain about being in trouble. He wanted to know why they couldn't see he has troubles enough of his own.'

'Did that sound as though he was referring to anyone in particular?'

'It may have done. He didn't refer to any woman by name, it seemed to be women in general or perhaps he was referring to several women. At the end of this ramble there was a long silence and I thought he had fallen asleep but he sort of started and shook himself and then he said "and she had to be dealt with, didn't she? It wasn't my fault, was it?" and then there was another silence and he said "Take my advice. You have to show them who's boss, you know. They take advantage of you otherwise." But I couldn't make out whether he was referring to women or his creditors. I waited a bit longer but then I could see that he was past talking so I asked one of the stewards to see that he got back to his lodgings and left. And that's it, old thing. I hope my sleuthing at the Club has been of use.'

'Enormously and I cannot thank you enough. It sounds as though you had a perfectly beastly time, especially on that last evening.'

'Absolutely vile. In order to avoid him getting suspicious and clamming up, I had to pretend to be as drunk as he was. He was quite incoherent at times and I had to lean in close to him to hear what he was saying so there we were, slumped together on a Chesterfield looking completely dishevelled and disgracefully under the weather and he was breathing whisky fumes all over me. I'm sure I looked and smelled as drunk as he was. I'll never be able to show my face in the Club again. That level of drinking is just not tolerated.'

'Definitely above and beyond the call of duty,' said Mr Harriman. 'I'll have to put in a good word for you with the committee.'

'What sort of a person do you think Hedley really is?' asked Eleanor.

'It's hard to say. He clearly feels sorry for himself. A bit of a sneak as well, I think, the sort who does things behind one's back. And he is genuinely afraid of these creditors, whoever they are, and I got the impression that physical violence might have been tried or at least threatened. I tried to find out how much he owes but I'm not sure he knows himself. They have probably added on a good bit of interest by now anyway. I do think he is the sort of person who doesn't take responsibility. The sort who behaves stupidly or recklessly and then blames everyone else for his misfortunes. One of the chaps at the Club told me that he was out on the moors at a shoot. Hedley was with the group and hadn't been performing particularly well. His aim was pretty poor and he kept blaming the chap next to him for crowding him. Eventually, this other chap got so fed up that he raised his voice at Hedley and told him his performance was down to his own blank, blank, incompetence. Hedley went into a rage and then turned on his loader, accused him of not knowing what he was about and blaming him for his own poor showing. He actually attacked the man and had to be restrained by the other loaders.'

'Goodness,' said Mr Harriman. 'I hope he isn't going to behave like that at Godwin Hall. It does not auger well.'

'It certainly does not,' agreed Eleanor. 'Philip, you have been enormously patient with this fellow and I really do appreciate all the trouble you have taken. It's not the sort of thing either Father or I could have done.'

'Well, my other assignment at St Anne's Hotel was compensation enough. Much less demanding and I think you will be interested in the result although I am not sure what relevance the information has.'

CHAPTER TWENTY-FOUR

After the fifth Duke of Devonshire died, The Crescent was divided into hotels. St Anne's Hotel, the first to be established, occupied the western arm of the building and now advertised itself as a family hotel.

'I was in luck at St Anne's,' said Philip. 'The barman on duty when I went to the hotel used to be an assistant at the shop where my father gets his wine. We recognised each other and it was easy to get into conversation. I observed to him that he had a good view of everyone who came and went in the hotel and that started him off on a topic he enjoyed: his favourite and not-so favourite guests. The conversation flowed on to the regulars and from there it was plain sailing. He confirmed that liaisons with guests are forbidden and when I hinted that, in a hotel the size of St Anne's and as busy, it would be difficult for the management to make sure everyone obeyed the rule, he agreed and said that he knew of several occasions in the past when the rule had been broken and at least one person who had recently been breaking the rule. So I ordered another drink and told him to keep the change. He said Mr Gregory, the manager, didn't know anything about it and he wasn't going to find out now because the person in question was dead. So I suggested that it might have been the waitress who was found in the lake and he agreed. He said it had been going on for a few months, since at least Easter, he thought. I asked him how he knew about it if the manager didn't and he said the customer in question, who was not a guest at the hotel, was a regular at the bar although he didn't come in every night but when he did he used to sit in the bar until just before it was time for the waitress to go off duty and then he would tip the barman to give the waitress a message. He would leave after about ten minutes and meet the waitress outside. The customer was in the bar the night before the waitress was found but he, the barman, hadn't been asked to give her a message that night. I asked how he could remember when it was and he said it was easy because the customer hadn't been in since that night and he still had two pounds on the slate unpaid. He had ordered quite a few drinks that evening.'

'Philip, that is brilliant. Absolutely brilliant. Maybe you should become a Miss Clitheroe after all.'

'I must admit I am getting rather good at all this sleuthing. I quite enjoy it except for the fact that it only seems to be required when someone has died.'

Mr Harriman said: 'I suspect that you may have had more success with the barman that one of the Superintendent's officers would have had.'

'I think it was a piece of luck that I was someone the barman knows. He would probably not have admitted to a complete stranger that he had been helping someone to break the rules. He would be afraid that it would get back to Mr Gregory and it might cost him his job. In fact, I hope it doesn't get back to Mr Gregory. And I also doubt whether the barman would have told the police officer the name of the customer, which by the way was Godwin, because his instinct, as with all well-trained servants, would be to keep confidential anything that he sees or hears in the hotel.'

'So that was the name on the slate?' said Mr Harriman.

'Yes,' said Philip, 'although I don't understand the relevance of that information. I hope that I found out what you wanted to know.'

'Oh,' said Eleanor. 'Yes, you have found out exactly what

we needed to know but I must admit I am surprised. I thought it might be the man we met on Broad Walk. Miss Clitheroe's quarry.'

'Philip, you have found out everything that was needed and more,' said Mr Harriman, 'and you have triggered a train of thought that I wish to follow up. I'll leave Eleanor to fill you in on the purpose of the enquiry at St Anne's Hotel. I'm just going to drop in at the Club and make an enquiry of my own. Thank you again for your help, Philip.'

Napoleon got up and supervised Mr Harriman's departure and Eleanor went to make them a cup of tea. She came back with a tray which included some of Mrs Clayton's biscuits. When she had served the tea, she said:

'Philip, I'm going to tell you something in the strictest confidence. I have made use of you dreadfully and you have been such a brick. You deserve to know.'

'Well, old thing, I always know that whatever you ask is in a good cause so you don't have to tell me anything but I must admit I am curious to know the full story.'

'Then you shall have it.'

O O O

Eleanor told Philip about Rose and Lily and the swap they had devised, but leaving out mention of Mary's involvement as she had done when she told their story to Mr Harriman. Then she said: 'So, what you have just told me fits perfectly with what we already know. Although, as I said, I was surprised to find that the man at the bar was Hedley Godwin. Just one more thing. When one is sitting in the bar at the hotel, is it possible to see the dining room?'

'No, so he wouldn't have known whether Lily was working there or not,' said Philip.

'And, obviously, he didn't send a message via the barman that night because he expected that Lily would be in

Manchester and not in the dining room.'

'So how did he find Lily, or rather Rose, on Broad Walk?'

Eleanor said: 'I remember that Miss Clitheroe said the young woman she saw was walking towards Fountain Street and she thought she was being followed by the man who spoke to her at the entrance to the Gardens.'

'The barman said as far as he could remember Godwin left some time around ten. He might have been progressing from St Anne's to the Club. So if he left the hotel at about the same time as Lily he may have seen her in the street and followed her.'

'Yes. I remember,' said Eleanor. 'That all seems to fit together, doesn't it. Although he was following Rose, thinking it was Lily.'

'Yes, it does seem to fit together but, you know, if you had seen him last night you wouldn't think he'd have the backbone to take any direct action, let alone kill someone. He was just sorry for himself and all he could do was blame everyone but himself.'

'People do behave out of character when they are angry though. If he thought that Lily had tricked him, taken his money and not gone to Manchester after all, he would have been angry. And don't forget he was trying to court heiresses to get himself out of debt. He would have wanted Lily out of the way, especially if she was insisting that he ought to marry her.'

'But would that have made him angry enough that night?' said Philip.

They sat in silence as they considered this question and then Eleanor said: 'There is one thing that we haven't thought about. Based on what Miss Clitheroe told us, we have assumed that the man and woman she saw at the entrance to the Gardens actually did go into the Gardens. Let's assume that it was Hedley and Rose. What we haven't thought about is the time between them entering the Gardens and reaching the ornamental lake. It takes a minute or two to walk that distance. He had spoken to Rose at the entrance so was he then still just following her or did he talk to her? Rose is unlikely to have gone into the Gardens voluntarily so he probably was steering her into the Gardens rather than following her. If they were talking, Hedley would have thought he was talking to Lily. He probably would have accused her of tricking him or disobeying him. Rose had never met Hedley but what he said to her at the entrance might have been enough for her to realise who he was. How would she have responded? Would she have continued to pretend to be Lily? Or would she just have remained silent, thinking it was better not to give Lily away?'

'Yes, I see what you are driving at. Judging by what I have seen of him, if Hedley was acting true to his character he would have been blaming Lily for getting him into this mess. He wouldn't have been taking responsibility for it himself. Also, I'm pretty sure he would have had to borrow the money he gave Lily and that would have made him angry if he thought he had paid her off and she hadn't stuck to the bargain. He would have felt that he had been tricked, yet again, I can imagine the sort of things he might have said.'

'I think whatever happened, it would have been difficult for Rose to keep pretending she was Lily. If Hedley was accusing Lily of things she hadn't done, surely Rose's instinct would have been to defend her sister. She knew the risk Lily was taking in seeking an abortion, and she must have been worried for her. Hearing her wrongly accused, would have made Rose angry. Perhaps she told Hedley the truth. That she was not Lily and that she knew all about Hedley and told him he was to blame.'

'He would have been very surprised, if not angry, to find that Lily had a sister. Also he would have suddenly realised that there was a witness to his behaviour towards Lily.'

'Would that have made him angry enough to react? To

attack Rose in a fit of anger? Or frightened of being found out, perhaps?'

'Yes,' said Philip. 'I think it could have. That incident when Hedley attacked the loader is an example of what he is capable of. Another thing we haven't taken into account. Hedley had been drinking at the bar at St Anne's Hotel for quite some time that evening before he encountered Rose so that may have impaired his judgment and caused him to over-react.'

'There is another problem, though,' said Eleanor, 'and if Hedley Godwin was charged with murder a good defence counsel like Sir Giles Benson would be able to get the charge reduced to manslaughter.'

'How does that work?' asked Philip.

'Well, the defence counsel would certainly be asking the jury to consider what the intention of the accused was when he half-strangled the deceased. It is one thing to half-strangle someone in a fit of anger intending to harm them or frighten them but not to kill them, more particularly, drown them, and quite another thing to cause someone to be unconscious with the intention that they will then drown.'

'I see, so if Hedley got angry, half-strangled Rose, and walked away not caring too much what happened to her and she then fell in the lake and drowned, that might not be regarded as murder.'

'Yes. He might still be guilty of a lesser charge but not murder because the cause of death was not strangulation.'

'So, imprisonment instead of hanging?'

'Correct,' said Eleanor.

'So if the defence counsel could sow enough seeds of doubt into the minds of the jury as to his intentions, he would live, but in prison?'

'Yes. There is no evidence so far to suggest whether she fell, slipped or was pushed into the lake. He may not have intended her to drown. Our theory as to what might have happened may well be correct but to take this any further, we need to know where Hedley was on that particular night between about ten o'clock and about ten thirty or eleven.'

Napoleon got up from the hearth rug, having heard the front door open, and stood, head on one side, listening intently as Mr Harriman came upstairs.

O O O

'Well, that was a useful exercise,' said Mr Harriman. 'Have you finished bringing Philip up to date, Eleanor ?' Eleanor nodded. 'Right, well my first port of call was Mrs Broomhead's in The Square. She was a client of mine some years ago, before your time, Eleanor, so I needed no introduction. She is not overly pleased with her lodger and would be very happy if he left her and went somewhere else so she was quite voluble when it came to describing his faults. There is quite a catalogue which I shall not bore you with. What she did say of importance was that one night recently she heard him come in swearing and the worse for wear. It was quite late, between about ten thirty and eleven, she thought, and she went out into the hall to see what the fuss was about and noticed that his shoes were wet, they left a trail of footprints on the floor and also the bottoms of his trouser legs were wet. She could not be exact about the date. She thought it was about two weeks ago.'

'So that suggests,' said Eleanor, 'that Hedley Godwin may have walked into the lake with Rose.'

'It does seem a likely explanation. One does not normally get wet in that way late at night, even if it has been raining, so something untoward had certainly happened. Then, she heard him go out again about fifteen minutes later.'

'To have more to drink, no doubt.' said Philip.

'She does not know what time he returned because she had gone to bed shortly after he left,' said Mr Harriman.

Eleanor said: 'Philip and I were just discussing the difference between manslaughter and murder and the question of Hedley's intention, if indeed, he did cause Rose's death. I suggested that, because the cause of death was drowning and not asphyxiation, he might admit that he became angry and rendered Rose unconscious without intending to kill her and deny that her drowning was caused by any act of his. However, the wet trousers and shoes do suggest that he entered the lake so he would need to explain them away in order for a jury to accept a verdict of manslaughter instead of murder.'

'And I suppose,' said Philip, 'Hedley's explanation might be that he found Rose in the lake and his purpose in entering the lake was to rescue Rose from drowning.'

'Or,' said Eleanor, 'after attacking Rose realised where Rose had ended up and, in a fit of remorse, went into the lake to try to save her and found that he was too late.'

'It would all depend on how plausible his explanation for the wet shoes and trousers is,' said Mr Harriman. 'But I agree with Eleanor's suggestion that he could be found guilty of manslaughter rather than murder. Now, let me tell you about my second port of call this evening which was to the Club to see the Secretary. He has had one or two complaints about Hedley Godwin, chiefly from the Club servants but also from some members and is considering withdrawing Godwin's membership. He was only admitted as a temporary member and, by some oversight, has remained so. His behaviour is quite unacceptable and not in accordance either with the Club's purpose or its rules.

'One of the complaints the Secretary received was from the hall porter. He reported that, early in the morning one day last month, two men came to the Club asking for information about Hedley Godwin. The porter, quite properly, refused to answer their questions. They then offered him money to do so, and when he refused the money, one of the men grabbed him by the arm and was about to twist it behind his back when, fortunately for the porter, a member arrived and the two men faded away. According to the porter, they were men not gentlemen and probably crooks. He could tell by their accents that they were not locals. Southern accents, apparently. As far as the porter could recollect. they came some time in May, he thought towards the end of the month but he was not sure. And that may have been just before Miss Godwin died. So, I think, Philip, when Hedley Godwin said he was in danger, he was not exaggerating.'

'That sounds like representatives of his creditors, don't you think?' said Philip.

'It does,' said Mr Harriman, 'and I think that the law needs to take over before they do. I shall speak to Superintendent Johnson tomorrow and put before him all of the information you have gathered.'

'I doubt if he will be appreciative,' said Eleanor. 'He is always cross if he thinks I have been meddling.'

'He will have to carry out his own investigation, of course,' said Mr Harriman, 'but I shall make sure he follows up all of the information you have uncovered. I think, also, he will want to speak to the young woman who contacted Catherine. Perhaps Catherine can reassure her that she has done nothing wrong.'

'I shall telephone to Catherine and let her know.'

'I'll be off then,' said Philip.

As Philip stood up, Napoleon got up, shook himself, and then stretched. Eleanor said: 'Yes, Leon. It's time for your walk, I know. We'll walk you to the end of Broad Walk, Philip. I assume that you are going that way.'

'Yes, I didn't bring the motor.'

Philip accompanied Eleanor and Napoleon along Broad Walk and, as they were approaching the end of Fountain Street, Eleanor noticed someone in an overcoat and hat, standing a few yards away in the shadows under the trees.

Eleanor called to Napoleon, who returned obediently and stood patiently while Eleanor attached his lead.

Eleanor said: 'Leon would definitely recognise that person and give the game away.'

As they passed, Eleanor and Philip gave a barely perceptible nod and the person returned their greeting by touching the brim of the hat.

'I did consider Miss Clitheroe's quarry for the role of Rose's assailant,' said Eleanor, 'but obviously his attention is elsewhere.'

'Yes, unwittingly providing evidence for one of the first applications under the new law.'

CHAPTER TWENTY-FIVE

On Tuesday morning, Eleanor and Catherine had arranged to meet at nine o'clock at Hall Bank before Harriman & Talbot's office opened and before Catherine had to be at her surgery.

Eleanor took Catherine up to her office and when they were seated and Napoleon had resumed his post at the window, Eleanor said: 'I know you went to Miss Godwin's funeral. Do you know if her doctor was there?'

'Dr Morley? Yes, he was. Why?'

'I just wondered if you had spoken to him at all about the cause of death.'

Catherine narrowed her eyes as she looked at Eleanor. 'Yes, I did. I'm not even going to bother to ask why you want to know.'

'I understand he signed the death certificate and there was no need for a post mortem.'

'That is correct.'

'I have been told that Miss Godwin was very rarely ill and that she had not seen Dr Morley recently, in fact, not for some time. Does it surprise you that he felt able to sign the death certificate?'

'No, not if she was his patient.'

'And he didn't think it necessary to report the death to the coroner?'

'Doctors are reluctant to do so unless there is clear evidence to justify reporting the death. It upsets the family if the funeral is delayed because of an investigation or, even more so, if a post mortem is ordered. Relatives are not keen on having them for obvious reasons.'

'And his diagnosis was respiratory failure, I believe.'

'Acute respiratory failure, yes.'

'Which means what? If it's acute and not just plain old respiratory failure.'

'Acute simply means there was no history of respiratory failure. That was the first known episode.'

'And the cause of the respiratory failure was not stated.'

'No, because it was not known.'

'You mean that the cause of the respiratory failure hasn't been specified so, in that sense, the death certificate is incomplete.'

'No, it is a perfectly valid certificate. The cause of death was acute respiratory failure. Why do I feel that I am being cross-examined?' said Catherine, in the blandest of tones.

'Because you are my expert witness,' laughed Eleanor. 'Did Dr Morley happen to discuss his diagnosis with you, at all? While you were at the funeral, I mean?'

'And now, why do I feel I am being led into a trap?'

'I just need information.'

'That's what you always say.' Catherine sighed. 'I don't want to get involved in questioning another doctor's diagnosis so if that is where this is leading, I refuse to answer any more questions.'

'No, I'm not questioning the doctor's diagnosis. I am just trying to understand it. I accept that the cause of death was acute respiratory failure. What I want to understand is what might have caused that failure.'

'Well, clearly nothing obvious or it would have been stated on the certificate. None of the usual causes: pneumonia, choking, strangulation, lung disease, smoke inhalation, gunshot wound, there's a long list. Do you want me to continue?'

'No, I only want to know about the not so obvious causes.'

'What condition was Miss Godwin in when she was found?'

'She was found sitting in her chair. She looked peaceful, as though she was asleep.'

'What had she been doing in the preceding few hours?'

'I believe that she'd been to a meeting at St Peter's in the morning to discuss a fundraising event and she had driven herself there. She had lunch and then went into her business room to check the monthly accounts. She was last seen just after lunch and was found by the housekeeper about four, or maybe four and a half hours, later.'

'Hmm,' said Catherine. 'So we can safely rule out food poisoning. The symptoms of that are all too evident. I suppose it is safe to rule out myocardial infarction, that's heart attack to people who cross-examine. One might expect evidence that the person had suffered pain but I suspect a post mortem might have been requested if that were the case. Also, a heart attack severe enough to cause death suggests a sudden onset but from what you tell me of Miss Godwin's condition when she was found, I suspect that the respiratory failure manifested itself gradually rather than suddenly.' Catherine paused while she considered further explanations. 'I read an article some time ago in The Lancet describing a case of botulism. It's a condition caused by a type of bacteria, which can be ingested with food. It was first identified towards the end of last century but I've not actually seen anyone present with botulism. It is a form of poisoning.' Catherine paused again and then shook her head. 'No, I think we can rule that out as well. I'm sure one of the symptoms is vomiting or abdominal pain and there was no evidence of that. Another factor to consider is that botulism is not necessarily fatal.'

'So,' said Eleanor, 'respiratory failure may be due to a number of causes, all of which would normally produce symptoms and those symptoms would allow the doctor to identify the likely cause of the respiratory failure. And the word "acute" means that the respiratory failure was sudden or of short duration. So, essentially, Miss Godwin died as a result of a sudden or short term failure to breathe.'

'Put like that I suppose it does appear a bit lacking in medical expertise. You lawyers have such a flair for stripping things bare and exposing the underbelly. Dr Morley did admit that he was puzzled by Miss Godwin's death and he said that he had been at a loss as to what to put on the death certificate but as he could find no evidence of any other cause, he was left with respiratory failure. Anyway, where is all this leading?'

'I'm not sure.'

O O O

As soon as James arrived to open up the office, Eleanor asked him to have the motor car brought round from the garage. Leaving Napoleon supervising Mrs Clayton, she went downstairs, put on her hat and coat and her motoring coat, and said to James: 'I'm going to Godwin Hall, James. I'm not sure how long I shall be.'

'Very good, Miss Eleanor,' said James. 'It's threatening rain so I hope you manage to avoid getting wet.'

'I hope so. We have been lucky with the weather so far, haven't we, so I suppose we shouldn't complain if it does rain but I do hope it stays fine long enough for the visiting cricket team, don't you?'

'Yes. It's creating a lot of interest. Good for the town,' said James. 'And I believe the North of England Croquet Tournament begins today so let's hope the weather holds for them.'

'Yes, in the past, visitors have been very uncomplimentary about our summer climate here in Buxton but I doubt whether it is any more unpredictable than elsewhere in

England.'

'Well, you only have to read the London papers to know that it always rains in the summer for the tennis or the cricket there. There's nothing wrong with our Buxton weather,' said James, proudly. 'Some folks just like complaining.'

'Especially when they go on holiday and the weather isn't fine every day just for them,' added Eleanor, laughing. 'Right, I'll be off.'

As she drove to Fairfield in a pensive mood so different from her previous visits, her mood matched the weather. The sky was a dull grey and James' prediction of rain looked like being fulfilled.

Her visit to Godwin Hall was unannounced but the dogs came out as usual and so did Mrs Lomas when she heard the approaching motor car.

'Good morning, Miss Harriman. This is an unexpected pleasure.'

'Good morning, Mrs Lomas,' said Eleanor and she got down from the motor car and took off her motoring coat. 'How are you getting on here at the Hall?'

'Very well, thank you, Miss Harriman, and we haven't seen much of Mr Godwin these past few days.'

Eleanor assumed that the contrast between those two facts was as close as Mrs Lomas was likely to get to expressing her opinion of the new owner. Eleanor had heard a rumour that there was growing ill-feeling in the local farming community towards Hedley Godwin and his supposed plans for Godwin Hall.

Eleanor followed Mrs Lomas indoors and when they were settled in the housekeeper's sitting room with a cup of tea, she said: 'Mrs Lomas, I need to ask you some questions and you may find them a little strange. I'm afraid I can't explain at the moment but I am sure all will become clear. What I should like to ask you about is Miss Godwin's last day.'

Mrs Lomas was clearly not expecting this. 'Of course, if

it's important.'

'It is very important, Mrs Lomas. You told me before that Miss Godwin was perfectly well during the morning and that she had driven herself down to Fairfield for a meeting with the vicar of St Peter's.'

'That's right.'

'And after the meeting, she came back here. What time was that, do you recall?'

'At about half past twelve, I should think. It wasn't long before lunch.'

'And I think you said that Mr Godwin was here that morning.'

'Yes, he was.'

'What time did he arrive, do you know?'

'If I remember rightly, it would have been about half past ten, or perhaps earlier than that because he came to ride the horses and he was out a goodish while.'

'I'd like you to tell me everything you can remember Mrs Lomas, if you wouldn't mind, from the moment Mr Godwin arrived, even details that might not seem important.'

'I see,' said Mrs Lomas, and she frowned as she concentrated on a mental image of that morning. 'Mr Godwin had taken Bursar out and Winton was still in the paddock. We've only got the two horses now and Mr Nall had let them out into the paddock. Mr Godwin wasn't expected you see and Miss Godwin wasn't intending to ride that day. When Mr Godwin arrived, he went straight round to the stables and then to the stockyard to find Mr Nall and told him to get Bursar in and get him saddled. Mr Nall was busy with something else and wasn't best pleased.'

'And what time did Mr Godwin get back from his ride?'

'About,' Mrs Lomas paused to reflect, 'about half past eleven. It was certainly before Miss Godwin got home. I didn't see Mr Godwin when he arrived back from his ride. I only remember hearing him call out for Mr Nall to come and walk Bursar and then groom him.' Mrs Lomas displayed a rare moment of annoyance towards Mr Godwin. 'As if Mr Nall didn't have enough to do. Of course in the old days, we had grooms to do that but those days have gone. And Mr Godwin knows that. He is perfectly capable of walking Bursar and grooming him but he expects Mr Nall to do it.'

'And what did Mr Godwin do instead of looking after Bursar, do you know?'

'Well, he must have gone back into the fields because I'd been down in the cellar checking some of the stores and I was just coming up to the kitchen ready to start getting the lunch because it was Cook's day off and there at the kitchen door was Mr Godwin with a great bunch of Cow Parsley in his arms, joking about how he was bringing flowers for Alice. Doris was telling him not to bring it into the house and I asked him what he thought he was doing and he said he'd brought it up for the horses. He said in Kent, where he comes from, it's considered good for them. I told him to take it away immediately. I won't have it in the house.'

'It is considered to be back luck, isn't it?' said Eleanor.

'Yes, it is. That's why it's called Mother Die. I don't usually hold with such things but Cook did remark, when we were preparing food for the mourners after the funeral, that Mr Godwin shouldn't have brought Mother Die into the house. She'd heard the story from Alice. And Doris said Mr Godwin had told her that in Kent it's called "break your mother's heart" so he should have known better.'

'Did he bring it into the house?'

'That I'm not sure about. I have to keep my eye on him when he's at the house because he's always larking about with Alice, the kitchen maid, hanging about near the kitchen door, and distracting her from her work. Quite a ladies' man is Mr Godwin. And, like I said, I was down in the cellar most of the morning doing some sorting out.'

'And I think you said that Mr Godwin didn't stay for

212

lunch?'

'That's right. Miss Godwin got back just before lunch so, naturally, she asked him to stop but he had something or other to do in Buxton and said he couldn't.'

'And what did Miss Godwin have for lunch?'

'Well, I'd put out cold meat and salad, just in case, as well as the soup.'

'Miss Godwin had soup? In summer?'

'Oh, yes. Miss Godwin always had soup for lunch, rain, hail or shine. Sometimes she only had a bowl of soup and some bread. Then, she'd have her meal at night. She was always busy during the day and didn't like to stop too long at the table. She only had proper lunch if someone was coming. That's why I put out the cold meat and salad thinking that Mr Godwin would still be here when Miss Godwin got back and she'd have that. I knew she'd invite him even though it wasn't very convenient. When it was the day for checking the monthly accounts she liked to get on with it as soon as possible after lunch and she avoided inviting guests on those days. And the local folk knew not to ask her to lunch or to go out on those days.'

'So it was common knowledge, then. I mean, everyone knew what day she would be doing the accounts.'

'Oh yes. Always on the same day of the month.'

'I see. And what sort of soup was it that day, do you recall?'

'Parsnip soup.'

'But I didn't think parsnips were available at this time of year?'

'At Godwin Hall they are. We grow our own vegetables here,' said Mrs Lomas, proudly. 'We leave it as late as possible to lift the parsnips and then we store them in the cellar. As I said, I'd been down in the cellar that morning checking to see what needed to be used up and I brought up the last of the parsnips. They were only fit for making soup

213

and needed to be used up that day.'

'And you mentioned that it was Cook's day off, did you prepare the lunch that day?'

'Not all of it. I left Doris to get on with making the soup while I saw to the ham and then went out to the kitchen garden to gather the vegetables for the salad.'

'And what time do you have lunch at Godwin Hall?

'Always the same. Twelve o'clock for outdoors, one o'clock for indoors.'

'Did everyone have soup or just Miss Godwin?'

'Just Miss Godwin. There was only enough for one. If Mr Godwin had been stopping I would have served the cold meat and salad instead.'

'So, there was no soup left over?'

'No.'

'So Mr Godwin left before lunch and Miss Godwin just had soup?' Mrs Lomas nodded. 'And how was the soup served?'

'Just with a little cream and a garnish of parsley and some of the bread made that morning.'

'And after Miss Godwin had had lunch she went to the business room to look over the accounts. Do you remember how long it was between Miss Godwin finishing lunch and going into the business room?'

Mrs Lomas said: 'I'm not exactly sure, about half of an hour, maybe an hour.'

'Would you think back to that time between lunch and Miss Godwin going into the business room. Was there anything at all unusual or was it just the same.'

'No, it was just the same as usual,' said Mrs Lomas, shaking her head slowly, 'although, now that I think on it, I do remember Miss Godwin saying that her feet were cold. It was a very warm day and she said she thought she must have been sitting in a draught during the meeting in the morning.'

'When you found her in the business room can you

describe for me exactly how she was.'

'Well, sitting up in her chair but sort of slumped to one side. The chair in the business room used to be a hall chair, one of those chairs with a tall back and wings at the side, and her head was resting to one side against one of the wings just as if she had fallen asleep. Very peaceful, she looked.'

'And can you try and picture the business room for me, was everything just as usual? Nothing out of place.'

Mrs Lomas thought for a minute. 'No, just as usual. There were papers spread out on the table, of course, but that was all.'

'And the door into the yard was closed when you looked through the window and saw Miss Godwin.'

'Yes. It was closed.'

'And you went into the room by the yard door. Then what did you do?'

'Well, I spoke to Miss Godwin thinking she was asleep and she didn't move. I called her name again quite loudly the second time and then again. When she still didn't move I sensed something was wrong but I wasn't sure what to do so I went into the yard to call Mr Nall. He came in and saw Miss Godwin and went over to her and felt for a pulse. Mr Nall's very good like that. He's often had to deal with accidents with the farm hands so he knows what to do. He said we should call the doctor but he didn't think it would be much good because she was already gone. There's a telephone extension in the business room so I telephoned to Dr Morley's surgery but he was out and I left a message for him to come. We just stood there for a bit and Mr Nall said perhaps we should pull the rug up over her face, being more dignified like, but we didn't like to disturb anything until the doctor had been.'

'Which rug was that, Mrs Lomas?' asked Eleanor, keeping her tone perfectly neutral although her mind was racing.

'Well, she had a rug over her, pulled right up to her chin.

There's one kept in the business room because it gets perishing cold in there in the winter even with a fire going. There's such a draught. It's always too hot in summer, mind.'

Eleanor decided not to comment on the fact that the day in question was a very warm day in May. She did not want to attract any more attention to her investigation than necessary.

'Can you recall what Miss Godwin had done on the day before she died?'

'Yes, I can. In the morning, she rode Winton over to Wormhill, Winton's her horse, to visit one of the farms that wanted to take some of our lambs for breeding. Then in the afternoon she took the motor car and went to Ashbourne. The son of one of our neighbours is there and he was being presented with an award. Miss Godwin offered to take his mother to see him. She got back about five o'clock and then she had a rest and after dinner she sat reading until it was time for bed.'

'And did she seem perfectly all right.'

'Oh, yes. Her usual self. She told us all about the present-ation, of course. Very entertaining. She was a great mimic.'

'Well, thank you, Mrs Lomas. You have been a great help. Now I must get back to the office.'

'Can I just ask, Miss Harriman. You were asking about what Miss Lomas had for lunch. Were you thinking there was something wrong with what Miss Godwin ate?'

'You are very astute, Mrs Lomas.'

'Well, I shouldn't like to think that our cooking was to blame. The parsnips were last season's I grant you, but they were perfectly all right to eat.'

'I can assure you that there was nothing wrong with what you cooked so please don't be uneasy. I can't take you fully into my confidence at the moment, Mrs Lomas, but I can tell you that I am carrying out an investigation and it is not anything to do with what you did in the kitchen that day. I don't want anyone to know what I am investigating just at the moment.'

'Is it to do with Miss Godwin?'

'Yes, it is and it would be very helpful if you would avoid saying anything to anyone, not even Mr Nall, about this conversation we have just had. You can just say that my visit was about the probate application, as usual.'

'Certainly, Miss Harriman.'

'Thank you, Mrs Lomas. I know I can rely on you. Now, there is just one more thing. I should like to look at the accounts in the business room, the ones Miss Godwin was looking at.'

'Of course,' said Mrs Lomas as she stood up and led the way to the business room. As she opened the door she said: 'Everything's just as she left it. We always had to be careful not to move any of her papers when we went in to clean so I haven't liked to interfere with anything.'

'That's excellent. Thank you, Mrs Lomas. I shall let you know when I have finished.'

O O O

When Mrs Lomas had left, Eleanor sat down in Miss Godwin's chair and contemplated the papers spread out on the table. She wasn't sure what she was looking for but she wanted to see if there was anything unusual, anything that looked as if it was out of place. Several account books lay open and on top of one book there was a handwritten note. Eleanor picked it up. It was headed "Anomalies" and under the heading there was the word "cheque" followed by a number and then under that the words "amounts drawn unaccounted for" and three dates were listed with figures next to each date: £10 March, £20 April, £40 May. Eleanor assumed that this note had been written by Miss Godwin as she was checking the accounts. Next to the account book was a cheque book. Eleanor picked it up. The first cheque was dated the twenty-fourth of April. She found the cheque butt which corresponded with the number written on the piece of paper. The details of the cheque had not been filled in on the butt. The butts on either said of the incomplete one had been filled in correctly. Eleanor took out a notebook and pencil from her bag, copied the words on the handwritten paper, and made a note of the number of the cheque butt. She decided that there was no point in her looking through the account books themselves to see if she could make sense of the three amounts listed on the handwritten paper. That would be a task for the accountants, in due course. She rang for Mrs Lomas and now that she was no longer concentrating on a task noticed how hot it was in the business room.

'Ah, Mrs Lomas, I wonder if you can help me. This cheque book on Miss Godwin's desk. Can you tell me who normally signs the cheques? There is a space for two signatures.'

'Oh, only Miss Godwin. No-one else.'

'What about Mr Nall?'

'No. He keeps the wages records but he doesn't have anything to do with the accounts or the banking. None of us do.'

'I don't suppose Miss Godwin mentioned that there were amounts she couldn't account for?'

'I don't remember her doing so.'

'Well, I think that's everything, Mrs Lomas. I shall trouble you no further. I must get back to the office. Thank you again for your help.'

CHAPTER TWENTY-SIX

On her way back from Godwin Hall, Eleanor called in to Catherine's surgery. The waiting room was empty and she asked Mrs Ardern if it would be possible to speak to Catherine.

'How long would you need, Miss Harriman?'

'Only about ten minutes. I just need to confirm something.'

'Very well. If you would care to wait until she has finished with her current patient, I shall ask her if she will see you.'

'Thank you, Mrs Ardern.' Eleanor picked up a magazine and flipped through it while she waited. Catherine's next patient arrived and, fortunately, it was not someone Eleanor knew. A few minutes later the door of the consulting room opened and Catherine showed her patient out. Mrs Ardern went across to speak to Catherine, and then asked Eleanor to go in.

'Hello again. What's all this about? I know you too well to think that this is a purely social visit,' teased Catherine.

Eleanor laughed. 'Oh, I say!' How unkind.'

'Nonsense,' said Catherine. 'In my defence, I plead truth. What do you want to know?'

'I'm really sorry to bother you when you are working, but I do need to ask you for more information.'

'Go on.'

'Well,' said Eleanor, 'I've been thinking about Miss Godwin. I haven't met anyone yet who hasn't expressed surprise at the suddenness of her death.'

'What are you driving at? Is this one of your theories that is going to lead to an arrest?'

'I don't know. I might be wildly off the mark but several pieces of information have assembled themselves in my mind, like a jigsaw puzzle, and I don't like the picture that they are making.'

'Right. Describe the pieces and let's see what I make of them.'

'First of all, Miss Godwin had been remarkably healthy all of her life and had no known medical problems. The day before her death she was well enough to ride over to Wormhill to see someone there and then in the afternoon she drove a neighbour to Ashbourne and back. She returned home perfectly well and in good spirits. The following day, she drove down to St Peter's for a committee meeting at which she took an active part and again, when she returned home, she was perfectly well and in good spirits. Between about half an hour or an hour after a lunch, which consisted only of soup and home-baked bread, she went to her business room to check the accounts, a routine activity. Before going to the business room she mentioned that her feet were cold, even though it was a warm day, and she put it down to sitting in a draught during the meeting she was at that morning. When the housekeeper found Miss Godwin later that afternoon she was in a chair looking as though she had fallen asleep and she had wrapped a rug around her as though she was cold, even though the weather was still very warm. No-one else had the soup, by the way. Last time we spoke you ruled out all the more usual causes of respiratory failure.'

'And you want to suggest one I didn't consider?'

'Yes.'

'Which is?'

'What about Hemlock?'

Catherine's eyebrows went up as she said: 'What!'

'Poisoning by Hemlock.'

Catherine looked at Eleanor and Eleanor steadily returned her gaze. 'You're serious, aren't you?'

'Yes.'

'But this is England, not ancient Greece.'

'I know, but in 1923 Hemlock is still a poison and, as Buxton and Fairfield are surrounded by fields and lanes, Hemlock is readily available on any grass verge that a murderer might care to choose.'

'Whatever made you think of Hemlock poisoning?'

'First, the absence of any other explanation together with the cold feet and the need for a rug on a warm summer's afternoon in a room, which I can testify gets very warm, the appearance of having just fallen asleep, and, the absence of symptoms suggestive of any other cause of death.'

'That's not much to base a diagnosis on.'

'I agree,' said Eleanor. 'But the same might be said of Dr Morley's diagnosis.'

'So, how was it done?'

'I've been out to Godwin Hall this morning and spoken to the housekeeper about the day Miss Godwin died and what she had for lunch. The soup was parsnip soup with a little cream and a parsley garnish, prepared in the kitchen.

'And did anyone else have the soup?'

'No. There was only enough for one.'

'Hmmm,' said Catherine, 'that was convenient. And you are thinking that Hemlock root might have been mixed in with the parsnip, possibly even mixed with the parsley garnish?'

'It's possible.'

'Possible, yes. Probable? That's another question. It's a plausible theory, I grant you. But, only a theory. All right, suppose it is murder. There has been a death certificate, all legal and above board. What are you going to do with your theory?'

'There's not much I can do, I admit. But, as a starting point, I did want to know if Hemlock in soup would be detectable and fatal.'

'Detectable? Unlikely. As only a very small amount of Hemlock is required, a small piece of root or a few leaves, it could go undetected in soup. And fatal? Yes, it can be fatal if not detected in time. The person who ingested Hemlock would begin to feel cold, first in the feet and then muscular paralysis would set in and gradually ascend, spreading to the rest of the body. When the paralysis reaches the respiratory muscles, the person would experience difficulty breathing and eventually would cease to be able to do so.'

'And the cause of death would be registered as respiratory failure?'

'Yes. If nothing further was known or suspected.'

'And can you see a parallel between that and Miss Godwin's last moments as I have described them to you?'

'I can.'

They sat in silence looking at each other. Then Catherine said: 'It was quite fortuitous that there was no soup to be tested in the event that someone thought to do so.'

'Yes. The other thing I forgot to mention is that Cow Parsley grows in abundance at Godwin Hall and that morning Mr Godwin had brought a large bunch of it up for the horses. Apparently, they feed it to horses in Kent. And where there is Cow Parsley there is generally Hemlock and Mr Godwin knows enough about horses not to feed them Hemlock and he was larking around with the kitchen maid with the Cow Parsley.'

'And I suppose you're also going to tell me he went to a good school, studied Greek, and knew all about Socrates.'

'I hadn't thought of that.'

'Hmmm, even if it was Hemlock,' said Catherine, 'I don't see that there is anything that we can do or even need to do.'

'No, not at the moment,' said Eleanor, in a tone that did

not bode well for Mr Godwin. 'I'm going to have to talk to my father. But thank you for sparing the time to answer my questions. I do appreciate your help. I shall let you get back to your patients.'

o o o

When she got back to the office, Eleanor asked James to put in a telephone call to the manager of Chillingham & Baynard, the bank that Miss Godwin used. It was the same bank that Harriman & Talbot used and Eleanor knew the bank manager. He had replaced Mr Sutton, the previous manager, whom Eleanor had found dead in a barn at Clough End Farm.

When the call came through Eleanor said: 'Good morning, Mr Critchlow. It's Miss Harriman from Harriman & Talbot speaking. I wonder if I could ask you to check something for me?'

'Good morning, Miss Harriman. Certainly. Is it something in relation to the Harriman & Talbot account?'

'No, it's the Godwin Hall account. We are making the application for probate.'

'Ah, of course. How can I help?'

'I need to clarify the presentation of a cheque drawn on your bank. It's number 1617. I'm not sure of the date but it would be some time in the middle of May. I should like to know in whose favour it was made out and the amount, when it was presented, and if possible, whether anyone at the bank remembers who presented it. If they do, could they describe that person. I hope that is not asking too much.'

'Not at all, Miss Harriman. Leave it with me and I shall telephone you back when I have the information you require.'

'Thank you, Mr Critchlow. I'm most grateful.'

Eleanor put aside the Godwin file and took out a file on

which she needed to draft a claim in relation to some goods which had not been delivered. After half an hour, James put a call through from the bank.

'I have Mr Critchlow on the line, Miss Eleanor.'

'Hello, Miss Harriman. I have the information you required. I have had cheque number 1617 traced. It was made out to Cash and it was for forty pounds. It was presented on the fifth of May this year. I have spoken to the teller on duty and he tells me that a gentleman presented the cheque. He was not known to the teller. He was tall, early twenties, and he recalls that the person in question said that he was calling on behalf of Miss Godwin.'

'Thank you very much, Mr Critchlow. I really appreciate your help.'

'Is there any irregularity regarding the cheque, Miss Harriman? I am most anxious to know if there is.'

'No, not at all Mr Critchlow. Just a routine enquiry. I needed to clarify some missing details and you have done that for me. Thank you. Goodbye, Mr Critchlow.'

'Goodbye, Miss Harriman.'

Eleanor went over to the window and stood beside Napoleon, staring out without really looking at the scene before her and mentally sifting through various facts and trying to assemble them in their proper place.

For the rest of the day, she disciplined herself to concentrate on her files and then spent an almost sleepless night trying to ignore the ideas that were whirling around in her head. Napoleon was grumpy because he felt that he too was being ignored.

CHAPTER TWENTY-SEVEN

'Good afternoon, Mrs Clayton. How are you?'

'Good afternoon, Mr Danebridge. I'm very well, thank you.' Mrs Clayton was carrying a tray of cups and saucers she had just collected from Mr Harriman's office.

'What have you got planned for this afternoon? I notice *The Sheik of Araby* is playing at the Picture House.'

Mrs Clayton was known to be a keen film goer. 'Oh, no, not this afternoon. My sister-in-law and I are going shopping this afternoon. We're going to the matinee on Saturday.'

'Jolly good. I hope it's up to scratch.'

'Miss Harriman's in her office if you'd like to go up. It's early closing today so I expect she's nearly finished for the day. Ah, here's Napoleon. He must have heard you.'

'Hello, old chap. Come on, where's your mistress?'

When Philip and Napoleon entered Eleanor's office, she was at her desk writing.

'Hello, old thing. If you're busy I can go and annoy someone else.'

'Hello, Philip,' said Eleanor, looking up from her work. 'I'm just finishing drafting a claim. Have a seat. I shan't be a moment.'

Philip picked up a copy of the previous week's *Buxton Advertiser* and said: 'Carry on. I'll just sit quietly and read the paper.' Philip browsed through the pages, looking occasionally at Eleanor with concern. After a few minutes, Eleanor put down her pencil and said: 'That's done. I'm a bit behind at the moment.'

'Yes, I was just thinking you looked a bit . . .' Philip paused. '. . . deflated is the word I'm looking for, I think. Here, this will sort you out. This is the very thing.' Philip pointed to an advertisement at the bottom of a page of the newspaper. 'Mental inertia. That's probably what you are suffering from. The pale and pasty complexion, the dull eye, the listless step. According to Dr Cassell's advertisement, all of that can be exchanged for vigorous health. A vigorous nervous system, that's the key. He promises to provide you with one if you will only purchase a bottle of his patent medicine tablets.'

'Dull eye and listless step. Is that how you describe me?' Eleanor laughed. 'You're probably right. But I don't need Dr Cassell's potions, I can always guarantee that you will tease me into a good humour. I've just been spending too much time on Hedley Godwin lately and the news is not good.'

'Ah, understood. Do you still want to play tennis? Definitely a preferable alternative to Dr Cassell's Tablets. But, if you're not feeling up to it, I don't mind.'

'Oh, no! I'm so sorry. I had forgotten all about tennis. My brain is not working very well at the moment. I am desperately in need of advice and Father and Edwin have agreed to go through my ideas with me. We can still play tennis afterwards though if you don't mind waiting. I shall probably need the exercise by then. And, of course, you're welcome to join in the discussion. You know most of the facts already.'

'That suits me. And if you get too much of a mauling from Messrs. Harriman & Talbot, we can abandon tennis and drown your sorrows with afternoon tea at The Crescent Hotel.'

'I shall take you up on that.' Eleanor laughed as they went downstairs to Mr Harriman's office.

Napoleon, sensing a long conversation before there was any chance of a walk, settled himself down beside Eleanor's chair and drifted off into his dream world.

Eleanor said: 'I'm sorry to burden you both with this problem but I really need your advice. I think we are more or less agreed that Hedley Godwin may be implicated in the death of Rose Penlington and that he may need to be questioned by Superintendent Johnson.' Mr Harriman and Edwin nodded agreement. 'I suspect that Hedley Godwin may be involved in another crime and I am not sure how to proceed.'

'Oh?' said Mr Harriman.

'Really,' said Edwin.

'I don't think Miss Godwin died of natural causes.'

Two pairs of eyebrows shot up as Mr Harriman and Edwin both looked at Eleanor with concern.

Eleanor continued: 'I know it might seem as though I am pointing the finger at Hedley Godwin just because he is suspected of committing another crime but Miss Godwin's death was unexpected. I believe that she was poisoned and I think I know how it was done.'

'This is a very serious accusation to make, as I am sure you appreciate,' said Mr Harriman, frowning.

'Yes,' said Edwin, 'I have to confess that I find your suggestion rather startling.'

'I know,' said Eleanor, 'it is difficult to accept and I admit that, at the moment, the evidence is very thin but if my suspicions are correct, there really should be a further investigation into Miss Godwin's death. Obtaining proof might require an exhumation because it involves poisoning and I know how you hate all the bother and publicity that goes with having to make such an order, Father, and having it carried out is rather gruesome but, if I am right, I owe it to Miss Godwin not to give up just because things are difficult or unpleasant.'

Edwin said: 'I know from experience that you always think very logically and you are not given to creating wild theories. Your suspicions may very well prove to be facts and, as you say, we owe it to Miss Godwin to be certain we have the truth. I am sure you have very good reasons for making this accusation and you have my support.'

'I agree with your observations wholeheartedly. Knowing you, Eleanor, I am sure you have not reached this conclusion lightly,' said Mr Harriman. 'We both know how capable you are and if you think there is something wrong, then we should not let the matter rest. It does need to be investigated.'

'So tell us what you know so far,' said Edwin.

Eleanor set out logically, in careful detail, the events of the day before Miss Godwin died and the day of her death. Then she said: 'There were facts which made me wonder whether Dr Morley should have requested a post mortem or at least asked a few more questions. I know he has a busy practice and doesn't need to be spending time finding problems where there may be none but there are some facts which made me question Dr Morley's diagnosis. There were no warning signals of any kind of illness and when Miss Godwin was found there was no sign of pain, or distress, or illness of any kind. Nevertheless, there seems to me to be something unaccountable about the way Miss Godwin died. One stops breathing for a reason and, so far, no-one has suggested one, or even thought that it might be necessary to find one.'

'But how on earth did you come to the conclusion that the cause was poisoning?' asked Mr Harriman.

'I had previously spoken to Mrs Lomas at Godwin Hall about the day Miss Godwin died and without my realising it something she told me must have stayed in my mind. Then there was an incident on Sunday involving Cicely's maid, Ellen, when Richard tried to bring some Cow Parsley into the house. The following morning I had a conversation with

Mrs Clayton which provided some more information about Cow Parsley and that connected with the information already in my head. Then I remembered something I learned at school. It all started me thinking about a possible cause of death not so far considered. I consulted Catherine and gathered some more facts from Mrs Lomas. Everything seemed to fit. You see, the only unusual thing about the day Miss Godwin died was the fact that she said, shortly after lunch, that her feet were cold. It was quite a warm day. She put it down to possibly having sat in a draught at a meeting that morning. However, when she was found she had a rug over her as though her body was cold, not just her feet. Bear in mind that it was a warm day and she was in her business room. When I was in the business room looking at the accounts, I noticed how warm it was in there. These two facts struck me as odd and, possibly, relevant. They reminded me of my school history lesson about the death of Socrates.'

'Socrates!' said Mr Harriman, Edwin, and Philip in chorus.

'You will recall the legend that, after ingesting Hemlock, he began to grow cold from the feet upwards.'

'Hemlock!' was the chorus.

Eleanor nodded and then described the process of gradual paralysis that Catherine had explained. She then related the account given by Mrs Lomas regarding the parsnip soup. By now, Mr Harriman and Edwin were frowning. Philip, the neutral onlooker, was observing everyone's reaction.

'Well,' said Edwin, 'I think it is a plausible explanation of Miss Godwin's symptoms but, you must admit, it does seem rather outlandish, dramatic even, to have taken place at Godwin Hall.'

'And, even supposing that you are right about the poisoning, what motive could Hedley Godwin have had?' asked Mr Harriman. 'He knew he was going to inherit

Godwin Hall eventually.'

'I wondered that. I don't think he cared about Godwin Hall at all and, according to Mrs Lomas he was intending to put a tenant in rather than live there himself. No, I think he would have been motivated by something else. When I considered the timing of Miss Godwin's death, I realised that it happened on the day she intended to check the monthly accounts. It was common knowledge that she checked them every month on the same day of the month. Yesterday when I went back to Godwin Hall I decided to look through the books of accounts which are kept in the business room. The books have been left just as they were when Miss Godwin died. I found a handwritten note which suggested that Miss Godwin had discovered anomalies in the accounting records.

'It seems that, in relation to three cheques, she had not been able to work out the reason they had been drawn. I suspected that Hedley Godwin had been helping himself to funds from the bank account by presenting a cheque made payable to himself. Quite substantial amounts and he could not expect that to remain undiscovered for much longer. I telephoned Mr Critchlow at our bank and he confirmed for me the details of one of the withdrawals made by Hedley for forty pounds. The cheque was made out to cash. It's possible to enter the business room at Godwin Hall from the yard and the door is not locked so anyone could easily enter the room without being observed from the house and could get access to the cheque book.'

'So, you think that Hedley Godwin has been helping himself to Miss Godwin's money for the last few months in order to pay his debts?' asked Edwin.

'Either that or he wanted to have money to spend. We don't know if he had an independent income and you said, Philip, that you had heard that his father had died and left him nothing.'

Philip nodded. 'From what I can gather he pretty much

sponges off everyone else for his daily needs so it's more likely that the money went to pay his creditors. A sort of goodwill gesture to show that he hadn't forgotten them.'

Eleanor continued: 'He must have realised that sooner or later someone, in particular, Miss Godwin, would notice. Perhaps she had said something to him or hinted that she knew money was missing. I know she saw him just before lunch on the day she died because she invited him to stay for lunch.'

'But surely, you are not suggesting that Miss Godwin was killed for the sake of forty pounds?' said Mr Harriman.

'No,' said Eleanor. 'Not at all. I don't think the amounts were important enough for him to commit murder. Besides, if he was afraid of Miss Godwin finding out, he probably thought he could talk his way out of it. He seems to have charmed Miss Godwin to some extent but I got the impression that Mrs Lomas didn't trust him. No, I think he was afraid of something more sinister. You know yourself that there is gossip about Hedley Godwin having to leave Kent to avoid his creditors. He came to Buxton hoping to be able to clear his debts and he has not been able to. I think his creditors have lost patience with him. After all, it is almost six months since he came here. They will not wait forever and we know that recently two men had come to Buxton to look for him and threatened the Club porter with violence.'

Edwin said: 'So you think Godwin might have been given time to pay and then, when he proved unable to do so, his creditors thought they had been cheated or tricked out of their money and they have now turned nasty?'

'Something like that,' said Eleanor. 'I think that, when he came to Buxton, Hedley was under the mistaken impression that if he inherited Godwin Hall he would have access to ready cash enough to pay his debts. Then he realised that Godwin Hall was not that kind of inheritance and that there was no large fund of money that he could tap into to pay his debts. So, if he thought his life was in danger from these creditors, he may well have decided that he needed to inherit Godwin Hall so that he could sell it and save himself.'

'Well, I suppose that is one explanation but is there any proof?' asked Mr Harriman.

'About Hedley Godwin's intentions and motives? No, only what Philip managed to find out from Hedley himself. And, I think, when Hedley Godwin said he was in danger, he was not exaggerating. We know he asked for an advance of fifteen hundred pounds from the estate, which probably provides some idea as to the scale of his debts, because I don't believe he wanted it to build stables. Certainly not if he did not intend to live at the Hall.'

'Supposing your suspicions as to a motive are correct, Eleanor, there remains the question of how Miss Godwin died,' said Mr Harriman. 'If it was as you suggest, why did Dr Morley not detect any evidence of it?'

'Because he was not looking for it. There was absolutely nothing in the circumstances of Miss Godwin's death to hint at a cause of death other than a failure to breathe. Dr Morley diagnosed the cause of death as acute respiratory failure and, apparently, did not ask himself what had caused that failure. I was surprised that he was willing to issue the certificate without further investigation given that the death was so sudden and he had not seen Miss Godwin for some time but, as Catherine pointed out, doctors do not wish to be thought over cautious or officious and prefer not to burden relatives with needless bureaucracy. But, you see, I asked myself why a seemingly healthy woman of fifty-four would just fail to breathe. Catherine and I discussed this and it seemed to her that there was no evidence to suggest that any of the usual reasons were the cause of the failure. But there must have been a reason. Just as there was a reason why Rose Penlington drowned, even though no reason was immediately apparent. There has just been an acceptance of the facts as stated without any thought as to whether or not there is a valid explanation.'

Just then the telephone on James' desk rang. Napoleon sat up to attention as Mr Harriman said: 'I'll go. James has gone home already.'

CHAPTER TWENTY-EIGHT

The three people left in Mr Harriman's office listened to Mr Harriman's side of the conversation.

'Yes, Mrs Lomas.'

'Godwin Hall,' said Eleanor to Philip.

'I see. When did they arrive?' There was a pause. 'Three of them, you say. And one says he is an accountant.' There was a longer pause. 'I see. And Mr Godwin, where is he?' Another pause. 'Right. I'll telephone Superintendent Johnson now. In the meantime, I shall send someone out to talk to these people and explain the situation. I'm sure when they understand the position, they will be prepared to be reasonable. All right, Mrs Lomas. No, not at all. I'm pleased you rang. You did exactly the right thing. Yes, I'm sure he will. I shall send someone immediately.'

Mr Harriman returned to his office and said: 'As you will have gathered that was Mrs Lomas. Apparently, three people arrived at Godwin Hall about a few minutes ago saying that they had a warrant to remove goods from Godwin Hall. One of their number is an accountant and says that he is there for the purpose of advising as to the value of the goods to be removed. I doubt very much that their warrant is valid. Mrs Lomas doesn't like the look of them. Mr Nall is currently keeping them at bay. Hedley Godwin is apparently at the Hall but out riding at the moment. He is not aware that these people have arrived.'

'From the work I have done on the probate file, so far,' said Eleanor, 'I don't think Miss Godwin had any major outstanding debts and there is no paperwork relating to any claim that would justify a bailiff's warrant. This sounds more like Hedley Godwin's creditors.'

'I shall telephone to Superintendent Johnson. He was intending to speak to Mr Godwin today in any event and if these men at Godwin Hall do intend to harm him, taking him to the police station may be the wisest course. I think the best thing would be for one of us to go and look at this warrant, ascertain who the alleged creditor is, and explain the situation to whoever is there intending to execute it.'

'Yes, I agree,' said Edwin, 'it will be a good opportunity to find out just exactly how much he owes. I think we should get there as soon as we can and sort this out.'

'My bus is outside,' said Philip. 'I'll drive you there, that will be quicker than you going and getting your motor car.' Philip looked at Eleanor and knew there was no chance she was going to be left behind. 'There won't be room for you I'm afraid, Napoleon.'

'So, if you'll telephone the Superintendent, Harriman, I shall telephone you from the Hall when I know what the story is.'

Mr Harriman nodded his agreement and Edwin, Eleanor and Philip put on hats and coats and went out to the Bentley. Philip started the motor car and drove off as fast as the traffic of pedestrians, carts, and other motor cars would allow. No-one spoke and Philip concentrated on driving. They reached Godwin Hall in twelve minutes. Philip stopped the Bentley at the edge of the large circular area in front of the Hall and surveyed the scene.

There were two motor cars parked on the circular area; a black Crossley at the farthest side of the circle, and a green Crossley in the centre of the circle closer to the front door.

'That's Hedley Godwin's car,' said Eleanor, quietly. 'The black Crossley.'

Two men were sitting in the green Crossley. A third man

was standing beside the motor car holding a clipboard on which were several pages. The two in the motor car were large and had rather ugly faces which looked as though they had been battered on more than one occasion. Eleanor guessed that the man with the clipboard was the accountant. Mr Nall was standing a few paces away from the man with the clipboard between him and the front door of the Hall, as though he intended to bar the way of the accountant if at all possible. Eleanor noticed a pitchfork leaning up against the wall beside the front door. Mrs Lomas was nowhere to be seen and Eleanor guessed that, after alerting Mr Nall, she had retreated inside with Doris and the kitchen maid ready to defend her territory and had telephoned to Hall Bank. Two of the farm hands were leaning on a fence near the edge of the driveway and watching proceedings with a keen interest.

Philip, from long experience of working with Eleanor and from natural prudence, drove around the circle so that the Bentley was facing towards the lane leading from Godwin Hall. Philip and Edwin got out of the motor car. Philip stood beside the door and Edwin walked over to Mr Nall, saying: 'Good afternoon, Mr Nall. What seems to be the trouble here?'

'Good afternoon, Mr Talbot. This gentleman here says he has a warrant which allows him to take items of plate from the house to the value shown on his document. I said I doubted that were the case so, as you see, we have reached a stand-off.'

'I see,' said Edwin. He turned to the man with the clipboard. 'Mr Talbot, Harriman & Talbot, solicitors. How do you do? May I see this warrant? I am sure there has been some mistake.'

The man did not introduce himself. He reluctantly handed a document to Edwin. Edwin read it carefully and turned it over to read the second page.

'No,' said Edwin, 'I'm sorry, this won't do at all. This

warrant is incorrect and invalid. It refers to a debt owed by Mr Godwin who is purported to be the owner of the premises described in the warrant. Mr Godwin may well owe a debt of two thousand and twenty five pounds, ten shillings and sixpence but he is not yet the owner of this house. So your warrant will have to wait, that is, if this genuinely is a warrant which I very much doubt. It looks to me like an attempt to create a document which might be mistaken for a warrant. I do not think any English court has issued it.' He handed the document back to the accountant. 'I suggest, therefore, that you take your document and return to wherever it is that you belong.'

Sensing the need for some persuasion to be applied, the two men sitting in the motor car now got out and stood, like a pair of bookends, on either side of the man with the clipboard, barring Edwin's way back to Philip's motor car. Edwin was eyeing them steadily and Mr Nall was edging towards his pitchfork. Eleanor heard the noise of an engine approaching but the three men were too intent on their confrontation to notice.

The man to the left of the accountant said: 'That's as maybe, mister. Court or no court, legal or not, we're here to get what's owed, the money or the goods and that's an end of it. We've waited long enough.'

Before Edwin could reply, two things happened at once. A black Model T Ford pulled up behind the green Crossley and a police sergeant got out. At the same time, there was the clatter of hooves on the cobble stones and a horse came round the opposite corner of the Hall. As the horse pulled up, Hedley Godwin recognised the two men standing either side of the accountant, and then saw the policeman. He immediately spurred the horse to a canter, dashed through the space between the Bentley and the black Crossley, and galloped up the lane away from Godwin Hall. The policeman, seeing Philip standing next to the Bentley called:

'If that's Hedley Godwin, get after him. The Super wants to speak to him.'

Philip leapt into the Bentley, started the engine, and sped off up the lane after Hedley. The three men left standing looked at each other, undecided as to what to do next. The policeman felt much the same way. He took out his note-book and pencil and walked towards the trio.

'Who's in charge here?' he asked.

'He is,' chorused the two bookends.

'Names!' said the policeman.

He took the names of the three men, purloined the false warrant, took out some handcuffs, and said to the accountant: 'You'd best come with me.' Then he looked at the two men and said: 'Clear off!'

Edwin watched the green Crossley depart and then said to Mr Nall: 'May I use your telephone?' Mr Nall motioned for Edwin to follow him to the business room.

O O O

Meanwhile, the Bentley had sped up the lane from Godwin Hall towards Waterswallows Lane, Philip keeping his eyes on the lane and Eleanor looking out for Hedley Godwin.

'I can see him!' she said. 'He's over to the right, cutting across the fields. He's taking a short cut through Orient Lodge. He must be heading for the railway bridge. Turn right when we get to Waterswallows Lane.'

Philip did as Eleanor suggested and, having left the lane, was now able to increase speed. They crossed over the railway bridge and Philip slowed the motor car.

'Where is he now?' he asked.

'There he is!' said Eleanor, as she twisted to look backwards. 'He's heading back south on the lane that goes to Great Rocks Farm. Perhaps he's going to double back to Godwin Hall.'

'There's no way I can follow him. That lane is fit only for carts. If I tried it, I really would need that new Bentley. But why would he be going back to the Hall?'

Eleanor who had not taken her eyes off Hedley, said: 'He's not. He's changed direction. He's left the lane and is heading east across the fields.' Just as she said this, they heard the sound of a train in the distance and then a whistle. Then she added, excitedly: 'I think he's heading for the station. There's a through train to London from the Miller's Dale station in the afternoons.'

'Right,' said Philip. 'Hold your hat, Lella. He'll probably be taking the short cut towards Wormhill. This old girl will give him a run for his money.'

Philip pressed down on the accelerator and the motor car shot forward. The land on their right sloped down towards Great Rocks Dale and horse and rider disappeared from view. They reached a T intersection and skidded round to the right. Now the road followed a gentle curve in the form of an S and the Bentley reached sixty miles an hour. Then the ground to the right of the road levelled out and it was now possible to see the fields.

'There he is,' said Eleanor as, in the distance, she saw horse and rider clear a dry-stone wall and then disappear from view behind a thicket of trees. Philip slowed the motor car as they neared Hargate Hall and another intersection. He took the right hand turn as fast as he could and headed downhill towards Wormhill. He sounded the horn in warning as they passed through the hamlet at speed. The road was edged with stone walls and trees and Eleanor could not see the surrounding countryside. The road surface was rough and in need of repair. The Bentley was shuddering over the uneven surface and Philip had to slow down.

'Really, the state of this road!' he said. 'It's no wonder the A.A. has blacklisted our roads.'

The road began to descend, gradually at first and then

steeply, as it headed towards Miller's Dale and the railway station. They were now clear of the trees and Eleanor could see horse and rider, much closer to the road now to avoid the steep valley sides of Chee Dale and the small quarry just north of the station.

'He'll have to come right up to the road to skirt the quarry,' said Eleanor, 'that will cost him a bit of time.'

Philip had to slow right down to take a hair-pin bend and then sped up again as they raced down the hill over the last hundred yards and reached the station yard. They saw the horse, steaming from his exertion and, as he was loose, Philip slowed down to avoid startling him. He pulled up outside the station entrance. They leapt out of the motor car and heard a whistle and then the sound of a train pulling out.

'Damn!' said Philip. He walked towards the horse, took hold of his bridle and tethered him to one of the posts of the awning at the station entrance.

The station master who had seen the motor car entering the station yard came towards them through the station entrance. He was putting his watch back into his waistcoat pocket and he said, with apparent satisfaction: 'You're too late. All our trains run on time.'

Philip said: 'Good afternoon. Did the man who arrived on that horse just get on that train?'

'He did.'

'Where is the train going?'

'Bakewell. The 3.15 and on time,' said the station master with satisfaction, his thumbs anchored securely in the armholes of his waistcoat.

'Did the man say anything to you?'

'He did.'

'May I ask what he said?'

'You may. "Is this the train for London?" is what he said.'

'And you replied. . .?'

'It is the through train to St Pancras.'

'Did the man buy a ticket?'

'He did not.' The station master sounded affronted and the passenger's flouting of proper railway procedure provoked him into a longer sentence. 'Opened a door and leapt aboard before anyone could stop him.'

'And can you tell me where the train stops next?'

'I can.'

'And where is that?'

'Bakewell, 3.47 p.m.'

'And after that?'

The station master recited the timetable: 'Rowsley, 3.54, Matlock Bridge, 4.04, Matlock Bath 4.07, Ambergate 5.54 where the train will wait for four minutes.'

'I need to get that man off the train, you see.'

'As do I. He's travelling without a ticket.'

'And after Ambergate?

'If you want to apprehend your man, I'd advise you to do so before Ambergate.'

'Why is that?'

'Ambergate is a junction station.'

'So he could change trains there. When did you say the train reached Matlock Bath?'

'4.07 p.m.'

Philip looked at his watch and then at Eleanor: 'That gives us forty-eight minutes.' He turned back to the station master. 'May I use your telephone, sir?'

'That's railway property,' said the station master, firmly.

'I need to contact Superintendent Johnson at the Buxton police station. It is a matter of some urgency.'

'Go to the post office. Platform One.'

Philip and Eleanor looked at each other, rolled their eyes.

'I suspect him of being a Yorkshire man,' whispered Eleanor, as they went on to Platform One.

'I'm surprised he didn't insist we buy a platform ticket,' said Philip.

When they entered the post office, they were disconcerted to find the station master behind the counter, now in his role as sub-postmaster. They waited in silence while the call was put through, the station master hovering within earshot.

'You'd better speak to the Superintendent,' said Philip.

Eleanor explained to Superintendent Johnson where Hedley Godwin was, giving as few details as possible for the station master to gossip about. She was careful not to mention Hedley Godwin's name as the station master would certainly be familiar with the name of Godwin. She gave the Superintendent the list of stops the train would make and the time that it was due to arrive at each station. Philip thanked the station master who said: 'And who's going to remove that horse? That's what I'd like to know.'

'Don't worry. I'll deal with him,' said Philip.

As they walked back to the station yard, Eleanor said: 'Superintendent Johnson said he would contact each of the station masters with a description of Hedley Godwin and he's going to radio to the police station at Matlock Bath. He will also alert the London Midland railway police.'

'The railway police? Oh, wouldn't it be ironic if Godwin was arrested for fare evasion, after all this! If he's on the London train, perhaps he is hoping to get back to Kent. Instinct makes the fox head for his den.'

'Or in this case, the criminal head for his lair,' said Eleanor. 'I suppose that means he won't try to leave the train when it reaches the next station or any of them before Matlock Bath so there is a good chance they will catch him.'

Philip said: 'He should be pretty easy for the police to spot. There won't be many people travelling in boots, riding breeches and a hacking jacket.'

'And smelling of sweaty horse.' added Eleanor. 'I'm afraid we've missed that game of tennis we had planned.'

'Oh, but this is far more interesting and I did enjoy that drive. Perhaps Richard was right. I should try Le Mans next year.'

As they turned their attention to the horse, Eleanor said: 'The horse that Miss Godwin rode is called Winton and Mr Nall won't let Hedley Godwin ride him so I assume this is Bursar.'

On hearing his name, the horse whinnied. Philip stroked his shoulder and said: 'We need to get you rubbed down, old chap.' He turned to Eleanor and said: 'He needs to walk about a bit after that hard ride. I'll take him back up to Glebe Farm. We can get him some water there as well. I'll ask them to look after him until Mr Nall can send someone over to fetch him.'

'Right. I'll drive up to the farm and meet you there.'

Glebe Farm was only a couple of hundred yards back up the road so Eleanor knew that Philip would trust her with the Bentley that far. Philip mounted Bursar and they began walking slowly up the hill towards the farm.

O O O

Philip drove back from Glebe Farm to Godwin Hall at a sedate pace. The driveway area outside the front door of the Hall was empty except for the black Crossley and there was no sign of the group of men they had left there. They went round to tell Mr Nall about Bursar. He expressed his thanks for their care of the horse and said that he would send one of the farmhands over to fetch him. He then directed them to the business room where they found Edwin. Mrs Lomas, having been alerted to their arrival by Mr Nall, brought them all a cup of tea and some biscuits and stayed to hear their account of what had happened to Hedley Godwin and Bursar. Mrs Lomas did not look at all distraught at the thought of him being arrested for fare evasion but was concerned that it might interfere with his return to the south, where she hoped he would remain. Eleanor and Philip had not mentioned the other reasons for the police's interest in him.

When Mrs Lomas and Mr Nall had gone, Edwin said: 'The police constable was sent by Superintendent Johnson to deal with the false warrant and has taken the accountant back to Buxton. The other two were told to clear off. The Superintendent didn't realise Hedley Godwin was here otherwise he would have sent someone else to arrest him.'

'There's a very good chance that he'll be arrested at Matlock Bath,' said Philip. 'The Superintendent was going to radio ahead.'

'Shades of the arrest of Dr Crippen,' said Edwin. 'Now, Eleanor, I've been looking at these accounts and you were quite right. It does seem that sums of money have been diverted for the last few months, no doubt by Godwin. I think we shall ask Mr Nall for permission to take these books back to Hall Bank and have the accounts scrutinised.'

CHAPTER TWENTY-NINE

After Eleanor, Philip and Edwin returned from Godwin Hall they described for Mr Harriman the events that had taken place. At ten o'clock the following day, Mr Harriman had a long conference with Superintendent Johnson and when he returned to the office, Edwin was sitting in Eleanor's office discussing the defence to a claim against one of their clients. Mr Harriman came up to Eleanor's office and sat down, rather wearily. Napoleon rested his chin on Mr Harriman's knee and Mr Harriman stroked him.

'Well,' he said, 'the Superintendent and I had an interesting discussion this morning as to whether the charge ought to be murder or manslaughter in relation to Rose Penlington and the wisdom or otherwise of ordering an exhumation in relation to Miss Godwin and before we had reached any conclusion, he received a telephone call and the argument became academic. It seems that your station master at Miller's Dale took matters into his own hands and notified the London Midland railway police that Hedley Godwin had boarded the train without a ticket. Because it was a through train, there was already one of their officers on board, which your Miller's Dale station master was probably aware of. He also contacted the Bakewell station master and when the train stopped at Bakewell, the station master passed the information on to the railway policeman on board. As you rightly observed, Hedley Godwin's riding clothes made him easy to identify and he was approached by the officer shortly after the train left Bakewell. He rushed out into the corridor and then made his way through several interconnected carriages until he reached the rear of the train and could go no further.

'When the policeman approached him, Hedley opened the carriage door and jumped out of the train. The train was passing over the Derwent viaduct on its approach to Rowsley station at the time. The railway policeman got off the train at Rowsley and the station master there contacted the Bakewell police station. A search was made along the river below the viaduct but without success. Hedley's body was finally located late last evening, some distance downstream. No-one knew the name of the passenger at that stage, hence the delay in reporting to Superintendent Johnson. The railway police contacted the station master at Bakewell and he referred them to your station master at Miller's Dale. He told them to contact Superintendent Johnson. The Superintendent received the call while I was there.'

Eleanor and Edwin were silent for a minute or so while the news sank in.

Then Eleanor said: 'And now there will no longer be the need for difficult decisions about murder charges or exhumation orders.'

'Why do you suppose Hedley jumped?' asked Edwin. 'Surely, before taking any kind of action, the London Midland officer would have simply asked to see Hedley's ticket. He must have realised that it was fare evasion that the officer was pursuing. He would only have been fined so that was no great cause for alarm.'

'One would think so,' said Mr Harriman. 'I suppose he may have mistaken the London Midland policeman for a civil policeman. Perhaps that, in itself, suggests a guilty conscience.'

Eleanor said: 'It is hard to make sense of what happened. He was safely on the train and, once the issue of the unpaid fare had been sorted out, he would have been able to get to London. When he came around the corner of Godwin Hall and saw the three men there, he clearly recognised them and he seemed to panic and just to react without any particular plan. But if he feared for his safety, he could easily have ridden into Fairfield, or even gone back to The Square. And yet he didn't. He headed in the opposite direction as though his only thought was to get away from everything as fast as possible and then, I suppose, the opportunity of the train presented itself. Or perhaps he had always intended to get the train back to Kent. I saw the way he was riding on the way to the station though. It was reckless as though he had no concern for his own or the horse's safety. Perhaps he was already trying to flee from what he had done and while he was on the train, he had the opportunity to reflect on it and realise the hopeless situation he was in.'

'And I suppose being accosted by someone in uniform might have just tipped him over the edge,' said Edwin. 'He would have had time between Miller's Dale and Bakewell to reflect on his position. Perhaps he was overwhelmed by the realities of the situation he had got himself into.'

'Yes, that's possible, I suppose,' said Eleanor. 'Philip did say that Hedley Godwin blamed everyone else for his misfortunes and that he did not seem to be the sort of person who took responsibility for what happened.'

'And all our careful consideration of the facts and speculation as to what caused the death of Rose and Miss Godwin are now completely irrelevant,' said Mr Harriman.

'But there are still two innocent people who are dead, probably because of Hedley Godwin,' said Eleanor. 'Well, three people, really. I think we were entitled to know the truth for their sakes. I know this sounds silly but I feel cheated.'

'I know what you mean,' said Edwin. 'On the other hand, Hedley's death saves us from the possibility of an unsatisfactory verdict. I know we were fairly certain that he was guilty, at least of Rose's death, but would a jury have been satisfied beyond reasonable doubt?'

Mr Harriman said: 'I have to admit that the evidence was slender and there was a real possibility that the prosecution may not have been able to make out the charge against him in relation to Rose.'

'If he had pleaded not guilty, a really capable defence counsel, such as Sir Giles Benson, might have been able to sway the jury in Hedley's favour,' said Edwin. 'For every piece of evidence we have in relation to Rose, it would be possible for his defence to provide an innocent explanation. The cause of death was definitely drowning but there was simply no evidence that Hedley or anyone else caused her to drown. We are looking at the difference between accident, manslaughter and murder. Defence counsel would be bound to point out that there is a world of difference between "she drowned" and "she drowned because of something he did" and "he intended to drown her" and so far we have seen no evidence of any such intention. I fear that the evidence we have might not discharge the burden of proof. I fear that we have only just reached "on the balance of probabilities" rather than "beyond reasonable doubt" so it is possibly not a bad thing that this has been taken out of our hands.'

'And imagine what would have happened if he had been charged and acquitted,' said Eleanor.

'It does not bear thinking about,' said Mr Harriman.

'And now,' said Eleanor, 'we shall never know the truth about Miss Godwin's death.'

'There is perhaps one thing which might ameliorate that feeling of disappointment. Godwin Hall has been saved from ruin.'

'That's true,' said Eleanor. 'Miss Godwin's legacy will be preserved and Godwin Hall will retain the benefit of all Mr Nall's hard work. I think we should let Mr Nall and Mrs

Lomas know about Hedley Godwin's death as soon as possible. They will be very relieved, I'm sure.'

'And we must now locate the new heir,' said Mr Harriman. 'Let's hope he shows more promise than the last one.'

O O O

Later that morning, Mr Harriman came upstairs to Eleanor's office and stood in the doorway. He said: 'Eleanor I have some news to share with you and Edwin.'

Eleanor got up from her desk and went into Edwin's office. Mr Harriman said: 'You may recall that, four years ago, when I first received notice of Hedley Godwin's claim to Godwin Hall, we discussed the merits of checking the validity of the claim. As he took no further action, neither did I. However, when Miss Godwin died, I retained the services of a genealogist. I asked him to provide a full family tree and, two weeks ago he provided me with the details of Hedley Godwin's claim and said he was still working on the rest of the details. Hedley Godwin's claim was based on his descent from George Godwin, who was Miss Godwin's grandfather. George Godwin's line ended with Miss Godwin. The genealogist assured me that Hedley's claim was valid. The claim to Godwin Hall had to be traced back to George Godwin's younger brother, Charles Godwin. Hedley was the great-grandson of that younger brother, Charles. Hedley's grandfather was Charles' son, Thomas, who was born in 1850 in India, was sent at the age of eight to a boarding school in Kent, and chose not to return to India.

'I telephoned the genealogist this morning to see if he had been able to complete the full family tree and he has. He is sending the details by post but this is what he told me. George's brother, Charles, had a second son, Felix, who was sent to the same boarding school in Kent but, unlike his brother, he returned to India. He established a business as a spice merchant and then, in 1892, he opened a second office in Liverpool so that he could return to England with his young family, not wishing to send his own sons to boarding school. He is now seventy-one years old, retired, and living in Southport. His eldest son, Leopold, who is now forty, with a family of his own, is the managing director of the business and he lives in Cheshire. So we now have a more promising lineage for the inheritance of Godwin Hall.'

Eleanor said: 'Oh, I am so pleased. That does sound much more promising.'

Edwin added: 'Yes, for one thing, if the family runs a profitable business and has its own source of income there will be no need for the heir to depend on Godwin Hall as Hedley would have had to do and for another thing, they will understand how to run a business, which Hedley certainly would not have done.'

'With any luck,' said Mr Harriman, 'they will leave Mr Nall to get on with running the farm and just concentrate on maintaining the Hall and perhaps enjoying it.'

'Let's hope so,' said Eleanor.

CHAPTER THIRTY

During that day, Buxton had been enjoying beautiful summer weather and it was exceptionally warm. As Buxton's weather was notoriously unpredictable, Cicely decided to take advantage of the opportunity for a picnic in the Pavilion Gardens when Richard came home from school. She telephoned to Philip and to Eleanor who persuaded Mr Harriman to join them. Edwin had already gone home intending to take his boys swimming.

Mr Harriman and Philip carried the picnic hamper and two deck-chairs between them and, as they walked, Mr Harriman told Philip about the death of Hedley Godwin. Eleanor and Cicely each had a deck-chair and Richard carried a rug. Richard's school friend, Thomas, carried a large ball and Napoleon walked ahead, unburdened and carefree as usual. They settled on a grassy knoll a short distance from the banks of the river. From there they could watch the ducks dipping and diving in the water which was rippling in the sunlight. The river flowed in a wide shallow curve before tumbling down a cascade a little further downstream. When the hamper was opened, they all exclaimed at the variety of the food prepared by Cicely and Ellen. Cicely poured them all some of the elderflower cordial she had made, the first for the summer, and they then spent a leisurely hour enjoying a little of everything that was offered.

After thanking Cicely for organising such a wonderful meal, Richard and Thomas asked if they could paddle in the river and the party broke into two halves. Mr Harriman and Cicely sat on the riverbank and watched as the two boys splashed about in the water and tossed Thomas' ball to each other. Napoleon, unable to resist the temptation of a ball, careered down the bank to join them, entering the water with a huge splash. There followed a boisterous game as the boys tumbled about in the water trying to play football. Napoleon alternated between jumping into the river and vying for possession of the ball and then climbing out to loll on the bank, dripping wet, to watch the action while recovering his energy. Cicely and Mr Harriman cheered from the side lines.

Eleanor and Philip, languishing in deckchairs, watched the river scene too lazy to move.

'You're quiet today, old thing,' said Philip. 'You're still fretting about Hedley Godwin, aren't you?'

'Yes and no,' said Eleanor. 'I am relieved it is all over but still sorry that we were not able to establish the truth about the death of Rose and Miss Godwin.'

'In Miss Godwin's case it is probably for the best. Imagine if there had been an exhumation and then a trial. How she would have hated the sordid publicity, not to mention having to be dug up and disturbed.'

'Yes, that is a rather horrible thought. People would remember her for all the wrong reasons. And it is possible that even if the police found enough evidence to charge Hedley Godwin, the prosecution would not be able to make out its case and then all of that unpleasantness would have been for nothing.'

Philip said: 'And it wouldn't bring Miss Godwin back.'

'No, so it's much better to leave everyone with the memory of her as the successful owner of Godwin Hall.'

'And I doubt whether anyone will remember Hedley Godwin for very much longer. What's going to happen about Lily and Rose?'

'Well, there will have to be an inquest for Lily but

Superintendent Johnson is not continuing with the investigation of Rose's death. Father thinks that, on the evidence so far, an open verdict will be justified and that means that the story of the swap won't have to come out. Rose's death with soon be forgotten about.'

'Have the police been able to locate any relatives?'

'As far as I know, no. Mr Gregory told Father that all the girls employed at the hotel have a penny insurance policy so that will cover Lily's funeral costs and Mrs Clayton's brother Alf has said that he will look after both Lily and Rose for the cost of one, so at least they will have a proper funeral.'

'That's good of him.'

They sat in silence for a while and Eleanor said: 'And the rosewood games table?'

'Safely at the very back of the showroom until I can display it properly. I've decided to take the lease on Mr Sutton's old house, Thornstead, on Burlington Road. My mother heaved a sigh of relief at the news. She is getting a bit tired of tripping over my bits and pieces.'

'I think that's an excellent...'

'Oh, no!' yelled Philip, as Napoleon thoroughly wet, tongue lolling, and mouth grinning, was heading towards them from the river-bank and giving every indication of being about to shake himself. Eleanor leapt up, grabbed Napoleon's collar, and steered him away from Philip's immaculate flannels and blazer.

'Well saved, Lella,' said Philip. 'Thank you. I am as fond of Napoleon as you are, but not when he is wet.'

As Eleanor was laughing and towelling Napoleon dry, Cicely and the boys came back from the river. 'Father's gone to look in at the cricket. I'm going in search of ice-cream,' said Cicely, reaching into a bag for towels for the boys.

Philip extricated himself from his deck-chair and said: 'I'll go. I prefer to be in drier company.'

'Can we come and choose what flavour we want?' said Richard. 'Please,' he added.

Philip looked at Cicely and, as she nodded approval, said to the boys: 'All right, come on then.'

When they had gone, Eleanor released a still damp Napoleon from the towel and resumed her seat. Napoleon shook himself and flopped down beside Eleanor satisfied with his afternoon's exercise. Cicely folded up the boys' towels and then sat down in Philip's deck-chair and said:

'Philip is very good with Richard, isn't he?'

'Yes, they get on well.'

'You and Philip were deep in conversation.'

'We were mulling over the facts about the girl who was found in the pond.'

'Ah, that is still puzzling you, isn't it? Perhaps we shall never know what happened.'

Cicely had not been burdened with all the other information about Hedley Godwin and would remain in ignorance of his affairs.

'No, we probably never shall know,' said Eleanor, as a picture of Hedley Godwin jumping out of the train carriage flashed through her mind.

O O O

Two days later, James Wildgoose opened the latest edition of the *Buxton Advertiser.* At the request of the Kent solicitors, he had sent an announcement for insertion in that newspaper and he wanted to check that it had been published. He took up a blue pencil and circled the notice which announced the death, as the result of an accident, of Hedley Godwin of The Square, Buxton. James, remembering his encounter with the unmannerly Hedley Godwin, had been most particular about the address of the deceased which was strictly accurate and avoided any mention of Godwin Hall. Later he would add the notice to yet another file labelled Godwin, which marked one more chapter in the long history of the Goddwynes of Fayrefeld.